THE TRUE MEANING OF TROUBLE

JP ROSSELLE

ISBN   978-1-953821-48-5 Ebook
ISBN   978-1-953821-47-8 Paperback

The EC Publishing LLC books may be ordered
through booksellers or by contacting:

EC Publishing LLC
116 South Magnolia Ave.
Suite 3, Unit F
Ocala, FL 34471, USA
Direct Line: +1 (352) 644-6538
Fax: +1 (800) 483-1813
http://www.ecpublishingllc.com/

Ordering Information:
Quantity sales. Special discounts are available on quantity purchases by corporations, associations, and others. For details, contact the publisher at the address above.

Printed in the United States of America

TABLE OF CONTENTS

CHAPTER I
MEETING THE PRESIDENT

We had just taken of from Davao airport, the Captain of the Hornet didn't say much. I was well strapped in with my headgear on. I asked where we were off to and the pilot said my final destination was Andrews Air Base. This was the fastest way we could get you there, he said. You will make three transfers, I hope you made a bathroom stop before the flight, we will be in the air for 135 minutes before our first stop. In seconds we were airborne. I could hear as the Captain spoke with ground control and then a ship picked up the comunications where the ground crew voice left off.

We landed on the Island of Guam, where the Captain said he would refuel and return to his ship. On Guam I was allowed a 15-minute break and then boarded another Fighter. Next stop Hawaii another 15-minute break then on to California. From California it would be the last leg to Andrew Airforce Base.

Once we landed at Andrews, as I exited the jet a Lieutenant handed me five envelopes; one had the seal of the President of the United States, you guessed it, of America. One was marked "Traveling Cat", one from the Admiral, one from Langley and one from Bob. Guess which I open first? The first one was Cat's, it read, "My love I'm at the Jefferson hotel waiting with your 007 suit. Come by and get a hot shower signed Cat" Of course I read this as we walked, I say we because I had an escort. We walked to a waiting limo where, once seated, my escort said we were to first visit the Admiral. By now I was opening Bob's envelope which only read "I hear you have made it to the BIG TIMES, be careful, Bob" Bob's envelope smelled of a Cuban cigar. I then opened the Presidents envelope and it was an invitation to dine with the President and his wife at 8:00 p.m. tonight at the White House, the invitation had listed Cathren Johnson and Myself. Wow I thought, I wondered if Cat knew? Her comment about the 007 suit and her being here said it all. The escort had what looked like a much fancier cell phone than I had seen. I asked for him to make the call to the hotel which he obliged, I asked for my room and Cat answered the phone. Cat, I said we've been invited to dinner at the White House. Cat said that she had received word yesterday afternoon and had been in DC since last night. Cat asked what time I'd be there? I said I guessed by 6:00 p.m. I 'll be ready she said, and we hung up.

The limo dropped both myself and the escort at the Department of the Navy. The escort had me bring my briefcase with us. He said we'd be going by helicopter to Langley and then the hotel. I was escorted right in to see the Admiral.

Ah Captain he said glad to see you could make it. I trust your trip was comfortable, oh yes Sir I said, first class all the way. Well he said. I will get right to the point. I have been ordered to turn the project of bringing up that Vessle in the TOTO Channel over to you. Why me I asked? Seems the powers to be are weary of my efforts. What's the hurry I asked? The facility to receive the vehicle won't be ready to receive the vessel for at least another year. The Admiral said that too, we need that time to be cut by at least six months. The President wants that vessel available on the deck by early next year. I'm to assist by any means possible the Admiral said. The Navy is at your service. Now then the Admiral said, that being said, my job is on the line here, so don't spend too much time with your other projects, I want your full attention. I stood up and said that I understood. We shook hands and he said that the Director was also waiting to see me, remember young man he said, your full time. He then smiled and asked if I had seen it? Seen what I asked? This month's Playboy man, its Karen he said. Oh no Sir I haven't. It's quite impressive the Admiral said.

I was then escorted to the elevator which we took to the top floor. There a helicopter was waiting. My escort and I got aboard and we were off to Langley. We were dropped off at the helipad pad with just a short walk to the side door. Here the escort said I could leave my briefcase and guns. The escort asked to look in the case and I warned him to do so at his own risk, be careful of the rat trap I stated. I unlocked the case and he examined some of the contents. There was a box inside that I was sure he would open. In the box was only a black cloth, and I knew he would squeeze on it. The escort then closed the box and gave his ok. I placed my guns inside the case and relocked it.

I went in to see the Director and he was very friendly, Jim how have you been, he asked? He also asked about Salinas and Michelle. All is good I said and you? Fine he said just fine. Jim he said, the Colonel and myself will be joining you and Cat for dinner tonight. The President wanted to meet you and say how much we need you and your groups support on our efforts to stop the communists. On the other hand, he said, I'm sure the Admiral informed you of the President's decision to give you full control of the Andros project. What do you think? Think I asked? As far as the support, I'll do what I can with you understanding that I don't trust you to do what's right. Especially where your personal are concerned. Whatever I say now about the Andros project would be without consulting my people. To cut the time in half, more than doubles the work. Two men can't stand in a one man's space and working at night is slow going. We will cut the time and do the best we can. The situation on Andros involving the 4 sailors that raped one girl and murdered the other has slowed us down. People won't work as well that have grievances on their minds. Inviting Cat to the podium we could all get an ear full. If it's brought up at dinner I will complain of the Navy's attitude with the locals, I said. We're lucky that any of the locals are still working on the base. They don't work they don't feed their families the Director said. I smiled and said, that's the problem with you politicians, you don't read the fine print. Your land contract that's probably 40 years old says that 80% of all labor, will and must be performed by Bahamians. With regards to contracts for services Bahamian companies are to receive priority. It also has a clause about Bahamian law must be followed and that any and all crimes committed against Bahamians must be brought to justice by a Bahamian court. Time served for any conviction would be served in a Bahamian jail. I wonder what smart man wrote such a contract I asked? And that part about feeding their families, people living by the ocean usually don't have problems getting food. The education the Navy is giving them about how we treat others doesn't look very good, I said.

The Director didn't like anything he heard so he quickly changed the subject. One of your C-130s should be taking off right about now he said. They will make a short landing in Limon, Costa Rica and then flying back making a quick in-air drop of supplies to our Contra's. That's fine I said but remember, No passengers under any circumstances.

Well the Director said I know you have to get ready for your big night. The escort will accompany you on the helicopter to the Hotel. A limo will be waiting at the hotel at 7:15 p.m. to take you to the White House. I don't think the escort will feel like flying, I said, he was looking alittle ill. He looked good to me the Director said.

When we stepped out into the reception area the escort was gone. That's strange the Director said. It would have been strange to me if he would have been there, I was sure the rat trap had got him. The rag that the escort had touched had a little of that dose of that special mix that Carson had given me.

I went alone on my trip to the hotel, I knocked on my hotel room door and this most beautiful women, not girl, women, opened the door. Cat had her hair up and was wearing just a nighty top. Her wearing her hair in a bag in the shower didn't bother me a bit, in fact seeing that back line right up to her neck was great. Cat's sister Deanna at 15 wasn't built like Lori but, for a then 16-year-old boy Deanna was quite something else. Lori's body had a better shape and tone as she had worked hard from a child. Cat and I dressed, Cat wearing and open backed dress that showed that nice back and neck line. I zipped up the short zipper of the back of her long black evening gown. She then handed me the diamond neckless that I purchased so long ago. The engagement and wedding rings were no longer on a chain around her neck, but on her left hand second finger. I had never seen her wear any other rings, this even though she was married to Jacob. Her last touches were those golden shell ear rings that I liked so much and my favorite perfume. Cat looked, well like a million.

I felt much different without my hand guns on but that was part of the price of dinning with the President. Once Cat was ready she pointed to the box on the dressing table, Cat said to open it. I did and inside was one of Cat's favorite necklaces. It was a large ruby encircled with diamonds on a gold chain also incrusted with diamonds. Cat said she wanted the President's wife to have it. I asked if she was sure? Cat said that we could have many more precious items that we had never even looked at. Cat was describing the latest treasure that we had brought up from the second ship, and as she stated, not even looked at. Cat took the small box and put in her purse.

We were out front at 7:15 p.m. where the limo was waiting.

At the White House gate, we presented our invitations along with our passports. This brought back memories of when Rusty and I visited Bob's house in Nassau for the first time. Then it was a horse and carriage instead of a limo. Other than that and the house back then being much smaller with Rusty and I dressed in jeans, it was much the same.

We were greeted by no less than the President's wife. I was astonished at how good she looked. She asked Cat if she would like a small tour while we waited for the President. Cat said yes of course, as we started to walk the Director stepped out of a doorway and motioned me toward him and the Coronel. The President's wife notice them calling me and said, yes by all means Captain go be with the boys, Cat and I will be just fine.

The director didn't look happy and said my escort had been admitted into Walter Reed for detox. The director asked sternly what I had done to him? Your man, I said stuck his hand where he shouldn't have. I gave him a clear warning about the rat trap. It's nothing that 24 hours won't cure I said. The Director looked at the Coronel and said he's reckless! I looked at him and said again, I did warn him!

At that moment a house man brought us drinks. Mine of course was a chivas on the rocks.

The Coronel said our bird, as he called the C-130 got off on time without a hitch. Cat had gotten that call just before we left for dinner. The cargo, as I suspected was weapons. I said I knew it was a little too late but asked if the Nicaraguan's had anything in that zone that could shoot down my bird, as they called it. The Director said not that we know of, the Coronel said hell no. The Coronel said that our people, meaning the Contra's, held all the South East ground.

The house man returned and said we needed to go in now. We walked in and there was Cat sitting with the President's wife, what a sight it was. The first thing I thought about was the first time I laid eyes on Cat. I could tell that Cat was thinking the exact same thing. The President's wife said as we waited she wanted to hear the story where Cat had saved my life.

Cat didn't get to even start when the President came walking in. Everyone except his wife stood, please, please the President said, be seated. Well Captain, we finally get to meet, I hear so many of your stories. I believe Cat was about to tell one of hers as I came in he said. Please continue he said. Oh no Cat said it was nothing. The Presidents wife said go ahead Cat, tell us the story. Cat was too nervous to talk so I jumped in telling the story how even with the man holding a gun and trying to shoot me, Cat ran straight at him and hit him like a linebacker. Cat then said she didn't know who Dick Butkus was for several days. What happen to the man the President asked? Jim, Cat said finally got to his leg holster and shot out both of his knee caps. The President's wife asked, did he recover? Well Cat said, he used a wheel chair until. Cat, I interrupted. No go on the Presidents wife said. Well supposedly the man owed money to the Colombians and three weeks ago they threw him out of an airplane. The President said his wife was looking for a happy ending. I made the coment that for me it was just that.

Wine was served with dinner and the President did most of the talking. We could clearly see his interests were the vessel in the channel, the Cubans and Soviets in Nicaragua and even El Salvador. I understand your men had a run-in with the communist rebels down in General Santos. You going to counter attack with your people he asked? Well Sir, the intelligence you received on this one requires some updating. It wasn't the rebels that attacked, it was the nationals dress as rebels with three Japanese nationals. All 13 nationals were killed along with the three Japanese. The Pilipino Coronel ordered a counter attack on the rebels and the Coronel lost an additional 17 men. How many rebels were killed asked the President? None Sir, I said. The rebels are well equipped and trained. Several of them, including their leader, are seasoned Afghanistan resistance who fought the Soviets.

What were the Japs doing there asked the President? They were after the Fruit company's prawns, I said. The Director jumped in and said that the Japanese Ambassador had complained that one of their fishing boats was sunk in the bay of Davao last week. The Ambassador said the Japanese said the attacked had the finger prints of the CIA because C4 was used. Well the President asked? No Sir, The Director said we didn't do it. Well then who the President asked? The director looked straight at me. There was no loss of life Sir I said, and the C4 was just being returned to the owners. The three Japanese we killed were from that same ship, and they had the C4 with them when they attacked us. Son the President said, the Japanese are our allies, we don't attack our allies he said. They killed three of my men and a friend I said. The President had walked in with a letter in his hand. Son, this letter is an introduction to a Japanese company looking for a partner to open a canned tuna fish factory in General Santos. Do you want it? I'd like to talk to them I said. And what if it's the same people that killed your friend he asked? Well Sir, they attacked us at Pearl Harbor and we bombed them at Hiroshima. Didn't you just say they were our allies? The President looked at the Director and said, you see, he is a fast learner and smiled.

The President passed the letter to Cat and looked at me. Now son, he said, I need that Andros facility finished and that vessel lifted where we can get to its secrets. The Coronel needs your help to keep the contras supplied and in your spare time keep those Damned rebels in check at General Santos. We can't afford to have any communist rebels running around in the Philippines.

Mam Cat said, handing the box to the President's wife; this is a token of our appreciation for the invitation into your home. The President's wife looked at the President as she took the box. She opened the box and took out the neckless. Oh my she said it's the most beautiful neckless I've ever seen. Oh Cat, she said, I can't accept this. It must be worth a fortune. Cat said that it was once owned by Sir Frances Drake. It was part of the first of two treasures that Jim found in our Bahamian waters. Please, Cat said, it was made for a Queen. The President took the First Lady by the hand and said its fine dear. The President then stood as we all did, we shook hands. Cat and the President's wife then hugged, and we were leaving.

The Coronel hadn't said a word all night. The Director and I didn't seem to do so good with each other. Looked like Cat and I had a new pair of friends.

The limo took us back to the hotel, it was probably one of our best nights out, ok so not everyone goes to the White House and eats with the President.

Once back in our room as I assisted Cat with her zipper, she said that the First Lady said behind every great man was a great woman.

I told Cat that Salinas was pregnant again. Cat said this time Salinas had to know what she was doing. Cat now under the sheets said that the next one was her turn. I mentioned that she was married and that I wasn't about to let anyone but me to be the father of my children. I couldn't remember when I had seen Cat cry but, tonight she did. She rolled away from me and cried. I tried to comfort her but she cried herself to sleep.

It was 4:00 a.m. when I felt her roll back to me, she asked if I could stay a few days? I said we could fly down to Andros together and meet with Lee and the men. Cat suggested that we could stop in Miami and eat at Joe's which was now open. Seemed the time passed by so quickly. I would be 34 years old in one more week.

The next morning Cat and I left via Tommy for Andros. Lee picked us up at the airport. He brought with him a copy of the subpoena that the Navy had sent me. Lee had sent the original to Jacob. We went to the house and first talked about the President's request of us taking over the project. Lee said as far as he was concerned we were already running the job site and received very little or no assistance from the Navy. Lee said we were ahead of schedule and could increase the size of our labor and bring in another loader and crane. He could see us being ready to house the vessel in February if we concentrated in that section of the building and postpone some of the other unrelated sections. Lee said the Diver's said that once the caves track was completed, then bringing up the vessel would be the priority. The Navy would need two of its large barges and two tugs. Lee said that Lusca would be the only problem. Lee informed us the stern of the fisherman's boat and tooth that we sent to the UM for research indicated that Lucas is a giant octopus. The divers had said that they figured that the last sub's crew that Lusca destroyed had gotten careless. They were most likely concentrating on the tethering operation and didn't notice Lucsa until it was too late. Since at that depth it is dark, the likely hood that Lusca is attracted to the lights is high. The UM Professors informed us that octopuses only had one eye and could only distinguish between dark and light, can see in the dark, and can change colors to camouflage themselves to their prey. The Professors went onto write that at the Miami Sea Aquarium they had witnessed a giant octopus swallow an 8-foot shark.

Last but not least, Lee said, an octopus can inject a paralyzing venom into their prey. As Lee finished I had an idea. We would build a small sphere with glass windows, the sphere would have battery powered lights. Inside we would fill the sphere with sea water and add live crawfish. The outside of the sphere would have pins like a World War Two sea mine. The octopus would see the light and crawfish and squeeze and swallow it or at least try to. Of course we knew there were other big fish down there that might like our sphere for a snack. We may need to build several spheres. I would make some rough drawings and pass my idea to the divers, Cat and Lee liked the plan.

Next, we talked about and looked at the photos that the divers had taken of the door they found embedded into the cave. We agreed that we would also send these photos to the UM. All I knew about Latin was that it was one of our first languages, my question was whom developed it? In looking at the photos I thought about myself and my booby-traps that I always installed into something that I didn't want others to open. No I thought we wouldn't attempt to open the door just yet.

Our divers had now gotten within 300 feet of the tunnel's sea entrance. We would stop there until we had the Lusca thing taken care of. The divers had decided and closed all the side caves as they went. The divers didn't want any surprises; I didn't blame them. No one knew where Lusca made its home and just the thought of it learking in one of those side caves was enough to think about, this without the thought of a 30 foot crockadile coming up from behind.

The underwater gear required to install the rails was quite sophisticated. Lee said we would need at least eight more divers to install the rails.

I really didn't want to go visit the base commander and certainly wasn't going to take Cat along. I wouldn't bring up the ongoing court case against their navy personnel unless he did. The subpoena that the Navy sent me had no meaning at all and if they wanted to talk about the jailed sailors, it would be with the Bahamian Government in Nassau.

The commander was very business-like and did not mention what I didn't want to talk about. He did mention, and I didn't like it, that his people would not be going back down there to tether the vessel. I wasn't looking for a fight so I didn't give him any reply. The visit was short, him offering assistance where he could. I was glad that I hadn't taken Cat because she would have jumped all over him for the Navy's abuses of and toward her people.

Fernando was in Haiti recruiting 20 more men to start training. He was sad about our loses in General Santos but proud that his men stood their ground and that he had some part in their revenge. The four remaining Haitians on Andros wanted to hear the story of the attack from me first hand. They too were sad about their friends but stood proud that they had eliminated the threat.

Our divers returned from their day's work and we sat with them as they ate and relaxed. We talked about my plan for Lusca and all agreed.

Jack said he would take a few days and travel to Miami to recruit more divers. He was correct in saying that it would take a group of special men to do the job ahead of us.

It was after 8:00 p.m. when Jack, Cat and I took off for Miami. Jack went on his way and Cat and I would go directly to the apartment, shower and get ready for a visit to Joe's Stone Crab on the beach. Cat again talked about getting pregnant and having a child of her own. Cat said if the only way was to divorce Jacob then so be it. I reinforced the fact that I would not be leaving Salinas. Cat said then Salinas would have to learn to share. I said she already was.

I had called Bob and would meet him tomorrow while Tommy flew Cat back to Nassau. I met Bob and with him doing the new Philippines Lines business numbers, Bob said going out with a full load should net the line almost $800,000.00 per month. We talked about the possible joint venture with the Japanese. Bob said that, should that become a reality we would need an additional ship from Robin's Sea Containers fleet. Bob's import export business was doing lots and lots of business. Durning the next few months' we would switch shipping agents for the new line from the Fruit company's agent to Bob's agency.

Bob, as was everyone, was impressed with the way Karen had tied her playboy story in with giving Omni such good publicity. Our Miami terminal was mentioned along with photos of Karen driving the lifts wearing her hard hat.

I handed Bob the photos of the door in the main cave under the base on Andros and asked that he pass them to his colleges at the UM. Bob looked at the photos and without asking what I was thinking said that I could just be right.

From Bob's I went and visited with Tim, this to coordinate the change of the group of the men we had sent to work at General Santos. Two of the 14 men wanted to stay as they had found women that they didn't want to leave, this plus the good money that all were making. These men were training the Philippinos while working the containers and the ships.

Tim had picked out a terminal sight for the new container yard. The newest Sea Container depot would be located in Roebling New Jersey. Yes, just 51 miles from New York's and the Philadelphia's harbors.

Tommy was about to return to Opa-Locka's airport and I would meet him there just as soon as I made two more stops.

My next stop was to visit and old friend that had retired from the original container business that I had sold. He retired saying that after working with me he couldn't work for the new owners. Chubby as I called him lived in a small house in little Havana. He had reached out to Lourdes looking for something to do. He and his wife of over 43 years had never had children of their own. I tracked down Chubby selling cars at a used car lot on SW 8th street. When Chubby saw me he almost cried. Please tell me boss you have something for me. I talked to him about my needs and how I saw it working. Chubby said he'd speak to his wife and let Lourdes know. I had asked Chubby if he and his wife would take on Lori and the two little ones.

From there I went by my bothers shop, yes that third generation business that my grandfather had built was still going strong. I sat with my brother Bob and told him about Lusca. I then told him what I wanted. Bob made hand sketches of what I described. When we finished, I asked him to build me one.

From there it was to Opa-Locka's airport. Tommy had been waiting and the moment I arrived we were off for Mandeville. Salinas got a heads up call and was there waiting at the airport. As we landed I noted that both of our C-130s were on the ground and quite a bit of our planned construction was underway. Things were looking good.

As the leer pulled up there was Jerry and Salinas, Salinas looked like a Godest! She was wearing a simple pair of black plaid shorts, with a low cut pullover and little or no makeup. She looked good enough to eat! She said, as she hugged and kissed me that they had missed me so much. I couldn't wait to get her behind closed doors. Jerry was there and looked like he wanted to talk but I asked if it could wait and he said tomorrow would do just fine. Welcome home Sir he said. On the ride home Salinas said she had met Jerry's wife and they had found a home for Jerry and his wife, not far from the airport.

It was good to see little Michelle. She was growing like a weed. Betty whom always said she didn't like kids was right there by Michelle's side doing everything for and with her.

Salinas and I spent the night in and the next morning we went for a long country horseback ride. Salinas asked what I wanted for my birthday. I said I'd like to spend it with her on the Hatteras that bore her name. Salinas said we would all go and visit our home on Paradise Island in Nassau. Lourdes sent word to Cat to have the house in tip top shape checking the phone service and putting the air-conditioning on low. It was late August and Nassau like Mandeville was hot.

When Betty got the word she let out a halleluiah! We would pack our bags and leave the next day.

Later that afternoon I went to the airport to meet with Jerry. Jerry said the cargo delivery had gone well and already there was more of the same type of cargo building up in our terminal warehouse in New Orleans. We would use the warehouse in New Orleans until our Mandeville warehouse was ready. Of course Jack would perform all the ground transport.

I told Jerry that we would make one Central America drop per month for the cause. Jerry was to figure the cost of each trip so that we could collect for any additional trips.

Before we left the next morning Lourdes said that Chubby had called and said they'd like to meet the children. I told Lourdes to find Jena and if her or anyone wasn't using the apartment next to mine that I'd like to borrow it for a month or so. If Jena had no problem with that then Lourdes was to contact Evette and get Lori, Samuel and Melody to Miami and into Jena's apartment just ASAP. Tommy could go and pick them up in Davao. Evette was to get passports and Visa's using whatever means necessary. Lourdes was to coordinate with Big Ted for a small security detail. Of course all this was a priority one and a top secret project!

It was now Saturday, we arrived in Nassau at 5:00 p.m. We arrived at the beach house on the Island just before 6:00 p.m. Salinas and I changed and jumped into the pool. From there we walked down the beach, going in and out of the water. I had almost forgotten the no see thems but they didn't forget us. We were back at the pool and then back inside before dark.

Sunday morning Salinas and I were down at the wharf eating from one of the small carts. You don't realize how much you miss this food until you taste it after not having it for a while. It was odd but I felt the same way about being with a woman. I didn't realize how much I missed them until returning to them. Salinas and I did some shopping and would head on down to the "SALINAS". Leaving out in the Hatteras wasn't like going out in the Hunter. The Hatteras could get us just about anywhere in a hurry. We weren't in any hurry and would just head east along the North side of Rock Island. We anchored at sun set and spent a quite evening just sitting and talking. We talked about Michelle and how we wanted her to be raised. Salinas wanted her to have everything, going to privet schools and traveling the world. Me on the other hand wanted her to go to a public school to insure she grew up with normal kids, not a bunch of spoiled rich kids. Salinas suggested I learn French as if Salinas had anything to do with it, Michelle's first language would be French. What you want, I said is a mama's girl, good luck with that I said. Salinas laughed and I followed. Next we talked about the boy Salinas said she was having. The list for him was, learns to swim before he walks, grows up on the Hunter with a Hawaiian sling in his hand, plays high school football, learns to shoot and runs all our businesses so I can retire. Oh and Salinas said he too was going to be a mama's boy. Fat chance of that I said.

The next morning, we reached Harbor Island and once again used the Valentin's dock for the boat. We carried just one small bag for the both of us as we walked to the Islands other side. Pink Sands hotel was where we were headed, we loved the place.

Salinas and I would celebrate my birthday with a specially cooked dinner for two. I drank all but one glass of the white wine they served us. Salinas was aloud that one other glass. I enjoyed Salinas's company as I always had. I knew that my extra activities and work load was not going to be good for the relationship. Salinas said she understood the work part of it. Salinas just didn't understand why I had to open a business on the other side of the world. Not often, but I to had asked that very question, mostly when I was sitting in an air plane for hours and hours at a time. My mother used to say that I had lots of good common sense but not too much patience. Salinas seemed to have plenty of what I was missing.

On the fourth day we headed back to Nassau with the "SALINAS". Salinas's mother had shown up in Nassau and she would stay with Salinas at the beach house. Salinas was aware that I needed to get back to work, she said they would stay in Nassau for least two more weeks.

I had received lots of information from Lourdes but nothing about Lori and the children. On the day of my departure from Nassau I visited the wharf having breakfast at Angee's with Cat. Cat and I then met with all three captains noticing that Maggie continued to go out with Otis even after their wedding. We then visited with Peter and the tourist as they came in from their night fishing trip on the "Nassau Queen". As Cat and I passed the city bar, I asked Cat what was going on with Willy? Cat said that Willy had been feeling poorly lately and someone was standing for him.

Cat then took me by to see Lucy. Lucy had been back and forth to Miami for the rebuilding of bone and plastic surgeries. She was in good spirits and seemed happy to see me. Lucy had also testified at a Nassau preliminary hearing on the two Navy men that had raped and attacked her. There had been a Jag attorney that wanted to talk with Lucy but her father said the attorney would have to go through me. I said, I wouldn't speak to any one from the Navy until the other two men involved were securely behind bars in a Nassau jail.

I had never been to Willy's house but remembered from the old days that he and Deanna used to call each other neighbor. We checked it out and went to visit Willy at his house. I hadn't realized but Willy was now seventy-two years old. We found Willy sitting on his front porch swing. When he saw us he jumped up and met us on the side walk. Turned out that Willy was being retired by the city. Willy said he never thought that he wouldn't being going to the bar every day. He always thought the bar as his own. We didn't spend much time with him but I knew that the only thing that could cheer him up was his old job back. Cat knew what I was thinking and before I said it, she did. Get Willy's job back!

From there Cat and I would make one last stop. We would pass by Martha's mom's house. Just as soon as Mary saw Cat and I she started crying. Its all your fault she said wiping the dripping tears, you and your launch business she said. Clam down mam she'll be back soon. No Mary said she's gone for good. I informed Mary that I was searching for the boat that Martha had left on and that once I found it, I would go and see if she's ok. Mary just stood and walked to her bedroom and shut the door.

From there Cat delivered me to the airport where Tommy was waiting with the news that Lori, with the kids were now in Jena's apartment. Big Ted had personally picked them up from the airport and got them settled in. That news was good to hear but I was bothered that even Bob couldn't find that Saudi phantom yacht. A yacht of that size shouldn't have been so hard to track.

CHAPTER II

THE ARRIVAL OF LORI

The flight from Nassau was short and Olga from our Miami Terminal was there to pick me up. She dove me straight to the apartment. Standing outside the door was one of Ted's men. I knocked and Lori opened the door. To tell the truth I hadn't remembered her beauty until that very moment. Lori waited until I shut the door behind me to jump into my arms. As she kissed me she expressed how scared she was until now. The children were watching their first cartoons on TV. They both walked toward me while not taking their eyes off the TV. That was until Lori scolded them. Lori said how beautiful my house was, I told her that we were barrowing this place until we could find something that met their needs. I explained about Chubby and his wife and they all would meet them tomorrow. Olga was kind enough to volunteer to spend tonight and tomorrow night with the children. Jena's closet was full of clothes, some I was sure she had never worn, the only pair of dress clothes Lori had were her black pleated pants. I opened Jena's closet and started looking. Who is this woman that has so many nice things Lori asked? Is she your wife? Actually she is a witch I said, but she's a friend and no she's not my wife. I looked through many of the dresses but none stood out or the ones that did, I figured the waist line was two sizes too big.

There was a knock on the door, Olga was here. We introduced Olga to the kids and I told the kids that their sister would be back in the morning. I took Lori's hand and went out the door. Lori started toward the elevator but I pulled her the other way. I pulled out my key and stuck it in the next door down. I opened the door and turned off the alarm.

Jena's apartment was nice but mine was nicer and bigger. I turned on the air-condition and opened the balcony doors and curtains. I walked to my bed and pulled back the spread and top sheet. I walked to Lori and started taking off her shirt and kissing her. Once I had her with just her bra and panties on, I walked showing her my second set of drawers and the closet. Then I walked her into the girl's room. Here I said we can find something you'll like for the night, tomorrow we will go shopping. Who lived here she asked? I use to live here I said. This was Karen and Evette's room and that's mine. And who lived with you she asked. A mix I said. A mix of what she asked? Girls I said. Three sisters, Deanna, Janie, and Cat. Jena for a while, and my first wife for a short time. Where is your wife right now she asked? I pointed to the clothes and said to try on something that she liked. I went to my closet and found a black suit and red silk long sleeve shirt. When I looked back at Lori, she had one of my all-time favorite long black short sleeved dresses. This dress would have been here since when Cat or maybe even Janie first came to live with me. Lori put it on and it looked like magic. Now I came to her and dropped the dress and took her hand and led her to my shower.

From the shower it was dress time, Lori found everything she needed. She tried on high heel shoes that she couldn't walk in. When she was ready and me only in my pants I walked her into the closet safe and started to open it. Once opened, I stepped back and pushed her inward. See if you can find anything in here that catches your fancy, Lori stepped in and I walked out. I then stepped back in and said not to touch the guns as they were loaded. I went to finish dressing and when I came back she was still looking. Is all this real she asked? Yes of course I said, Lori said she liked this one and held it out in her hand. Bring it here I said. She walked into the bathroom in front of the mirror. I stepped behind her and took the neckless and placed it on her chest and hooked it behind her neck. I then took a rubber band of some kind that the girls used and made a pony tail of her hair. It wasn't right so she removed it and did it again. Not perfect but it looked good. The gems and diamonds sparkled as did her dark eyes. As she looked in the mirror I could see the satisfaction with her new look. I went back into the safe and found a diamond solitary and put it on her Finger. That looks good for now I said. She looked at the ring and smiled. She put on her new black shoes and she was ready to go. I splashed on some lagerfeld and relocked the safe. Lori wanted the children to see her, she also wanted to use a dash of her perfume.

When we knocked on the door and went in the children said that Lori looked like a princess. Olga said her mother would watch the children while she worked tomorrow.

Lori and I would go down to the lobby where the valet would bring around my car. We would eat at the Studio while I explained to Lori what my plan for the children and her was. She would be working hard every day! She would have privet lessens for everything. Reading, spelling, writing, math, swimming, sailing, scuba diving, sports, and how to be when necessary a lady which meant walking in high heels. The children would be sent to public school and learn the American way. They will have everything they need. I told Lori about my plan of buying a house in which a friend and his wife, if they agreed, would be their care takers. The three of them would live there unless I was in town or sent for her. We had desert and went home.

The next morning, I got up and fixed coffee, as I sat out on the east balcony, Lori came to me and said that she would do as I asked. She said she would be my women and do whatever whenever I asked. I don't want you to lose your sprit, you are and will be your own person. You will be given all that you need to choose your own life when the time comes. You will still be a young lady when your brother goes into collage. It seems like a long time but we will keep you busy. Lori took my hand and pulled me back to bed.

We got the children ready, stopped at Denny's for breakfast and then dropped the children at Chubby's. We said we'd be back before 5:00 p.m. Chubby said to take our time.

First we drove through my Dad's neighborhood, we found a nice three bedrooms two bath home with a pool. The yard had space that one day if needed we could add on a room. The pool would need fencing until the kids, including Lori, learned to swim. The school zone was that of the same schools that I attended. Lori liked the house and I gave the realtor a cash offer. This was the house that I would buy. Lori then asked what if those people, meaning Chubby and his wife, didn't want them. I just said that things would work out. We then went to Levitz and purchased furniture for Lori's and the kid's bedrooms. I would let Chubby and his wife pick out the rest. Then we went to Burdines. We bought some clothes for the kids but most of what we purchased was for Lori. I didn't know too much about kids toys but we also bought some small items. We ate lunch at the 1800 club, it hadn't changed much but most of the girls that I knew had moved on. Billy and Jan were still there and both came and spoke with me.

From there we drove back to Chubby's and found that this seemed like it was going to work out. I would only be staying one more night. Tim's wife would be the one setting up things for Lori. The furniture and toys were on hold until the address was secured. That same evening Chubby and his wife followed us to the new house, the real estate women had called Lourdes saying the owners had accepted my offer. That same night I called Lourdes and told her to buy the house.

The kids stayed at Chubby's and Lori and I went back to the apartment, we showered and would dress for a night out. I had forgotten to call and cancel Olga, she showed up and I apologized and said we wouldn't need her. When I came back into the bedroom I saw this beautiful girl. The dress Lori had put on was satin red with a low cut front and back; she was a knockout. I wondered what she would look like coming from the salon. We didn't have any time for that this trip but it was coming. We went to Joe's and were going to have what I thought was a quite dinner. Just as we were seated at the table I saw a hand waving. It was the Iranian General Montibelli. I excused myself to Lori and walked over to his table. Please he said, be seated, I have some news. Thanks but I have a quest that's expecting me back. Mr. Montibelli spoke to the women that was sitting with him in Arabic and she stood and moved toward our table. Don't worry he said she's harmless. Please he said sit. I sat down and asked if she was Iranian? Lebanese he replied, they are the most beautiful women in the world he said. I see you have acquired an Asian taste he said, they too are beautiful. Ah the women of our world he said, what would we do without them?

Well he said I'll come right to the point. Marcos is losing support in Manila, there's a movement called People's Power that is gaining strength. Marco has used that terrible General Santos rebel attack to move his people's thoughts away from him to the Communist rebels. Marco is planning an attack on the rebels and will bring 5 or 6 farmers back to Manilla to stand a very public trial. Even if not guilty, they will be executed. Marcos's own troops will carry in and out a large stash of weapons that the army will say was delivered by Vietnam and China. Marcos hopes this will rally the people behind him.

Marcos like the Shah was, is ill. Montibelli said that Marcos is having dialyses almost daily. Like the Shah he has no clear leader to pass the Dictatorship's power too. It's only a matter of time and if the time was chosen then lives could be saved and the U.S. could look a bit better. Montibelli then set an envelope on the table, it's not tainted he said. I picked it up and put it into my inside jacket pocket. It's a short history of Marcos he said.

I then pulled out an envelope from my other inside jacket pocket and handed it to him. Enclosed is the name of a man and his yacht that I'm looking for. He opened the envelope and said, ha Rasheed, I know this family he said. The name of the yacht is in Arabic; it means King's Man. Rasheed's father was one of the Saudi Kings right hand men. The older Rasheed has passed and his children, that are many, have for the most part shunned their father's ways. This son is most likely in his early thirty's. He and the yacht will be hard to locate as the yacht will not be registered and only the Captain would know the next destination. I will put out the word he said, we will locate this Rasheed. Why do you want him he asked? Rasheed took a girl from Nassau and I want to make sure she is ok. You see he said, It's all about the women, they are all trouble. Please he said send Anna back to me. I stood and thanked him for the information. When I got back to the table Lori asked who the man was? Lori said the women was pleasant but asked a lot of questions. What kind of questions I asked? She asked where I lived and if we were lovers. What did you tell her I asked? I told her the truth, I told her that I live wherever you tell me to and that yes you are my only Love. I looked at her and repeated the word, Love, I thought you were only with me for my body. She smiled and said that too.

We did have a good dinner, Lori liked the stone crabs and the potatoes. We shared a bottle of white wine with me drinking the most of it. She didn't want desert but I had her try the key lime pie. She ate it all! We went straight back to the apartment and the plan was for me to leave the next day at about noon. I wanted to take Lori with me but knew that the children would need her. Besides I wasn't sure how long I would be where.

Things changed when we got home, there were three messages on the phone, first was Bob saying that the Latin professors had deciphered the writing on the door. Including Bob, all three of them had classes tomorrow until 4:00 p.m. Bob said to call him with where to meet. The next call was from Lourdes whom said that Roy's office had called and said the purchase agreements for the Philippines were ready. Roy's office wanted to know where to send the agreements. The third call was Lourdes again saying that a women named June was looking for me and left a phone number.

I listened to the messages out loud and Lori asked about June? I said she was an old girlfriend, how old Lori asked? We were 15 and 16 I said, she had a figure much like yours but not near as pretty. Lori smiled and asked if I would call her? I said no and erased the message.

The first two calls had changed things. I returned Bob's call and he said my apartment would be good, they'd be here tomorrow at 7:00 p.m.

I told Lori that we would, I would be staying at least another day. My first thought was a hair salon for Lori. I called Lourdes and asked her to get Lori an appointment for tomorrow morning.

Lourdes would call me back in the morning as the salon that she used closed at 8:00 PM. I then remember where Karen used to go and knew they opened early. My hair cut was never special, and after my barber, Dave, had retired and moved to the keys, Karen's girls would cut my hair whenever I showed up.

The next morning, we stopped by to see the kids. They were happy to see Lori but seemed to be enjoying Chubby and his wife Lilly. I hadn't ever known Chubby's wife's name but now it was definitely a must.

From there we went to the Salon, I wasn't surprised that it was still there and the girls remembered me. They were all interested in what Karen was up too. I told them that since she had become famous that I didn't hear from her much. The girls then turned their full attention to Lori. It was 9:00 a.m. and they told me to come back in three hours, oh yes and to bring some Cuban coffee. I said not to cut the hair to short and no coloring! I walked to the corner and called Lourdes to let her know that she didn't need to bother with the salon for Lori. Lourdes said that June had called again and this time said it was urgent that you call her. This time I noted the number and said I would call her. I then called the number and June answered. June asked if I was in Miami and with my yes she asked if

I could meet her at the sailing club. June said she had something to show me. I said I'd be there in 20 minutes.

I was there at the club out on the end of the dock when I saw June walking in. It was either my eyes or she looked pregnant. I walked toward her and met her at the docks beginning. She didn't stop, she went right for the kiss. When she stopped kissing me she stepped back, she paused and said she was looking for a boyfriend. I looked her and said it looked like she had already found one, yes she said I found him 18 years ago but lost him, then almost 4 months ago I found him again. I've been pregnant two times in my life she said, both by the same boy. The first time I made a mistake, if I would have kept that baby you would have come back from the military and married me. I love you Jim she said and we are having a baby. I stepped back and looked and then asked if she was sure? Sure I'm pregnant or sure it's yours she asked? Mine I said. She said she was sure. Do you need to sit down she asked? When are you due I asked? She said I'm four months and starting last week I'm on maternity leave. I looked at her and said that I was still married and had a little girl and another on the way. June looked at me and said nothing was going to stop her from having and raising our child. I'm going to move in with my parents she said. This was meant to be she said, I should have had the first child. My parents understand that I'm going to be a single mom. If you don't want to be the father you can be the uncle. But you are the father. June then came at me again and kissed me. I'm the happiest girl in the world she said. Any new girlfriend she asked? Why I asked? I just wanted to know where I stand in the line she said. Well it's nothing new that I do jump around a lot I said. In fact, I'm here in town with a friend. You'll never change she said, your just what my father said you were 18 years ago. It doesn't matter she said I love you and I'm going to have your child. He or she will have a child hood like we did except no privet schools. He or she will learn to sail and fish, maybe spend the summers with their uncle Jim. June started to cry as she talked. She hugged me and said that she hoped to hear from me whenever I could call or see her. With my arm around her we walked to her car. I asked if she needed anything, she looked at me and said that she'd like to spend a weekend just the two of us. Please give me that call, she kissed me again and drove off. I walked back to the end of the dock and just stood there thinking. If when I had got back from the military June would have been there waiting, maybe it could have worked out.

From there I went by Roy's office. Roy was in court but the girl said everything was good to be signed. They had spoken to President Marcos's attorney and they would be waiting for me and the money in Manilla.

My next stop was to buy Cuban coffee and go pick up Lori. When I walked in I couldn't believe my eyes, they, my eyes had to be playing tricks on me. Lori had turned into the most beautiful young lady I had ever seen! Her hair that had been long and stringy was now shoulder length. The makeup that they had put on her changed the way she looked. Her nails had been done with a polish without color. Her toes were now red. Lori looked at me and asked how I liked it. I couldn't help it, I said we were going straight home. She smiled and looked at the girls and said, he likes it. They all laughed. Me I wasn't joking; straight home we went. The afternoon went by quickly; it was almost 7:00 p.m. before we knew it. The knock at the door was at 6:55 p.m. Bob was there with two of his professor friends, all three were professors at the UM. They came right in and I introduced them to Lori, Bob said I was the Devil himself.

The Professors had brought two books with them, one looked every old. The one Professor opened the book and turned to a marked page. There on that page was a drawing of what appeared to be similar to the drawing on our Panther skin. I stood and went to my safe and brought out the rolled up material. I then separated the panther skin and rolled it out. The drawing on the Panther skin almost matched the drawing in the book. In the book the drawing had the Latin word for Teacher written under the drawing. There were many strange drawings in the book but the one besides that one was of a sphere or object that appeared to be suspended in air.

The next book was used for translations. In short the professors said that the Latin translations were directions on how the cell as they put it, should be opened. It seemed that there were two connecting rooms, the second, maybe to be used in case of some kind of an attack. The valves had the words pressure which made me think that maybe these valves were meant to show whether there was water behind the door. Could be that the outside door would need to be open only when the first room was full of water. Once the outside door was opened and then closed, the valves would be used to somehow drain the water from the first room. Once, one was inside the first room and the water was removed, then maybe the second door could be opened. When the first room was without water, the inside pressure would not permit the outside door to open.

I told the professors my theory of these beings, being here for hundreds maybe thousands of years. My theory was that they had come here looking for some kind of sanctuary from some kind of threat. I mentioned the beings that had been discovered in Nicaragua in the Late 1970s. I then pulled out a drawing I had of one of them. I said that these looked to be much bigger, maybe meat eaters. The larger beings had lasers, one for sealing wounds, the other weaponized. I thought that the smaller beings had a vehicle in which they had traveled and it too was weaponized. I said that I thought the smaller beings were not killed off by what they were running from but, were killed by humans.

Bob then said he didn't smell any cooking. Lori said she was sorry but that she would soon be taking lessons. Bob laughed and said it was too bad I couldn't send her to live with Angee. I looked at Bob and said I thought that would be a great idea. Bob said that Lori would have to learn to defend herself first. Lori said she was also going to learn to fight. Lori said that Jim says a good offence sometimes doesn't leave much for the defense. Bob laughed hard at that.

The two Professors looked at me and asked when they could see the inside of these rooms. Well I said they didn't look like they could reach where these rooms were located. However, I would fund any research that they could do to find more information on either being.

It was now almost 9:00 p.m. and we hadn't eaten, we invited Bob and the others to dine at a restaurant but they all said they had an extended school day ahead.

Me leaving tomorrow, we ordered pizza and stayed in. Once Lori had a nightgown on she came to me and showed me that the girls had pierced her ears. Lori said the girls said that if I didn't like it, the holes would grow back closed. I got up and went to the safe and picked out a set of earrings that I would first soak in alcohol and then put in her ears. These earrings don't match your ears, but they should do until we get some. The earrings were each a one-carat diamond that, with her hair the way it was cut, couldn't be seen.

We finally got to sleep and the next morning, while Lori was still sleeping, I called Cat. I asked Cat to travel with me to Manilla, I would sign the contracts, and she'd get the payments done. We had alerted our Cayman bank and Cat could do the transfer from Manilla. Yes, this could have been done in Nassau or states side, but I wanted Cat to also visit Japan with me. We planned to fly into Manila then on to Tokyo then back to Manila, and on to General Santos. Cat would be staying only one night in General Santos and taking Evette out with her. Evette said that she had now trained Nilo's son Erick to work the telex machine, do container controls and estimates. Tim had been working on a computer program that could communicate by telex and it could be ready soon. Tim and Lourdes would travel to General Santos with the computers and all the progrming the shipping line would need. Lourdes would stay in General Santos for a few weeks training Nilos's son and others on the computer.

I called Lourdes and sent Tommy to pick up Cat. I would meet them at Opa-Lock at noon today.

Lori was now up and we would shower, go eat and then stop by Miami Diamond. I locked up all the things that I had browed from the safe and we carried a small bag with Lori's new things.

Once at Miami Diamond I purchased some relatively inexpensive jewelry that was pretty yet wouldn't standout too much.

Lori was thrilled that she now had these items of her own. Frankly she looked to damn good with her new look and this stuff. I had taken a better than average looking teenager and turned her into his beautiful young Lady. Well maybe not the Lady part yet but she would get there.

I then dropped Lori off at Chubby's and Lilly's house. Chubby had all the contact information and money that he needed. Things would start happening quite fast for them. House moving and getting all three in classes.

I said my good byes with hugs and Kisses for all. Lori walked me to the car and was concerned when she would see me again. I told them not to worry, she'd be staying busy, and the time would fly by.

CHAPTER III

MY MARCOS VISIT

I then went to the airport where Cat, Lourdes and Tommy were waiting. Tommy wouldn't be taking us all the way, Cat, Lourdes and I would fly commercially from Chicago. Tommy would be needed to be close by.

We caught a flight the next morning from Chicago that would get us into Manilla by the next evening. We would stay at the Manilla Hilton and then Cat and I would meet President Marcos the next morning. This trip Cat had luggage. Lourdes would fly on into General Santos and do some additional training with Eric.

Cat said the she had spoken with and convinced the city that Willy was needed at the city bar. Willy could work the hours he wanted.

On the morning of our Philippines Presidential visit, Cat was dress as good as I had ever seen her, she had put on a few pounds but if you didn't know her you would have only noticed her beauty and great curves.

I did want to talk to Marcos about the rebels but not until our transactions had been completed. We met the Attorney first, signed the paperwork that was already signed by Marcos. Cat would then excuse herself and visit the bank, Cat had gone to this same bank not so long ago. I would wait for Cat to return with paperwork showing the transfer conformation.

While there waiting, Marcos appeared, Marcos was being pushed in a wheel chair and looked pale. I stood and introduced myself. Marcos said he was expecting someone much older. He said he was young once but was now getting old. He thanked me for purchasing his company and hoped that I would stay with the same name. I told him I had no intentions of changing the name.

Marcos talked about his people, he sounded sincere but I thought from what I had seen and read that he was a good talker. Actions I thought worked much better than words. When I got my chance, I asked if he would let me speak with and maybe negotiate with the rebels. He shook his head no. No he said, what they need is a good lesson he said. Don't worry young man he said we won't let them block your fruit from reaching the port. I asked again this time in a different manner. You might be seen as a wiser man if peace could be made without any further loss of life, I said. No he said. I will crush them once and for all, you will see he said, I will crush them. Well he said I must go take care of important matters. He wished me luck and was rolled away.

It was another three hours before Cat returned. The transfer had been made and we were given our originals contracts with what was a box of signed deeds. It was quite a bunch of paperwork that Cat and I hadn't planned on moving around. I decided rather than move this box with us to Tokyo we'd drop the boxes to DHL. The contracts we would keep with us.

Our flight out to Tokyo wasn't until tomorrow, we'd go back to the hotel and go for a swim. Cat didn't seem to have that normal pep in her swim but I nor did Cat mention anything. We ate there at the Hotel and visited the Hotel's disco after dinner. Cat looked tired so we made an early night of it. There was no question about my shower.

The next morning, we flew to Tokyo where we checked into the Hotel and later would be picked up by our Host and taken to a fine restaurant. Mr. Micthocomi had brought his wife and oldest son along. He said we would not talk business but wanted for us to get to know one another. Cat looked exceptional and did most of the talking pleasing Mrs. Micthocomi but not Mr. Micthocomi. The son said that in his father's world women were to be seen but not heard. The son and Mrs. Micthocomi smiled at that but Mr. Micthocomi scolded both of them in Japanese. We had a nice dinner and Cat and I were dropped back at the hotel. Tomorrow a limo would pick us up at 8:30 a.m. and take us to their fish plant.

That night we had our great shower and went to bed. It must have been 5:00 a.m. that I heard Cat vomiting in the bathroom. She and I had eaten the same meal so I thought it was something else. I checked her forehead and ruled out a fever. Cat said she would be fine. Cat came back to bed but for only a short time and right back to the bathroom. Cat didn't look well but we both were ready for the 8:30 a.m. ride.

Once at the plant, just as soon as we got out of the limo and the fish smell hit us, Cat started to have the dry heaves. I asked if she was ok and she now didn't say yes nor did she look good. I asked the driver to take her back to the Hotel.

Young Mr. Micthomoi was the one that walked me through the plant. They also canned tuna along with other products. In my mind, I pictured their machines working in our General Santos Factory. From the tour we were driven back to town to the main office. Everything was impressive. Mr. Mitchomoi seem much friendlier. His son committed that it was because I hadn't brought Cat along. Mr. Mitchomoi had lots and lots of numbers. We did a lot of talking, at one point he stopped and pointedly asked if I was responsible for the sinking of his fishing vessel in Davao? Without hesitation I said yes. He smiled and told his son in Japanese that I was an honest, honorable man. His son then looked at me and told me what his father had said. The Father stood and extended his hand and said we have an agreement. It was September, according to my partners we should be shipping our first canned tuna from General Santos by March or April of 1986. Our plan would be to ship 20 20-foot dry containers per week. Sales should be right at $3,000,000.00 per month.

I left their office by 4:00 p.m. and went straight back to the hotel. What a day Cat had missed. When I open the hotel room door Cat looked like the cat that had the canary in its month.

Cat was only wearing her nighty, I asked if she was sick she stood and came to me and said she was pregnant. His or mine I asked? Ours she said, ours. She then came in my arms and hugged me not letting go. Still holding on she asked if I was mad with her. Well I said just as long as you're willing to share, all will be alright. Of course Cat had no idea what I meant by share but she would understand soon enough. I then kissed her and carried her back to bed. I told Cat that I didn't want Jacob or any man to be with her again. Cat said she would move into the Nassau apartment that was over our Nassau's store, this until she settled things with Jacob.

Once things settled down I told Cat that we were now partners with the Japanese in the canned tuna business. I told her that to make all this work we would need to help settle the conflict between the Marcos Government and the rebels. Cat asked if I had a plan and I said yes but I hoped that I had enough time. Cat said she didn't want to see a Doctor and I wasn't sure I wanted her to reach General Santos. Cat chose to go. The next morning, we were on our way back to Manila. The not so good part about this was the travel delays. We missed our flight to Cebu and would need to stay overnight in Manila. This would put us a day behind schedule.

The next day we arrived in General Santos at about 4:00 p.m. Nilo was there at the airport to get us. We dove straight to the factory so that Cat could lie down in the air-conditioning. Since I was there last, the office or apartment now had a bathroom with hot water. Nilo then drove me to the office where Evette was getting ready to leave. Eric was there with Lourdes, they would be there for some time as we had a ship that would be docking the next morning at 2:00 a.m. I spoke to the men, and they all agreed that we needed another ship, now not later. Last week we left 24 refrigerated containers with fruit. This week that number would grow to 40. By next week we could be short on equipment and electric. Evette was still here, and I had her send a telex to Robin asking about the availability of another ship, maybe 150 more reefers, and six more ISO fuel tanks. The extra equipment could cost well over $500,000.00 per month. I had Evette also send caterpillar a telex requesting three more generators.

Evette didn't seem happy with Cat being here, seemed I had promised her something that I could now not deliver. Cat didn't tell Evette she was pregnant but Evette figured it out. Evette and Cat would leave the following day just as I had planned. The ship was here working and only Nilo took them to the airport. Cat said that she may stay a Few days in Miami. Evette said she'd be glad to get back to New Orleans. A good meal and men she said. While Cat was sitting in the rover, I kissed Evette and gave her a pat on the rump. You deserve a big fat raise and a paid vacation. Where to Evet asked? Some nice Caribbean Island I said. Cat said ok girlfriend get that butt of yours in this rover. Evette looked at me as if I hadn't kept my promise. If we would have been alone as I was sure she would have gotten what she wanted. I smiled as they drove off, I thought of me having four children all within a year of each other. Then I thought, and four women too. Then the thought hit me, four women and sleeping by myself again. Not every well-coordinated of me. I would go in and change my clothes and walk to the port.

Everyone seemed glad to see me, most called out, Captain Jim. Once in the Container yard I started checking refrigerated container temperature settings and temperatures. Most of these containers were loaded with fresh fruit such as Bananas and some, a greater number each week were loaded with prawns. All the cargo I checked were either good or our people were working on them. Even new units sometimes had problems. Of the 72 units we originally found that had been cannibalized we either changed out the refrigeration unit with a new one or rebuilt them, only 5 of those containers were unsalvageable. Those 5 had physical damages that were too costly to repair. Those five containers would be used to build offices or storage boxes.

I worked the entire ship and was exhausted. By working alongside the men, one could see how hard they all worked.

Once the ship was loaded and had departed, myself and Lourdes got some sleep. The next day I would get up early and wash the blood from the exterior office wall. Joe-Anne had paid the heaviest of prices.

I would cross the river to find Ninong. I rode across with a truck transporting an empty reefer to a farm. We crossed the river by means of men helping by tying lines on to the bumper and pulling us across through the river's moving water. The truck that I was traveling in was not stopped at the first rebel post nor the second. As we passed through the second post, I asked the driver to stop. He did and I got out with my hands high in the air. I immediately got lots of attention. They took both guns and pointed me to that same big tree. I sat there for most of the day, I watch as the trucks passed full to the south and empty to the north. I kept a mental count of how many rebels and what kind of arms they each were carrying. I hadn't ever traveled any further to the north except to visit the farms, but it seemed that at least in the day time the rebel's numbers were limited, fewer than 50. I saw no big guns other than one 50 Caliber that was sitting within the tree line covering the road coming from the south.

It was after 5:00 p.m. when Ninong showed up by much the same means that I had arrived. A truck with a loaded reefer container stopped and he jumped out of the passenger side door. There was a women sitting in the middle of the truck that I thought I recognized, it looked like she was talking with Ninong when he exited the truck. It might have been chit chat but it looked like more. Ninong was still wearing that mask of his.

I hadn't seen Ninong since I crossed the river that night and met him in the fishing village, he spoke with the guard and walked over with my guns, one in each hand. He then turned and yelled to bring water. As he got close to me he apologized for the wait and handed me one gun then the other then held out his hand. We shook hands and then I received a surprised hug and pat on the back.

I told him that the Coronel and the Japanese were no longer a threat but that Marcos was planning something big. Ninong said that removing one Coronel for another would not solve the problem, maybe only slow it down. The same with the Japanese he said, they will still come and rob our fishermen of their catch.

You are correct about the Coronel I said but the Japanese will not be back, at least not to rob your people of their catch of prawns. I told Ninong of the agreement that I had made with the Japanese. The old fish factory will be rebuilt and enlarged I said. This will create 100s, if not 1000, jobs for your people. The water came and Ninong sat on the ground with his legs crossed. As I drank water, Ninong pulled out a pack of Lucky cigarettes. He shook the open pack against his hand and out jumped a few. He held the pack out to me. No thanks, I said; he put one in his mouth and then lit it using an old steel case lighter. Ninong then looked at me and said our people. He gave me one of those rough smiled and said he knew that I had taken Lori, her brother and sister. You must educate her and bring them back one day Ninong said, maybe with a son to keep your name living. Lori is a hard working girl that will make a good leader one day. Do bring her back he said.

I did not talk of Lori, I changed the subject back to Marcos's plan. Ninong didn't seem worried, let them cross the river he said and we will crush them all. Their army is not well trained and the soldiers have nothing to gain by fighting us. They know that their leaders are corrupt and only care about money. I said we should concentrate on a solution, he interrupted and said that Marcos must go. I told him that Marcos was sick that I had seen him the week before. Ninong said Marcos's death wouldn't come soon enough. Ninong repeated his promise not to go south across the river but he said Manilla was to the north. As Ninong talked there was clearly a hatred in his voice. I reached into my pants and pulled out the first pack of money, as I handed it to him I said it was the third month's farmer's money. He most likely didn't want to hear it but I told him anyway. Marcos no longer owns the farms I said. I will keep my word about the land I said. I then took out the last pack of money and said it was to be used to open some kind of clinic. Before he could take the money I warned him not to use the money for the fight against Marcos. I told him that within the coming weeks there would be a clinic in the city. It would only be staffed with a Doctor and one nurse. The service would be free to anyone that couldn't afford it.

I could tell Ninong didn't know what to say, he did smile and say that he hoped that my car didn't run into a tree. He then smiled one more time. Ninong yelled to one of his men to stop the next truck, this to give me a ride back to the city.

We worked all the week and serviced the next ship. Eric was working the telex almost all day, every day. Today one of our C-130s should arrive with Tim, Doctor Rodriguez, Nurse Rebeca and the replacement men. The C-130 would also have two more Generators, more parts, medical supplies for our new clinic and our new computer. I had rented a small older building in the center of town for the clinic. Nino had several volunteers clean and paint the place. Tim's computer would be permanently located at the fruit companies office on the port. Tim would join Lourdes and I in my apartment. Nilo drove to the airport and came back with Tim and Jerry. The bird had landed as they would say. Jerry would go back with Nilo with trucks following to load up the inbound men and equipment. The men that were going home were packed and ready. The C-130 was unloaded and the men returning home loaded up. Jerry again said he could stay but I sent him back. The plane took off and we were working to get things hooked up.

Having two new generators and me ordering more reefers meant that we could store up to 100 more loads. This would give us more time to get production up to what we would need to bring in that third ship.

The Fruit Company's prawn supply had jumped 10%, this without any increase in production. Mr. Partridge admitted that I was right about stopping the pirates. This 10% would enable The Fruit company to reach and exceed their goals. The Fruit company shipping one more prawn refer containers per week meant over $500,000 a month in additional revenue for them. Our only monthly prawn increase would be additional sales of just over $20,000. The $20,000 gain was nothing compaired to the sales increase that an additional ship would bring.

Mr. Partridge said that Mr. Bozzni of Standard Fruit wanted me to come to visit him at their U.S. headquarters in San Francisco during the third week of October. This was only three weeks away; I didn't see that happening.

Within a week Tim had everything wrapped up and was heading back. Lourdes said she would stay on but I didn't want her to be away from her children any longer, so I had her go back too. Besides I had been sleeping by myself for too long and she was starting to look good.

The Clinic had opened and was serving the general public. Every day there were lines of people.

The next morning Eric gave me a telex from Bob saying it was urgent that I catch the next flight to Washington DC, to telex him back and he'd meet me there.

That same afternoon I was on my way to Davao then Cebu. While in the airport waiting to catch my transfer flight in Cebu, I heard gun fire, not just a few rounds but hundreds of rounds. Seemed that the airport was under attack from someone. What I saw was the regular army retreating and what looked like the rebels walking right in. Just as soon as I heard the shooting and was sure what was going on, I went into the women's bathroom and took my guns off and put them in the trash can under a bunch of papers. I then went and sat where I had been. Within moments the rebels came taking everyone's papers and, of course, my passport too. The rebel's where not threatening, they were talking about how corrupt Marcos was.

The shooting now at a distance lasted another 3 or 4 minutes, then it stopped. Two minutes later, in came none other than that mask-wearing Ninong himself. Ninong came right to me and asked his men where my guns were? The men said I had none. Ninong looked around and told his men to look everywhere, they are here he said. I said they were in the women's bathroom in the trash rapped in paper. Ninong looked at his man and said go. The man brought my guns back and handed them to Ninong, Ninong then handed them to me. Ninong looked at me and said, go to your Washington and tell them that I can reach Manilla just as easily. Ninong then looked at the rest of the passengers and said that the rebels were the people's army who would rid the Philippines of Marcos. Almost interrupting his words, more gun firing could be heard in the back ground. Two of Ninong's men came running up and gave some kind of signal. Ninong then looked back at me and said, tell them it won't be much longer. All of the collected papers and my passport were then thrown on the floor. Then Ninong and his men trotted off. As they left a loud explosion was heard. I went to the pile of papers and retrieved my passport.

Within minutes the regular army was back at their posts.

A lieutenant came through asking questions, one of the passengers pointed to me. The lieutenant then came to me and asked for my passport and then asked if I was armed? I slowly handed him my side holster gun and then the man that had pointed me out yelled that I had two guns. I then gave up my leg gun and the Lieutenant asked me to come with him.

As we walked through the small airport I could see that the rebels had blown up a small army post. There was a jeep outside and the lieutenant pointed me to get in. I said that I wasn't to miss my flight. The drive was short and we arrived at a much larger Military office. A Major then questioned me as to what the Rebel leader and I talked about. If you ask your lieutenant I said, he should have told you that I didn't speak not one word to the rebels other than to tell them where my guns were. What did the rebel say he asked? Well, I said, much the same as he told the others, that Marcos wouldn't be in power much longer, that's all. You have business in General Santos he asked? Yes, I said I have business and farms. The witnesses said that the rebels seemed to know you, the Major said. I trust the witness that your lieutenant spoke with mentioned that the rebel that did the talking was wearing a masks. Now I said, I do need to make my Manila flight, if not please call my embassy and let them know you are holding me. You are carrying a large amount of money the Major said. Yes, I said, your ministry is aware of my money and my guns. I could see the Major didn't want to let me go but I was also sure he knew exactly who I was. He looked at the Lieutenant and said in Filipino to take me back to the airport. He handed me my passport and I was taken to the airport. Before exiting the jeep, my guns were also returned.

Turned out that I made my flight including the one out of Manilla that same night. Eric was the only one that knew that I was heading to Washington. I wondered if I could get Evette to come back as I needed someone here that I could trust.

Once in Manila after taxing from the National airport to the International airport I had called home and asked Salinas if she was up to flying to DC to meet me there. Salinas of course said yes. Salinas would also bring me some fresh clothes. Salinas and the family were still located in Nassau.

By the time I arrived in DC, Salinas was there already checked into the hotel and waiting. The reunion was great. Salinas was now well into her 3rd month and wasn't showing as I thought she would be. She did look great! I told her she better keep up with her food intake as that boy in there would be hungrier than Michelle was. I was only at the Hotel one hour before Bob called to see if I had made it in and to say we were to go directly to the White House. Salinas asked if she had heard me right? Your being seen by the President of the United States? Yes, I said. Why Salinas asked? What does he want from you? I'll let you know when I get back I said. We took a hot shower, I dressed, leaving my guns, kissed her and off I was.

Bob met me in the lobby, we got in the limo that was waiting, and headed to, Yes, The White House. Bob said that he was briefly briefed, that this was all about General Santos and the rebels. I told Bob about my Cebu experience and he said that the new news wasn't good.

Bob and I were received at The White House security gate and entered the White House, and escorted to the Presidents Waiting Room. Within minutes the Coronel appeared then the CIA Director. Business was not talked about. We talked about non-important things like fishing.

Forty-Five minutes down the line we were asked into the Oval office. The President entered at about the same time as we all did.

Be seated gentlemen the President said. He looked at me and said, Jim let's start with you. What's going on in General Santos? I suppose you mean with the rebels I asked? Yes, he said. Well on my way here, the Cebu airport was attacked by Ninong, them knowing that I was on my way here. I mentioned that Nino's son had received Bob's message and most likely he passed it to Ninong. The scary part, I said was how Ninong and his men could have gotten to Cebu so fast. They were, I said, only maybe an hour behind me. Ninong could have men stationed in Cebu, but I doubted that. There must be some kind of airstrip on one of the farms, I said. The Director said I should fire Nilo's son, I said I'd keep him to use for a later date. What I think, gentlemen is that Ninong was telling us that they could reach Manilla if they wanted. What do the rebels want The President asked? They want Marcos and the army out of their hair I said. Do you think we can trust this Ninong the President asked? Yes, I said. The Director then jumped in saying that even if we could, and he didn't believe so, what if Ninong was replaced with a more radical leader? My answered back saying that my Dad always said that if a frog had wings it wouldn't bump it's butt every time it landed from a jump. The President then laughed.

The President then said that Marcos is planning to go into General Santos and declare Marshall Law. Marcos has asked us for six tanks and air support. I didn't interrupt but when he finished I said that I had met with Marcos and he looked in poor health. I said that I felt the National elections in February if illegal, would go badly for Marcos and it would be a mistake for us to further back Marcos. I understand the importance of our two military bases that are supported by Marcos, however should he be overthrown by a group that didn't want us there, then what? The President asked what I suggested? Make an agreement with Ninong and if and when Marcos is voted out, we should move Marcos to retirement. The Director said making an agreement with a small group of communist rebels would send a poor signal to our allies and other rebel groups. The President then said he'd think about it and make a decision within two weeks. Jim he said I trust you can stick close by until then. Yes sir. Ok then how are we doing with our Andros project the President asked? I said that the construction was ahead of schedule and that the Navy was presently moving the first test design to Andros to see just how much Lusca likes Florida Crawfish. I explained how the lights could attract Lusca to his death by explosion.

What about this door your divers found that Bob has told us about? I looked over at Bob and said that due to the distance from the cave's entrance, going that route under water it could be some time before divers could be down there long enough to work on opening the door. I told the President that we would figure out something. The President then said he'd appreciate us letting at least one of the Colonel's men in on the dive when we opened that door. I looked at the Colonel and then back to the President and said that it had taken our men almost six months to prepare to get where we are today. Looking at the Colonel I asked if he did any scuba diving? I purposely did not answer the President. The President then stood and thanked me for coming on such short notice. We all, of course, stood when he did, and we all walked out after he exited.

Me, I was ready to go see Salinas, but I first wanted to reem Bob. As we walked out, Bob said it wasn't him. Bob then said that one of the newer divers had been keeping The Director informed. Bob said that Jack had already fired him. I then asked Bob if they knew about the Latin writings and what it said. Bob said that only he and I knew that part. And just why were you here I asked Bob? The Director wanted me here to help them with you he said. Big help I was Bob said.

I told Bob that we were just days from being able to work on opening the Door. I though you just said that it was just about impossible at this time. No, I said the distance from the entrance of the cave to dive that far was too much at this time, meaning, to scuba all that way it couldn't be done at this time. Lee has cut a hole directly over the cave where the door is located. The hole is now covered with a 40-foot container with a trap door in the floor. The hole has a ladder from the top ground to the bottom of the cave's floor. When we go in, it will be without any Government personal.

As we rode in the limo Bob asked when we would bait the trap for Lusca. I said that the Navy's ship had left Miami last night. Bob invited Salinas and I to dinner and I said I'd take a rain check.

When I got to the hotel room Salinas was sound asleep. I took off my suit and joined her in bed.

The next morning, she woke me up early. We showered and I asked her what she wanted to do. Salinas said she wanted to stay in bed all day with me. We talked about my presidential visit and the new Tuna business, and General Santos politics. I said I'd be closer to home for a couple of weeks, spending several days on Andros. I said she was welcome to come to Andros with me. Salinas asked if I could work days at Andros and fly back to Nassau at night. I said I'd do my best.

The next morning, we flew to Nassau with Tommy. I got to spent some time with Michelle. Salinas stuck with me like glue, even my visit to see

Willy, she went along. Somehow I just thought that she knew about Cat's pregnancy. At Willy's I was hoping that Willy didn't know about Cat's condition or at least he wouldn't mention it. Willy was his old self, only talking about the old days. I told him that I had just seen Bob dressed in a business suit. Willy said I should have taking a photo. I had told Salinas not to mention my visit with the President. Out of the blue Salinas asked Willy if he had seen Cat as of late. Willy said he had seen her just this morning doing something on the boats. She didn't stop in. Willy said she just waved as she passed by.

Salinas didn't have any complications this time, she said she would have this baby here in Nassau. That's what you would like she asked, a Bahamian son? I said anywhere her having another girl or boy will be great for me. Salinas saying it the way she did, I figured she had to know.

The next day I few to Andros, we would fill the trap for Lusca with live crawfish and see what happened when we dropped it over. It was 10:00 p.m. when the Navy dropped the trap over, not ten minutes passed when the trap exploded. The Navy ship's sonar had picked up something moving to the trap and whatever it was, after the explosion it disappeared. Within minutes there were sharks everywhere. Looked like they were feeding on something, I hoped it was Lusca.

It was midnight when I got back to the Hill Top beach house in Nassau. Salinas was still up when I got home, as I got in bed, she asked me if Cat's baby was mine. I didn't hesitate, I said yes. Salinas only said two words as she turned away, I only heard," That Bitch".

The next morning, I got up and returned to Andros. Not being sure of the results of the explosion, that same day, I called my brother and asked him to build another trap.

CHAPTER IV

BEHIND THE CAVE'S DOOR

Today Jack and I were going down to possibly open the cave door. The container used to disguise the access hole was perfect, it had a trap door and a side door. The trap door could be opened when needed it and when closed one wouldn't notice it was even there. Lee had now moved an additional 40-foot container next to the original one. Both containers having sliding side doors that faced each other allowing the access from one container to the other. The second container that was placed had all the gear that we would need.

Only Jack and I would suit up and go down the ladder. Jack was the first one down the hole. Then I passed what we might need down to him, I then followed. We both knew there was some risk but the thought of what might be in there overcame the fear. Besides, we didn't even know if it would still work whatever it was. Jack turned one set of door valves while I turned the other. As we turned the valves we could hear water moving. It wasn't like I thought. The room behind the door was apparently void of water, it was now being filled so we could open the door without pressure. Once the room was filled with water we felt the door shift. We then turned the biggest wheel and the door began to open. The only lights were what we had brought down with us. We entered the room, I knew that we would need to close the door so that the pumps wherever they were could then pump the water out. I was hesitant of closing the door behind us as we couldn't be sure it would or even could be opened again. The controls on the inside of the door were much like the ones on the outside. I closed the door and Jack and I again turned the valves. With the door shut, we turned the valves and water started to be pumped out, my ears popped as if I was diving deeper. I held my nose and blew out and again felt my ears pop. The water drained completely out. We had extra lights that we set up, before we stopped using our oxygen, I used a tester that indicated oxygen in the room at 20%. I took off my mask and Jack did the same. It felt strange to be able to freely talk with Jack. Our attention quickly turned to the next door. Here there was only one wheel that I tried but it seemed locked. I remembered the sphere that the Navy had asked Joe and I to open. I had brought with me a small tool pouch that I thought just might come in handy. I told Jack to watch the time and the oxygen level. We had taken down with us enough air for 1.5 hours each. We had told Lee and the other divers that we would come back up before that mark. We now weren't using our air but the men up top didn't know that.

I started poking thin rods into several holes that were near the wheel. When pushing the small rod into one such hole, I felt the rod push something in. I took a file and filed a cut into a rod that maybe just maybe this other hole had something that needed to be pulled instead of pushed. I tried but couldn't get it, I did some more filing and tried again this time catching something and when pulling it toward me, we heard a click. I looked at Jack and both of us started turning the wheel. The door seemed free and we pulled it open. To our surprise we heard some kind of, maybe electric motor start and lights came on in each room. As we stepped in we could see it was like a control room. It looked like some kind of flight control station. I knew right away what it was but didn't say a word. The room was small, there were selves of what looked like some kind of jarred food. There was what I was also sure was a small desalt plant. There was a canvas type cover that I pulled back. It was all hard to believe but what I now saw was so real. There were stacks of what I was sure were gold bars, hundreds of bars. Jack looked at me and asked if our original agreement was still good. I said yes and that he and the other three drivers could now be rich, well I said just as soon as we get this stuff out of here. The gold would have to be moved by hand into the center room then filled with water then carried up into the container. We had now been gone 70 minutes. I walked to the stacks and started moving bars. I figured we would see how much we could move in 15 minutes. Both myself and Jack moved gold bars. When our time was up we closed the door behind us leaving most of the gold, put on our scuba gear and turned the valves to refill the first room with water. As the room filled the electric motor stopped and the lights went out. When the room was full of water we opened the outside cave door and startling us was two of the other divers. They thought we were cutting it to close. We left the door open and all went up the ladder. I should have been tired but I wasn't, it was the adrenalin. We told the others of the gold and this time the five of us would go down and move all the gold out into the cave. We had two of our Haitian military dressed as locals guarding the doors of the container. Lee would go out and find something to use to bring up the gold. Jack and I changed our double tanks and were again ready. One diver would wait in the cave just in case. The rest of us did what we had to, to move the gold from the second room into the first. Once it was all in the first room the rest was easy. We all went up and rested only 30 minutes, changed tanks and were ready once again. Lee had now returned with baskets and line. We would do two men down and three up. Lee would also take a turn on the up side. In just over two hours we hauled the gold from the bottom of the cave to the container. The divers and I had now been working 11 hours. I went down and shut the outside cave door. This time we removed the ladder and sealed the hole with a pre-cut steel plate and shoveled dirt on top, and then shut the container's trap door. We still were not done, while the hole was being sealed the others were once again moving the gold bars from one container to the other. 3 hours later we were finished. We all walked out and shut and locked the container door behind us. Lee had the crane lift the container with the gold and set it on a flat bed. The truck then pulled out and headed to the house. Once at the house, I called Lourdes and gave the order to hire a tug from Miami, travel to Nassau and bring one of our barges to the house dock on Andros. Lourdes said that she had most likely made a terrible mistake but that Salinas had called in the morning and asked for Tommy to carry Salinas, Michelle and her mom to the Chateau in Paix. I hesitated and said to call the tug.

It was now almost morning. I walked to the couch and lied down and fell asleep.

I woke up with the smell of fresh coffee and bacon being fried. I got up and walked to the kitchen where the house woman was cooking up a late breakfast. I hadn't noticed before now but my entire body was sore.

Then I thought about how that happened and I walked out on the balcony to look for the container. No it wasn't a dream, then I thought the part about Salinas leaving wasn't a dream too. Once I had some coffee in me my brain started working again. My mind returned to the control panels in the second room. I had thought then and now that those controls could be used to move the vessel that was on the bottom of the channel. What if this is possible? I somehow knew that it was. The phone brought me back and it was Lourdes confirming that the Tug would reach Nassau by tomorrow evening and be here with the barge by the next morning. I had at least two days before the tug would be here. My four divers could now be very rich but any one of them could get greedy. I called Lourdes back and said that I wanted Tommy to again fly to Paix and retrieve all but two of the new recruits plus Fernando and bring them here with arms and ammunition. This would leave a guard of six men for Salinas and Michelle. Tell Fernando to have three guards on special orders, no one in or out of the Chateau until he returned. I knew that Salinas would think she was being made a prisoner but it would prove to be wrong once Fernando returned. I also asked Lourdes to contact Big Ted and get him here with two men. I then called Bob and told him that he was needed to be in Nassau in three days, no questions asked, it was urgent. Bob said he understood. Lourdes called back informing me that Tommy was in the air bringing Cat to Andros. Lee had gone in to work but the divers had taken the day off. Jack would drive and pick up Cat from the airport, bringing her here to the house.

Cat got here knowing nothing of the gold, only that Salinas had taken Michelle and gone to Paix. Cat said that Salinas told Betty to stay in Nassau but Betty called her and said she wasn't going to let Michelle go without her. Cat said she knew that this was all her fault. No it's not I said. The truth is I have a Philippine girlfriend and then I asked Cat if she remembered June from the sailing club? Well I said June got stood up at her wedding and she spent that night with me. Cat looked at me and said she's not. I said yes she is. And the Philippine Girl Cat asked? No she's good. What do you mean by good Cat asked? I mean she's not pregnant. Cat sat and put her head between her legs. Cat looked up and asked how I had gotten into so much trouble in such a short time. Do you realize you're going to have four children all within a year she asked? Yes, I said the thought has crossed my mind. Well she said the only one that could leave you just did. Now what are you going to do. I'm going to take one day at a time I said. You still going to be my friend and lover I asked? I'll have to think about it she said. I walked to the balcony and looked to the ocean. Cat came and said she thought about it and said she would go to Paix and bring Salinas back. I said if that happened it wouldn't be anytime soon. I looked at her and asked if she still loved me? Cat said she was only planning on sharing me with one not three. Then she said that maybe Salinas should stay in Paix. Then you'd have one in each location, Cat said. She then hugged me and said I should spend more time in Nassau and started to cry.

When Cat stopped crying I told her that the container in the yard had 316 bars of gold inside. The Bahamian Government would get 25%, the divers split 10% and the rest was ours. Cat asked what else was down there. I said I guessed if the cards were played out in our favor, maybe millions more. Cat then reminded me that Salinas wouldn't have any money over there in Haiti. I asked what about the million She had transferred last year. Cat said the money was transferred on Salinas's Hattian passport where her real age is 17, a minor. You are the trustee until she is 21 Cat said. Does Salinas know that I asked? Did you tell her Cat asked? No I said. Well neither did I, Cat said. Cat said the property was listed the same way, it was Salinas's on her 21st birthday. I then called Lourdes and said for her to have someone from Port-au-Prince take $5,000.00 in cash and deliver to Salinas.

I didn't have a copy of the Navy's land lease with the Bahamian Government with me but was sure that it was just that, a land lease with the Navy having zero rights to what was there when they occupied the property listing such as Natural Resources. I was sure that Gold that was put and left there by others would be considered the same as a sunken Treasure. Where there was a question in my mind was about the vessel on the bottom of the channel. To me again it could be looked at as treasure or salvage rights for whoever brought it up from the bottom. I didn't want to alert anyone until we had the gold safety in a Nassau Bank.

With Bob being there, and us having a good track record with the government, the gold should go our way. At this point Nassau didn't look well on how our Navy handled things. The wait made me restless.

I now hadn't seen Lori and the children in quite some time. June too was most likely thinking that I had forgotten her. The way it looked, it would be another 3 or 4 days before we got the gold to Nassau and in the bank. These 3 or 4 days would be spent with Cat, of course I still wasn't sure how that was going to turn out. Cat put in a call and had Mike bring the Chris Craft over to Andros, and I called Lourdes and had Jerry bring on over the C-130 with the big gun; both would serve as escorts for the barge's way back to Nassau with the gold. That night Ted and two men showed up. I told Ted that he was not to make a big deal of it but we would be moving this container to Nassau and it was not to be opened by anyone. For Ted that's all it took. Early the next morning, Fernando showed up with his Haitians, Mike with the Chris Craft and Jerry with the C-130 soon followed. The next afternoon the Tug showed up with the barge. The Tug pushed the barge up to the beach and then Lee had the crane lift off the twenty foot container that was sitting on the barge and then lifted on to the barge the 40-foot container with the gold. The container was locked down and we were ready to go.

After checking the weather we would pull out that night not to be noticed by the Navy. Cat, Ted, his men, myself, and 4 Haitians were on the Chris Craft while another four men were on the Tug. Fernando would go with the rest of his men on the C-130 as he was the only one that could with any accuracy use the 50 caliber gun. The C-130 would fly back and forth over us providing cover as needed. By morning we were half way to Nassau. At noon we had entered Nassau Harbor. The C-130 would now land in Nassau's main airport and once the gold was in the bank, the C-130 would take Fernando and his men back to Paix. Bob received us at the dock. The barge was tied off and the crane lifted the gold container onto the shippings line's dock. Bob almost fell overboard went he saw the gold. It took the rest of the day to move the gold into the bank. This time we didn't use safety deposit boxes as there just wasn't the space. The gold was stacked in the bank's main volt. We didn't lose not one bar.

Ted and his men would fly back the next morning.

Cat was now living between the apartment over the restaurant and or on the Hunter. She visited the children every day once Jacob went to work. I supposed that Jacob wasn't too happy with either of us. I visited Jacob in his office and first asked if they were thinking of a divorce? Jacob said that Cat would soon return to him, he was sure. Jacob said the baby was his, he was also sure of this too. We then talked about the Navy lease. Jacob said the Navy had no rights to whatever was found on or below the ground. Jacob said that whomever brought up the vessel would then be able to claim salvage rights.

I had spent three nights with Cat and things seemed good between us. Tonight I would head to Miami. Cat asked me to stay but she knew I would be going. Then she said the strangest thing, why not bring June here she said.

Bob had done the best he could with the Government for the lowest price. It wasn't much of a negotiation, the government had the weight and would use the current international price of gold. The government would settle for a sweet $9,000.000.00. Ouch! I had told Bob to go back in and offer $7,500,000.00 paid within two banking days. Cat and I would wait for Bob at Willy's. The government offices closed at 5:00 p.m. sharp but Bob was still in their office. At 6:50 p.m. Bob came walking over to the bar and said he'd just saved me $1,400,000.00. He laughed as he said it. I looked at Cat and said that she needed to make the transfer of the $7,600,000.00. Cat said she might have to travel to do such a transfer. I told her I'd take the Chalks morning flight and leave her Tommy. Bob said he'd have to stay until the transfer was completed. I told Bob that I wanted to sell the gold to the highest bidder and to get an appraiser over here to appraise the newest jewels that we had in the deposit boxes. Cat will open the small museum that we had promised and pick out what we wanted to keep for the museum. We would sell the rest. I said the original six deposit boxes with their continence we would also keep.

Willy said it was quite some time that he had seen Bob and I together. Bob still had that Cuban cigar in hand with that offal laugh.

Cat, Bob, Willy, the four divers and Myself would eat at the Bahamian Cuisine. After dinner Cat and I would sleep aboard the "SALINAS", ok sleeping on a boat with Salinas's name on it was strange.

The next morning, we were up early, we ate at Angee's and Cat drove me to Chalks. I told Cat that I would look for Mr. Montibelli to see if he had any information on Martha. I asked if she was serious about me bringing June. Cat said yes please bring her. You're not planning on hurting her are you I asked? That's the most stupid thing you've ever asked me Cat said. She then kissed me and said she loved me.

I hadn't flown Chalks in years, oh the memories it brought back, it gave me the best feeling in my stomach. In those days when I was a regular everyone knew me. Sometimes I would get on the flight straight from fishing and or pulling crawfish traps. I remembered there was this one lady that worked in Miami and Traveled to Miami every Sunday afternoon. I'd be traveling that same flight to make my MYF church meeting. Eloise was her name; she said she always knew when I was on board by the smell. The smell of fresh crawfish aint so bad she used to say. Oh the memories I thought. I also thought the flight used to be a lot shorter.

Once in Miami I caught a taxi to Chubby's house. Chubby and the kids had gone. Lilly invited me in for a cup of coffee. Lilly couldn't stop talking about the children and how much they were enjoying them. You're not thinking of taking them are you she asked? You mean Lori I asked? Any of them she said. We want them to stay together, here with us she said. Lilly then took my hand and led me into Lori's room. There on her dresser were photos of me from High school. My senior photo and football photos. Chubby had taken her by the high school, Lori wants to go there next year, she'll be ready too Lilly said. I looked around the room and then the children's room. You need a bigger house I said. No Lilly said this is perfect.

Where's Lori right now I asked? Lilly looked at her watch and said Shenandoah pool over at the park she said. Then she asked if I knew where it was? I learned to swim there at the age of 5, I said. Well Lilly said all the kids can now swim. I was anxious to see Lori swimming, so I said I'd be back and jumped in the taxi, and headed to the pool.

It felt strange walking into the pool area, Chubby was sitting in the stands. He stood and waved. There he said, there she is, that one. Chubby pointed and there she was. Lori was with a privet Tudor teaching her the art of swimming, not just swimming but all the strokes. Lori had on a one-piece speedo to include a swimmers cap. I looked at Chubby and saw this glow on his face, no it wasn't the sun it was pride. I sat there with Chubby until Lori noticed me. When she did there was nothing that could have gotten in her way, she got out of the pool and came a running. I made it to the deck where she latched onto me not letting go. Kiss me she said and don't stop. Needless to say we made a scene. Her teacher came walking up behind Lori and said so this must be Captain Jim. The teacher a 35 or so woman smiled as I shook her hand. Your all she talks about the woman said. I thank you from the bottom of my heart I said. Lori doesn't know but I learned to swim in this very pool. Lori did not let me go for one second. The teacher said that Lori and her still had another 45 minutes. I looked at Lori as she was shaking her head no. Go on I said and finish up. I got some things to do and I'll see you at the house. What time she asked? I'll be there at about 4:00 p.m. I said. I'll be ready she said. She kissed me again and went back with the teacher.

From the pool's pay phone I called June's parents' house. June was there and she asked if I was coming over. I asked if she had a car? She asked, doesn't everyone? I'll be there in 20 minutes and don't change from what you have on.

I gave the taxi driver the address and we were off to June's. As Lori, I hadn't seen June in weeks if not a month. June came to the door and wow, I was surprised. June was beautiful! She had that big belly but she was beautiful. Maybe I was too familiar with Salinas, but June made a much better-looking pregnant girl than any others I had seen. When she opened the door she pulled me in. Well she said are we going to be friends or can I jump you she asked? Today you better, she didn't wait for my answer. When we stopped kissing there was her mom looking from the kitchen door. Hello Mrs. K, I said. Hello Jim she said as she walked my way. June's mom stopped and looked at me, then said the time had treated me well. Yes, mam I said and you look the same. We didn't see too much of you back then Jim, her mom said. I hope under the circumstances we'll be seeing you a lot more. I took June's hand and followed Mrs. K back into the kitchen. Well mam, I don't know if June told you or even if she knows I'm working on a remote island in the Philippines. I have a shipping line, 2,800 acers of crops and we're building a tuna fish canning factory. Her mom looked at me and said she thought most of my business's were in the Bahama Islands. Well mam I said we are the largest fishing company as well as construction company in the Bahamas. Besides, when we have something special going on, those operations pretty much run on their own. You still work the water front these days her mom asked? Yes, and No I said. I still have a container yard here in Miami but I don't do any of its managing. We also have a large terminal and warehouse business in New Orleans but again I don't do much there either. Anything else I don't know about June asked? Well it's not much yet but we do have a small air cargo business based in Mandeville Louisiana. When will you heading out Mrs. K asked? I'm actually on a stand by, in a holding pattern waiting on a business decision, it could be one day or a week. Well June's mom said I trust you have some time to spend with June. Yes, mam. I will be heading back to Nassau in two days and if June can travel and put up with some connivances she is invited to come along. June handed me her car keys, oh no I said, I want you to come with me and help me pick out a car. June said, you said not to change my clothes. Yes I said, I wanted to see you as you are now. Well how do I look she asked? You're the prettiest pregnant girl I've ever seen I said. June's mom laughed. June and I left and as we drove June asked about the inconveniences that I mentioned, ones not your wife or that girl Cat right? Wrong I said Cat will be there and she's almost as pregnant as you are. Yours, June asked? Yes, I answered. June stopped the Car and said for me to get out. I opened the door got out and started walking. She drove the car next to me asking where I was going? To the BMW dealer I answered. She pulled up ahead and opened the door. I got in and she kissed me. You, she said are a SOB. None of this was planned I said, but I look forward to both of you having my children. I'm having the boy she said, that's for sure.

I purchased a nice four door BMW, the same car and color as my other only a newer model and a lot lighter. I told June that I had something to do that I couldn't take her along on and I'd pick her up in two days. At any given moment I'll have to rush to Washington, so she'd have to pack clothes for that trip too. For Nassau you'll only need a bathing suit, a long shirt and a hat to protect you from the sun. I kissed her once more and told her she was beautiful and patted her on the butt.

Still in my suit and running out of time, I drove my new car straight to the house in the roads. As I drove up in the drive way, Lori came to greet me. She again made quite a seen. What will the neighbors think I asked? They'll think my man is here she said. Come on she said the children want you to see them swim. And see them I did. Samuel and Melody swam like fish. They too, were happy to see me. Samuel said that Mr. Chubby had taken them to Disney World, it was the most wonderful thing he said. Melody said she liked Goofy the best. The children and Chubby and his wife were genuinely happy. Lori said that they had also gone to the football stadium where I used to play football. Yes, she said they had gone to a Miami High football game at the Orange Bowl. Lori said that they had gone to the school and spoke to one of my coaches that still coached there. Coach Shae Lori said. That coach said to tell you how sorry he was that they mistreated you. He said you would understand. Lori said my name was still on the roster written on the wall in the locker room. The coach said you were one of the most talented players that he had ever coached. The coach said you only followed two sets of rules, have a good time and win.

It was hard to believe that coach Shae was still there at Miami High. It was even harder to believe that Chubby had taken Lori by there and to the Stadium. Lori had other surprises too. She had met my brother Bob and seen the original sail boat the "Princess". The "Princess" was there in the side yard of my Dad's business. Chubby said he wanted to show Lori how I grew up. Chubby knew some of the men that still worked for my brother in the fabrication shop. My brother Bob had recognized Chubby's face and came out from the office and spoke to him and Lori. Lori said that by brother was very nice to them and said he hadn't seen me much over the years. Your brother said you were an adventurist. I asked your brother if he had ever gone to the stadium and watched you play football? Your brother said that yes, yes he had gone several times just to yell "that's my brother that made that made that tackle". Your brother said that you made it look like so much fun. Your brother asked me if I knew you? Chubby answered by saying that Lori was his adopted daughter and that you were my God Father. Your brother looked at me funny and asked if you were all right. I told him you were. Your Brother said to tell you he loved you and missed you she said.

Lori came to me and hugged me and said to please take her with me when I went back to General Santos.

It was now 6:00 p.m. and Lilly asked me to stay for dinner. I told her that I would love to but had made other plans. Lori had a small bag packed and was ready to go. We left saying that I was planning to be here in Miami for two days but that could be cut short but if so, that I would be back shortly after that. Lori was itching to get going. Once in the car and only a block away Lori had me stop the car, kissing me. We drove to the apartment and didn't go out that night. Lori and I spent the next day and a half together side by side.

On the day I was to leave her, I took Lori back to Chubby's where she would change into her bathing suit and I would drop her off at the Shenandoah pool for her daily lesson. Chubby was there with me as I watched her, I told Chubby I would be back within the week, thanked him for what a great job he and Lilly were doing and I walked out without Lori seeing me go.

I drove to June's house and there she was waiting. You ready for this I asked? She said yes I've been ready for 18 years. It's just that I'm a little nervous how I'm going to handle this. That makes two of us I answered.

Tommy was waiting at Opa Locka, we took off and in no time we were landing in Nassau. We didn't stop anywhere, we went right to the city dock. I stopped in at Willy's, Willy remembering June. June said her hello to Willy saying that it was a surprise to her too. Willy seeing June's belly understood what June was saying. I asked Willy about Cat's where abouts and he said that she was up at the Charity's office. You know Willy said, helping some girl that had got into trouble. He looked at June and said no, not that kind and smiled. Willy raised his eyes and asked if Cat was expecting us both? I looked at Willy and answered yes. Willy mumbled that this was going to be one of those days. I asked Willy to keep June company and would walk over to get Cat.

Cat was there working and stopped what she was doing and came to me, we kissed and hugged and she asked where June was. I said that June was with Willy. Cat took my hand and pulled me all the way there. Cat walked into the bar and up to June, Cat stopped and said, I'd hoped you wouldn't have looked so damn good! Cat then took two more steps and hugged June and welcomed her to Nassau. Come on Cat said, I'll show you our room. June looked at me as she and Cat walked by. Willy asked? Did I hear her right? Our room? I raised my shoulders and started walking after them both. As I almost caught up with them, they had stopped at the Hunter. Cat had mentioned that this was our sailboat. They both went aboard while I picked up the bag that June dropped and I then walked on to the "Salinas." The girls finally got there and said they wanted to start out on the Hunter. The girls said they would go shopping and meet me back in one hour; I was to get some fresh Crawfish.

In about an hour, we were all three aboard and leaving the dock. We would go with the tide that was coming in. While still in the harbor I raised both the main and jib. I stopped half way back on the side deck and looked back. They were both talking and looking like they were making a plan. I started walking again and stepped into the cockpit. It was Cat that came to me first. She looked at me and said she was in love with me and was going to have my baby. She then kissed me and grabbed my butt. Cat then turned and took the wheel. Apparently it was now June's turn. June now came to me and said the same and also kissed me. That was the beginning of a great trip. The three of us got along just fine. The girls where wearing a bikini bottom with a "T" shirt top. That was the only thing if anything they wore for the entire trip. We sailed until after dark. We dropped anchor over the first treasure sight. We cooked crawfish tails and ate them while we sat on deck watching stars. We did this until we went below and all slept in the forward stateroom.

The next morning all three of us put on skin diving gear and went for a morning swim. We caught a few more Crawfish and would cook them for snacking on during the day. The girls both cooked bacon and eggs for breakfast. We agreed what we would sail back and take the "Salinas "to Harbor Island. We pulled up anchor and headed back to Nassau.

Sailing back to Nassau, you won't believe it but I had the best time of my life! These two girls were crazy! They were either throwing a bucket of ice water on me, pulling down my pants or wanting to throw over the anchor. It was great! The girls got along better than any two people I had ever seen, the fun never stopped.

We arrived in Nassau and changed boats. The "Salinas" was basically ready to go. We moved some food and clothes and shoved off. Harbor Island would be a straight shot us only stopping once when we headed closer to shore and anchoring to avoid some bad weather. Not to worry the girls cooked something like the crawfish chelow that Rusty and I used to eat. It was good to remember the Rusty days until Martha came to my memory. Lori and I had visited Joe's on my last trip to Miami but without running into Montibelli. I prayed that Martha was alright and if not that she knew that she could always come back home.

The weather broke and we were off again to that beautiful Island where my grandmother had been born.

We arrived at Valentine's on Harbor Islands west coast. We left the boat and taxied on over to the Pink Sands Hotel. Mrs. King had remembered my last visit and looked at me rather strangely, but she shook it off and asked twice about our one-room request.

The beach, service and food were as always the very best. June unlike Cat was light skinned and couldn't take much direct sun. On the beach, there were plenty of big umbrellas to hide under. Our time here went by and before we knew it I got the call to return to Washington. We all knew it was coming; it just came too soon.

CHAPTER V

RETURN TO WASHINGTON

Tommy would get me in Eleuthera and fly me directly to Washington. On my way I spoke to Roy, him having met with the Bahamian Government, Roy was under the opinion that we had no problem with the whatever we had found in the cave including the gold and the rooms contents. The vessel he said was different as it could be concived that the Navy had contracted me to bring it up and deliver it to them. It seemed best to go ahead and make some kind of financial agreement for only the delivery of the vessel.

When arriving at the White House, the Secretary of State was the only man other than the President in the room. Both the Colonel and Director were not in attendance. I was introduced to the secretary of state as a friend of the President. First, The Secretary asked why I didn't trust The Director. I said it wasn't him, but my experiences with our Government weren't good in general. The Secretary asked if I trusted the President, and I answered yes.

The Secretary said we have a mission for you, We want you to take an offer to this Ninong. It's a peace offering, he said. I agree with you that the elections may go badly for Marcos and that Marcos will do everything and anything to stay in power. We will back Corazon Aquino, he said and remove Marcos. We want you to take Ninong a letter from the President. Talk to him and convince him not to interfere in the changing of power. Ninong must keep his men on the southern Island and not expand. They will be given latitude to manage their own people and have their own local elections. The national army would be removed from the island. Well, the

Secretary asked, what do you think? Well I said it sounds good to me; let's see how it sounds to him. We will need a signal the Secretary said. We want all the rebels to disappear from the day of the agreement until after Mrs. Aquino is declared President. We need this done by no later than the end of November. What happens if he disagrees, I asked? The President then spoke for the first time. Then we'll remove the rebels, the President said. Ok I said, I'll go and do this.

Then The President said they had heard that there had been some activity in the caves. Yes I said, we found a way into the room and have gone through the doors. There's more than one door, the President asked? Yes Sir I said, it's a bit tricky, but we have entered. Sir, my present agreement is cost plus 40%; we have found what I believe to be an incredibly advanced system that may move the vessel down there into place without tethering it. You mean like a remote control system, the President asked? Yes, sir, I think that this system could enable you to send a drone or missile anywhere you have satellite coverage. You do know drones have been around for years the Secretary said. Yes Sir, I said, JFK's older brother Josef was killed in 1944 on his way to deliver such a drone over Germany. The President asked the Secretary if that was true? The Secretary confirmed the incident. I believe that the vehicle not only holds the laser technology that you are looking for, but also has the technology to take off, complete its mission, and return. What is it that you want Jim the President asked? I want the government to stay away from it until I deliver the vehicle to you. When I do, I would like to be paid for the construction project as we have agreed plus if the technology is there and I can deliver it, I receive an additional $20,000,000.00 in non-taxable US dollars' stateside. The President said I was out of my mind, but the Secretary stood and said we had an agreement. I looked at the President, he stood and said yes. We all shook hands. The Secretary asked if I needed a ride anywhere? I smiled and said that had my own transportation. I looked at the Secretary and said all I needed was the letter to Ninong and for them to remember our agreement, that the government was not to be involved or interfere.

I left thinking that I had just made a business arrangement with the President of the United States of America, but could they be trusted? That remained to be seen.

Before I took off from DC, to return to Nassau, I had called Nassau for Cat, but got no answer, I called Willy and asked if Cat had gotten back from Harbor Island. Willy said that the "Salinas" slip was still empty.

I would fly directly to Paix to visit Salinas and Michelle. Fernando was back there doing his training thing and picked me up at the Paix airport. I had told Tommy that depending on how things went, I might be leaving within the hour or spending the night.

Salinas was happy to see me and treated me like nothing had happen, it had though. She basically had left me taking with her, my only child. I wasn't upset, but I put on like I was. She thanked me for the money I had sent and asked If I wanted her back? I said that the houses in Mandeville and Nassau were still empty but that I wouldn't count on them staying that way.

Salinas had one of those big bellis that I now had found quite nice to look at. Salinas didn't feel half as pretty as she really was. Salinas said she would take her mom, and they'd go back to Mandeville. I said ok, go but, I didn't want her mom there. That seemed to change things, and things seemed to get icy from there. I spent some time with Betty and little Michelle, Betty telling me all the new things that Michelle was getting into. Soon Betty said Michelle would be having a little brother. I said yes and maybe a sister or two also. Betty didn't catch my meaning. I asked Betty if they needed anything and hugged her good bye, I kissed Michelle and was on my way back to Fernando's truck when Salinas came running out of the house. Where are you going she asked? Back to the Philippines I said. Please she said take me with you. Sorry I said even if I wanted to you couldn't go on this trip. Then stay here tonight, she said. Why I asked? You don't want me because I have more than one woman, I said. I asked you to go to the Doctor and not to have another baby for a while, but you or your mother made that decision without me. Cat and June also made that kind of decision without consulting me. Who is June, Salinas asked? She's and old girl girlfriend that I ran into one night. Yes, one night that's all it took. And you, you left me hanging out there, I reminded her. No talking about it. You just left me. Salinas said she'd never leave me again. Do you love me I asked? Yes, she said. Well if you want to be close then go back to Nassau, be friends with Cat. She, too, is our family. If you can't do Nassau then go back to Mandeville, but if you come back to me don't bring your mother. I walked to her and scooped her up, and took her up the stairs to bed. One hour later I came down and found Fernando and asked to be returned to the airport. Within 30 minutes, we were in the air on the way to Miami.

It was late when I arrived at the house on the roads as I called it. The lights were out but I knocked on the door, Chubby came and opened it, Chubby said that Lori hadn't eaten a thing since I had left. I knocked on her door and she opened it; I stepped in and closed the door. By the next morning I had decided to take Lori with me back to General Santos. I just couldn't leave her. I could have said it was for her, but it was for me. I wanted her with me. I calculated that we might not make it back to the States before thanksgiving and maybe not by Christmas.

There were several things I had to do before heading west. Lori said her good buys to the kids, Chubby and Lilly. I then dropped Lori off at the apartment. I then called Tim and said I was coming by to talk. I also called Bob and said I needed Montibelli and that Bob and I needed to talk before I left.

Tim was first. I told him about the Vehicle at the channel's bottom and the story that went along with it. I also informed Tim of the room in the cave that led from the channel to one of the bigger Blue holes. In the room, I believed that the controls we found could remotely control the vehicle. Tim was to find some ex-Nasa engineers that had worked in guided missile technology, along with one ex-Nasa pilot. If they could read Latin, all the better. Oh yes they all had to scuba dive. I would put a start date on this project of January 5th 1986. Before I left Omni, I again called for Cat. This time Cat answered her cell, saying it had lost its charge. Cat said that she and June had a great time. June would be staying at least for a few more weeks before heading back to Miami.

Bob had said to meet at Joe's at 1:00 p.m., Montibelli lived two blocks away in some big expensive house; if he wasn't at Joe's, I could walk on over and visit him. He won't like being distrupted but then who does.

Bob and I met for lunch, me giving him updates on my second meeting with the President and me now knowing the Secretary. Bob said that once he told me I was playing with fire. Now you're sitting in a furnace with the gas on, he said. I then mentioned my three pregnant girls and my trip with two of them. Bob, while laughing as hard as I'd seen, called the waiter and asked for a match. The waiter brought over a pack of matches, Bob took it and lit one and threw it at me. The whole time laughing. Bob while still laughing asked me if I'd seen any of the lists of items that my C-130 had been dropping over Nicaragua? I said no, Bob said hell son there building a runway; what planes do you think their thinking will be landing there? Those big birds of your will make some offal nice targets when the time comes he said. Well I said I don't think it will happen without my permission, and I don't believe my pilots are so stupid to land in a hostile country where they know they'll be targeted. No it won't happen I said. Maybe not while you're alive Bob said as he lit another match and threw it my way, this time not laughing.

I didn't tell Bob that I was carrying a letter from the President, I trusted Bob but he didn't need to know; no one did.

As we were about to have desert, a beautiful young girl came to our table with an envelope. Written on the envelope were the words Major Jim. Before I touched the letter, I asked to see, then smell the girl's hands. Once I did take the envelope, I opened it and smelled inside. The girl looked at me strange and said the Mr. Montibelli said you would do exactly what you did. The girl stood by as I opened and read the note inside. The note said, "I heard you were promoted; congratulations, take extra precautions these days. Always have a planned way out. Rashid's yacht is docked on Kish Island just off mainland Iran. Only the crew is aboard, and there is no sign of Rashid or your niece. I will keep an eye on the yacht and keep looking for them" it was signed "your friend." I looked up and the young girl was still there, I glanced at her and thought about what Montibelli had once said about women and trouble. What nationality are you I asked? She looked at me and said, I'm a Jew, then asked if there would be anything else? Bob was quick to ask her if she would have desert with us. She smiled at me as she turned and walked away. Bob said, as she walked, that Montibelli would most likely die of heart failure caused by an overdose of something just like that. What a way to go Bob said. As we left, maybe for the first time, at least not in a long time I thanked Bob for being such a good friend. I told him that all of this fun I was having was his fault. This time I was sure it was the first time I hugged him.

I drove back to the apartment and had a heart to heart with Lori. I told Lori about the other three girls and how they all became pregnant.

I told her that Cat was my best friend and I would do anything for her or the other two of them. I told her I was no good for her and that she should go back to Chubby's and take care of her family and herself. I told her that taking her with me was selfish and only thinking of myself. Lori turned and walked to the opened baloney and looked out. I walked up and stood alongside her. Lori asked if I loved her? I said yes. She asked if I'd ever abandon her for one of the other girls? I said no. She then turned and faced me and said. I will always go with you wherever you take me. I will always be yours until you don't want me anymore. I asked only one thing for me that when the time is right that we have children, lots of children. Lori then slowly kissed me.

CHAPTER VI

DELIVERING THE PRESIDENT'S LETTER

The next morning Lori and I boarded a Chicago-bound flight to catch a flight that stopped in LA, then on to South Korea, where we would change planes for Manilla. In Manilla we would taxi to the National airport then fly on to Cebu, then Davao, then General Santos. The last time I left here it was raining and today the rain has covered all three stops so far. Lori said that the rainy season would be ending very soon.

It was a long drawn out trip that ended with our small four seater swooping down to chase the cows of the grass runway, then circling around to land. As usual there was no taxi waiting or car to meet us. Yes, it was also raining here too. I got out my poncho and gave it to Lori. Lori and I started walking toward town until picked up by a truck heading our way. As we passed through the center of the city, we noticed a heavy presence of the National Army. There were two tanks parked at the Y in the road that either went to the port or to the river. I could see the worried look in Lori's eyes. It was after 5:00 p.m. when we arrived at the factory. The construction crew working to get us ready for the canning operation were wrapping up, calling it a day. Our people were working the last leg of one of our ships. The guards said that all until now was calm but that the army was talking about them soon attacking across the river.

When I first met Lori this was where she and the children were living. Lori said with all the changes going on, she wouldn't have recognized the place. Lori smiled when she saw what they had done to rework our new apartment. A separate bathroom with running hot water, before living in

Miami Lori's water here would be hauled from the river in a bucket. While Lori looked at our room I walked through the factory out back. Where before I could see the river, now there was this reinforced wall. I imagined the wall had a dual purpose. I walked up the steps on the southwest guard tower, and to my surprise, there were Regular army troops stationed along the river. I counted 6 men, looked like one every 50 yards. The men concerned me but the river concerned me more. The river was much higher and moving fast, I knew I would soon cross it to reach Ninong.

As I was saying about the wall, it would now protect the factory from any flooding that the heavy rains would add to the river. The other reason was it would keep people out. I was sure it was an eyesore to the small fishing village on the other side.

I knew it would be tonight that I would need to cross the river and find Ninong. I went back up front and told Lori that I was going to visit the ship. I went out the Factories front gate and walked to the Port gate. From the gate I could see the three yard trucks going and coming from the ship's ramp. Yes, we had four yard trucks, but if everything were working as it should, one yard truck would be standing by to take the place of one if and when one broke down. Everything we did had a contingency plan. I was surprised to see Mr. Partridge's light on. I stopped in to let him know I was back. The first thing he said was that I hadn't gone to see Mr. Bozzni in San Francisco, the second, I was making him work more than he wanted to. Sea Container said you're looking at an additional ship he said. Don't you think you should speak to us about that before another ship comes in here he asked? It's nice to see you too I replied. My office nor myself have received one communication from your Mr. Bozzni to set up any meeting. As for an addition ship I said, we are leaving cargo on the port every week. It seems that all the cargo left behind until now is ours. We have increased your cargo in numbers and greatly improved the quality in which your fruit and frozen cargo arrives to its destination. How many loads have you lost since we started I asked? Mr. Partridge paused then spoke, It's not that we don't appreciate what you've done here he said. It was like working in the dark before you came. It's that we don't know what you will do next. The Tuna business for example, did it even cross your mind that we had the tuna business in mind or that we might want to be a part of that business? You purchasing all those farms, that too was a part of our expansion plans. We didn't know you were even interested in those farms he said. And that's what Mr. Bozzni wanted to talk to you about. There's plenty of business here for us all, I said. Mr. Partridge went on to say that they are the product experts and I the container and shipping expert. Mr. Partridge said that the Fruit Company has similar problems in other countries, well maybe not as bad as this was, but yes problems all around the globe. We need your assistance in other locations but we can't be worried that you'll go in there and buy up our future plans before we get to them. Can I think out loud I asked? Sure Mr. Partridge said. What you are saying makes perfect since. But since you said it so well, why would I have to fly to San Francisco to hear it. From the first day you came back from vacation I felt you didn't like me too much. I stayed away from you and you me, I said. You grew on me Mr. Partridge said. Ok I said I'll go visit your Mr. Bozzni but why not come along I said. You go and I'll go too. Mr. Partridge said that he would arrange that meeting with San Francisco with Lourdes. I stood and as I walked out Mr. Partridge thanked me for the clinic in town. He said it's made a difference.

I then walked down to the dock and up the stairs of the ship to visit with the Captain. Captain Berk was up in the control room planning the departure with his chief mate. Berk was busy but would stop to chat. He expressed his satisfaction with our operation and mentioned that London had inquired how things were going. Berk said, we took the liberty of working out a schedule that could include a third ship. I have a copy in my quarters he said, would you like to see it. Maybe another trip Captain I said, I know your busy.

I then walked the ship shaking hands with each person I reached. Even though soaking wet from a down pore they all seemed content.

By now I had run into Nilo, him apologizing for not picking me up at the airport, how could you have known I asked? I was sure that Lourdes didn't even know I was coming.

It was getting dark with the ship still working. Nilo took me back to the factory and I asked him to take Lori for something to eat. I told Lori that I had some work to do. Once they left I changed into my black leotards outfitted with my stainless steel Walter 9 mm in my front mounted black tourist quick zipper bag, my black running boots, a small water proof flash light, $30,000.00 in cash and the President's letter. With my face marked in black boot polish I exited the front gate and walked up along the edge of the road toward the bridge that the rebels had destroyed. There were of course no street lights and I was sure I was not noticed. Before I got to the river's edge, I watched the National army guards on my side of the river, when I saw a break I ran into the rushing water. The current was swift but I was able to make it to the north side. I must have gone 100 yards with the river before reaching the northern shore. Getting back was going to be much more difficult. I laid on my stomach and looked in all directions before I stood and ran into the woods. Once in the woods I would make my way to the road heading north. When I got to the first rebel post I walked around it without being noticed. When I got to the second post I sat in the woods until I recognized one of the men. From the edge of the woods I called out that I was a friend and needed to speak to Ninong. I had attracted a group and I walked into the light with my hands up. At first they were a little rough on me until they realized who I was. They of course took my gun and this time they posted two guards while I sat under that same big tree. Ninong must not live to close because again I sat under that tree for almost three hours. When he did come wearing that mask I asked how I knew it was really him. Well he said you ruined my best coffee pot. I smiled and I asked him to sit down. I started handing him the money and then the letter and my flash light. He didn't check the cash and opened the letter. He started to look at it then stopped and asked if this was from my President. I answered, Yes. Ninong read the letter and asked how was I so sure Marcos would go. I looked at him and said I would personally put him on a one-way flight. Ninong stood and walked into the dark. I waited 30 minutes and he came back and asked if the letter was his to keep. I answered, it was. Ninong asked if needed his answer in writing? I said that a hand shake and his word were good enough. Ninong held out his hand and said he would abide by the agreement. Well I said, I have a long trip back. Ninong had his men return my gun and said he would carry me to a place where I could cross the river shorting my trip. Ninong said there were fewer guards to the east of the bridge.

As we rode in this old beat up truck Ninong said he would disband his men at the bridge tonight and spread the word. He asked, what he should do if Marcos sent his army across the river. The only thing you can do I said, defend your people. I was now about a half mile up river from the bridge. I would cross back here. The next meeting, I said, you will have no cause for your mask. I walked down the bank and into the rushing water.

I was in the water again for about 100 yards or so when I reached the south side of the river. I started to jog at a slow but steady pace. All of the sudden there were lights turned on and the sound of dogs became very clear, I reversed my direction just as light caught me moving threw it, then sounds of rifle fire. I felt a sting in my left leg but I kept running until I hit the river. I knew two things as I was carried by the rushing river. I was now being taken by the rushing water that would take me under that mangled bridge. That sting in my leg meant that I had been wounded. The sting disappeared with my new worries. I could see the men with lights and the dogs running along the water's south side. The bridge was coming and as I looked I could see men on the south top of the broken bridge with lights shinning down into the water. As I rapidly approached the bridge, I took a breath and went under. It seemed a long time and when I came up I had passed under the bridge. There was one new problem. That same leg that had the stinging had been caught and sliced by a piece of exposed rebar or sharp concrete. As the water took me I reached down and felt the large wound in the back of my left calf. My next hope was to ride the river down to the fishing village and get help. As the current took me passed where the river turned south, I swam toward the west bank, reaching one of the small fishing village docks. I unhooked my gun belt and hooked it around one of the dock's posts at the water's bottom. I then pulled myself to shore. There were now two fishing village dogs barking at my face level. It wasn't long when someone came to see why the dogs were making such a racket. I could imagen that the dogs barking would also bring attention from the army on the other side. The old man that came to me then went back and got help. They helped me to the first hut where from the light of a small inside fire and my flash light, we could see what looked like three wounds. A bullet hole that went in one side and out the other and a 10-inch-long jagged cut running up the back calf of the same leg. Within minutes we herd more dogs, this time coming from the other side of the river. The older man said that if they crossed the river they could be here shortly. By now a woman was wrapping my wounds. The man said we would have to leave by canoe. He then helped me on my feet and we moved back to the shore where they placed me into a canoe and then with the old man sitting at the rear we were shoved off into the river. The rushing water was now moving us down river and shortly we would be in the large bay. The older man paddled to the east when I thought he should go west. I soon saw where we were heading. The General Santos fishing fleet was just starting to leave the docks. One of the boats saw the canoe and came to us. I was transferred from the canoe to the fishing boat. I thanked the old man as he disappeared into the darkness.

I was now in a lot of pain and had lost quite a bit of blood. The captain then headed our boat toward another boat and the two captains talked, one boat would go in and bring the doctor from the clinic while the boat I was on would stand by. The boat which went for the Doctor didn't return for two hours. It was 7:00 a.m. when the Captain said he saw the boat returning. The captain used his old pair of world war ll binoculars and said there were two boats on the way. At first I thought the other Captain was bringing the army or the police but it was not so. The first boat passed right by but the second bigger boat stopped. I wasn't doing so good until I saw whom was on board. It was Lori and Doctor Rodriquez. I was moved from one boat to the other, I was able to thank the Captain and his crew from the first boat. The boat that I was now on had a small cabin of which they brought me in and placed me face down on the table. I could hear the engine speed up and it seemed we were heading east north east. Lori was helping the doctor, as they hooked me up with some bagged liquid and that's when I must have lost consciousness.

When I opened my eyes there she was sitting there staring me. Where are we I asked? We're on our way to Davao Lori said. What's in Davao that I don't have here I asked? Looks like I have everything I need I said. Lori then came and kissed me. I'm the one that now has everything she said. Anyone call Tommy as yet I asked? Lori said he should be waiting on us. What's the verdict on my leg I asked? It's pretty banged up she said, the bullet passed right through breaking the bone she said, that cut you got took almost 100 stiches she added. I went to sit up and was reminded what pain was. What do we have for the pain I asked? Not too much for the pain or the possible infection she said. How much longer I asked before we reach port? About one hour the Captain said. I wondered if there looking for me. I will need clothes, did someone think of that I asked? Lori said she had brought my back pack to include my passport and shoulder holster. She mentioned that my smaller gun was not on the boat.

I somehow got into a pair of pants and would need to somehow walk on my own. The boat docked, I thanked the good Doctor and he and Lori got a taxi. I was dress and when Lori returned, I was at the boats edge looking at the space between the boat and the dock. The tide was low so the dock was higher than the boat. The distance looked insurmountable. I gritted my teeth and with the Captain on the boat side and stepping into Lori's and the Doc's hands, I went forward. I can't say I remember the pain, I do not. Somehow I walked the dock and got in the taxi. We had the taxi drive to a side gate at the airport where we paid for its opening and the taxi was able to drive right up to the Jet. Tommy helped me get up the steps without causing too much attention. Tommy was fueled and ready, we took off and headed directly to Guam. The fuel would be low before we arrived but Tommy said we would make it. Tommy had stopped and picked up a nurse that had brought the medicine that they believed was needed. The next thing I knew I was in the military base hospital in Gaum. Lori was right there; she hadn't moved from my side. Tommy was there too, he said there was news from General Santos. I took a deep breath. He said the news was it looked like the Army's show of force there had the rebels moving into the jungles. I let out the air that I had in my chest, both he and I smiled. I looked at Lori and asked when we could go home?

We spent a week in the hospital with the good Doctors here operating on my leg taking out a leg bone fragment that was not going to reattach. Once everything with my leg looked good Tommy would fly us to Tokyo.

Here in Tokyo using a cane to walk I met with my Tuna partners. They were both happy with the progress that we all had made and the news of the fleeing rebels. From Tokyo Lori and I would fly to San Francisco where Lourdes had made an appointment with Mr. Bozzni from Standard Fruit. Mr. Partridge was a no-show.

Our meeting went good, although Mr. Bozzni didn't quite approve or understand how we got things done, he was overjoyed with our accomplishments. He questioned me about the Tuna Factory and the market. He mentioned that Sea Containers had mentioned the possibility of a third ship entering into the service in April or March of next year. He noted that they had on the drawing table two super container ships of their own. These ships, he said, would be used in their Central American- Gulf Port service and their Ecuador-California service. The Fruit Company would soon begin returning their older Sea Container leased equipment and were looking into long term lease with a new company called Genstar. At present all equipment is leased through Sea Containers.

Mr. Bozzni's small talk led to what he really wanted. Standard wanted to buy the over 2,800 acres of land that I had purchased from Marcos. He hinted that they'd return my money plus ten percent. I told Mr. Bozzni that at present the land was not for sale but that I would keep them in mind. I thought him telling me that they were going to build two container ships was most likely true but it was said to somehow intimidate me. Presently the Fruit company was paying dirt cheap for my fruit and shipping it under their Fruit Company's flag.

Lori had waited patiently for my long meeting, she kept saying I was overdoing it on my leg. My leg was doing just fine.

From San Francisco we returned to Miami. We stopped by to see the children and then we headed to my apartment for some rest. I told Lori that her being off from classes was over, she laughed and said that Thursday was my thanksgiving day and that Cubby was going to cook a pig in the ground. Thanksgiving, I thought, where did the time go.

I called everyone to let them know I was back in town. June had just come home from Nassau the week before and she too had invited me over to her parent's house for thanksgiving. I said that I would stop over sometime in the late afternoon.

Lori and I spent some of the time mapping out her future. She wanted to start High School in late August of the coming year. To make that happen we would contract a full time teacher that would also serve as her director of activities. Lori was to stay quite busy learning to read and write along with her swimming, scuba diving, sailing, skiing, shooting, horseback riding, self-defense courses, driving and flying lessons. Lori was to master all of these things and more. Lori said I had forgotten to mention, first aid and how to give stiches, she said watching that doctor put in the 100 or so in my leg she thought she could do a fair job the next time.

I really didn't know what I would do while Lori was keeping so busy, but I was determined and committed to get her into high school in late August of 1986.

On Thursday we ate Thanksgiving dinner at Chubby's then I would leave Lori there and go to June's house.

Seemed June's family had waited until I got there to begin eating. It didn't look like Mr. K was to happy interrupting his pro football game. As we were eating Mr. K said that June said that I had quite a set up in Nassau. He asked if that's where June and I would be living after the baby was born. June quickly changed the subject. As I was still using a cane, June's father came back and asked just how I did hurt my leg?

Sir I said, I was delivering this letter from our President to the rebels in the Philippines and on my way back I was shot in the leg breaking the bone. I dove into the rapids to get away from the army and their dogs that were chasing me. While going down the rapids under the bridge that the rebels had earlier blown up, my leg got caught on a piece of rebar gashing my calf. June's brother said wow how cool. Mr. K said why didn't I just tell the truth. I then said I broke my leg skiing down the bunny sloop at Spokane. June's father laughed and said I had made up the other story but at least in the end we heard the truth. June pinched me under the table. June said that the only reason she excused me from doing kitchen duty was my bad leg. June and I went out to the pool area and sat. June said the only reason she returned this week was Thanksgiving. I'm going back to Nassau on Saturday she stated. I'm going to have our son here in Miami but within two months afterwards, I'll be moving in with Cat and her son or daughter. Cat will work and I'll take care of the kids June said. You girls got along that good I asked? Yes, June said but if you'd rather marry me before then she said that will be even better. I said I'm already married. June said, no you're not, Cat said you're married to a Bahamian girl of 19 years old that doesn't exist. Why not spend three days with me here at your apartment, just three days June said, and then if you don't want to marry me after that you and I can go visit Cat.

You go on and go I said, I've got business this week. That new Philippine girl June asked? I said yes. Cat and I want to meet her June said. Maybe another time I said. You didn't tell her about us June said. No I said she's heard about all three of you. Then what about it June asked? I'll call you I said. Here comes my father June said and then she came into my arms and kissed me. June's father said he wanted to see my leg, why I asked? Because I made a bet with June's mother he said. I stood and unbuckled my pants and they fell to, well my leg holster. June's father kneeled and looked. I pointed to where the bullet entered and exited, then turned and pointed to where the 100 stiches were. What a mess Mr. K said, that was one hell of a bunny sloop. I said, yes Sir it was quite a wild ride. Mr. K looked at June and then me and apologized the best he could. Then he asked where the patch job was done? I said the surgery was performed at the Navy base on Guam. June said to pull up my pants as her sister was watching. As we walked out I said loud enough for June's mom to hear, thank you, mam, for the fine meal. As June and I walked to my car June asked if the Philippine girl was here? I replied that her name was Lori and yes, she was here.

By the time I arrived at Chubby's I had made up my mind, the next morning Lori and I would fly to Nassau and depending on the weather take out the "Cat" or the "Salinas". From there we'd head west.

That night I made and received several calls attempting to clear out anything that couldn't wait until my return.

Lori and I would go to Nassau and take out the Hunter.

Once in Nassau we stopped in and I introduced Lori to Angee and Janie, Janie was again pregnant. We asked if Cat was around but Janie said she was visiting the children. Angee didn't look to happy but served us up some of her good food. Angee did some warming up when Lori said she had worked on the docks all her life and never tasted anything quite so good. Angee could tell that what Lori had said came right from,' the heart. You be careful not to get pregnant she said to Lori, we's got enough pregnant girls around here. Angee looked at me with a smile and said yes that Maggie was also with child. I gave Angee a big hug and said I knew that had made her happy. Tears rolled down Angee's face as we both remembered her Johnny.

Lori and I did some shopping and stopped to see Willy at the bar. Willy asked Lori to put her chin up on the bar and we, Willy and I laughed. Of course Willy told Lori all about the old days.

We were just about to throw the lines to the dock and pull out when I saw Cat walking down the dock. Cat stood on the dock's side walk and asked permission to come aboard. Cat threw her one leg then the other, over the Hunter's side cables, she came and kissed and hugged me. When she was finished she turned to Lori and hugged her too and said welcome to the family. Your welcome here just as long as you understand that we all love him. She turned back to me and again kissed me and said to watch the weather. She stepped off the boat and looked at us. She then said that Lori reminded her of herself 15 years ago. Oh to be your age again Cat said, she looked at Lori and said, Jim always says it's about choices. Cat looked at me and said I love you and walked off. Lori then came to me and latched on. Hold me she said and never let me go.

We eventually pulled out running against the incoming tides current. Once out of the Harbor I raised the sails, cut the engine and we were heading east. The breeze was out of the south, south east but the Hunter captured the wind it was given and we were moving at a speed of about 6 knots. Even though Lori didn't want to wear one she had on a red life jacket. I put out a tow line and explained why. Lori went below and came back with only the life jacket and her bathing suit bottom. She came and stood with me, me showing her how to handle the wheel. We sailed until almost midnight. Anchored and once ready to bed down for the night, Lori changed the life jacket for one of my shirts, we lied down on the deck and watch the stars. At about 1:00 a.m. the breeze had shifted around now coming from the north and the northerly wind turned chilly. We got up and went down into the cabin and fell fast asleep.

The next morning my eyes opened with the smell of coffee. I sat up and could see Lori, now in an old sweat shirt that she had found. The cabin door and hatch were closed. Lori brought me my coffee and asked about the weather. Lori had never seen it so cold, it was about 65 Degrees Fahrenheit. Wearing the warmest clothes, we could find we pulled up anchor and headed for Harbor Island. That afternoon we reached Valentine's dock, secured the boat and took a taxi to the Pink Sands. We were there for two nights and three days.

We then sailed back to Nassau where Lori met June whom was perched on the "Salinas" just waiting for us to come back. Lori got to chat with June as we got to see and meet our crawfish boats coming in with their catch. Lori got the chance to meet everyone.

June was a bit weird at first but when she saw how nice Lori was, June also became quite nice. June asked if she could take Lori to see the "Salinas", Lori said she wanted to go so, I said ok. They both walk off down the dock, both looking back at me for approval.

I walked over to sit with Willy, Willy said that he had just gotten a call from Lourdes. I used his phone and called the operator and she got me Lourdes. Lourdes said she was sorry to bother me while I was fishing but she wanted me to know that Salinas had arrived at the Mandeville house last night, bringing with her Michelle and Betty, no sign of Salinas's mom.

Lourdes said that Tommy said I had given him permission to move them whenever Salinas called. Lourdes asked If I wanted the rest of my messages? I said yes of course. Jerry is looking for you as there is a group at the Mandeville Airport that wants to install some electronics in both of the C-130s, Jerry has them standing by at the Motel 6, Jerry said that the Colonel had sent them. Tell Jerry that it is not authorized, I said. A Mr. Crowbe called from US Maritime and left a personal phone number. Do you want the number she asked? I told her to send it to my recorder at the apartment. The Colonel has called three times, Tim, and Jack from New Orleans are looking for you. Lourdes said she didn't have any more calls and wanted to know if she could tell Salinas when to expect to see me. Tell her, and before I could finish. Lourdes said that you're out fishing. Right I said.

While I was talking on the phone June and Lori walked in. Before I hung up June was already showing Lori the broken window, mirror and the bullet hole in the bar. June was telling Lori one of those old stories. I hung up and asked for June not to tell that story any more. Willy said that by the next week the glass and mirror were going to be replaced. Willy said they would leave the bullet hole in the woodwork.

Lori asked how old I was when I started causing trouble? Willy laughed and said women and trouble always seemed to be finding me.

I called Tim and he said that he had the personal that I had asked for. Since I was here and they were not working, Tim asked if the new people could start now. I asked Tim about the scuba part and he said all had scuba diving experience. I thought about it a moment and then said to move them to Andros but to make sure they had all signed their contracts and the non-discloser agreements. I then called Lee and said to do some house shifting as one of the flight engineers was a woman. Lee said he'd bunk on the couch. I thought about it and said we'd move the "Salinas" on over to Andros and leave it at the dock. Lee said taking into consideration that Lusca could still be out there he'd sleep on the couch. I then thought about opening up Lucy's families house. I mentioned that to Lee and again he said he'd still take the couch. Ok the couch it is I said. I looked at Lori and June and told them to go over and pick out something for the kids, Chubby and his wife. Something touristy I said. Lori knew that was my queue for her to move it.

I then returned Jack's call, Jack from New Orleans was calling to complain about how much freight we were receiving for Central America. Jack said the money was great but with the customer base he was building; they were running out of room. I told Jack I'd check it out and get back to him. I then called Jerry, he started on the group that wanted to install the new electronics. I stopped him and asked about the new hanger and warehouse. Jerry said the hanger was about 50% and the warehouse almost 90%. I said to have them concentrate on the warehouse and let me know a new time estimate of when he could start receiving cargo. Jerry said he'd do the numbers and let me know. I asked Jerry if we were receiving payment and Jerry said I'd have to ask Lourdes. My next call was back to Lourdes, Lourdes said she hadn't received any payment for our trips or the warehousing and or ground transportation, Lourdes said that we were making one free trip per month and charging for the others. I asked what they owed and Lourdes said it was just over $2,000,000.00. I told her to collect the money or I was going to take it out from her pay. Lourdes didn't say anything at first, then asked if I was kidding? I said to do what she could to collect the money.

By now Lori and June had returned with two bags each. I walked to the Hunter with Lori and grabbed our bags. I had told Lourdes to have Tommy pick us up. June asked when I'd be back and I said I be over on Andros. Lori asked what was going on over there? I said we were working a large construction project. Lori asked if she could go? I said her holiday was over until Christmas.

We said our good buys to everyone with June giving me a very conservative hug and kiss. Lori and I took a taxi to the airport where Tommy was there waiting.

During the flight home Lori asked if I owned the tourist shop's too? I said the shop next to Angee's restaurant belong to Cat and I and that the Thomson store belonged to Diane and the Johnson family, The Johnson family being Janie, Cat, their mother and father. Lori asked who was

Diane? I said that Diane was a bed time story that spanned over 10 years. Does the story have a happy ending Lori asked? I said she'd have to wait and see. One day Lori said, you should write a book.

We landed in Miami and were on our way to see the children. We all were happy to see each other. Everyone liked their gifts.

I took Lori home with me for the night and would take her back to Chubby's early the next morning. At the apartment Lori said she had the time of her life on that trip, better than anything, even Disney she said. Lori said that Cat and June were beautiful! She said it would be hard to complete with either of them. All you have to do is make the right choices, all the rest will come to you I said. Lori asked that I stop taking chances, what would happen if something ever happened to you she asked? I said that she and the children would be well taken care off. I don't want money she said I only want you. I got that hot shower and much more, it would be hard to drop her off tomorrow.

The next morning came and I did drop her off. I promised her I be back for Christmas. Lori's tears didn't stop and I almost changed my mind. I reminded myself about the choices.

I called Cat and had her speak with Lucy' parents about their beach house on Andros. I remembered it wasn't much but even if I could stay in the room that Cat and I had shared that would be fine. Cat spoke with Lucy's parents and Cat would fly over to Andros with Ida to see what could be done with the house and rooms. I would take a commercial flight to New Orleans while Cat and Tim would use Tommy for transport to and from Andros. I visited Salinas and little Michelle while Cat, Ida, and yes, even June worked on Lucy's small hotel on Andros. I was gone for four days seeing Michelle and patching things up with Salinas. Salinas and I celebrated her 17th birthday at her favorite French restaurant in New Orleans.

Tommy then picked me up at Mandeville. The airport here in Mandeville was coming right along. We would start receiving cargo here the first week of the new year. Jack said they could hold their own at the New Orleans terminal until then. As we flew out of Mandeville I noticed that one of the C-130s was gone, I didn't think anything of it. I still had not spoken with the Colonel and the contractors that were staying at the Motel 6 were still there waiting.

When we arrived on Andros, Tommy mentioned that one of our C-130s was parked at the end of the runway. As we taxied off the runway the C-130 took off.

Lee was there to pick me up saying that the C-130 had a group of Fernando's men that would be practicing parachuting today.

Our first stop was the Hotel. Cat had gone back but Ida and June were still there working with some of Lee's men and the locals. The place now would have its own small generator with some air-conditioning and hot water. The main house wouldn't be ready for another week but they now had three small hotel rooms ready. All three were with air-conditioning and had new beds and ceiling fans. The room that Cat and I had used on the beach was one of the three ready. It was now December 9th but that screen hanging over the bed reminded me that the no seems here were year round.

Tim had come with our new people and were now staying at the dock house as we called it. I threw my bag in the room where I had once stayed and told Lee that I wanted to meet the ex-Nasa people.

When we caught up with them, they were at the container with the trap door. Jack had ordered to move the diving equipment, three chairs and two cots to the container that was set over the hole. Food and water were also made ready.

CHAPTER VII

THE RETURN TO THE CAVE

With me there, it would be 8 of us that would go down the ladder. Two of our divers would stay outside the door, and six of us would enter the rooms. The two divers at the ladder would change every hour. The engineers were impressed with the system in which the outside door and the removal of the water in the first room worked. Once we got to the second room the engineers were flabbergasted? When we were in the room before, all I saw was the gold. I didn't pay much attention to anything else. There were two small control chairs built for someone about 4 or 5 feet tall with very small frames. There were two helmets that were just about the right size as the engineer's heads. My head was a bit too big to fit in. The engineers were amazed to hear machinery working and seeing the flashing lights on the panels. There were two small computers like screens and one large one. As the engineers started marking what they thought the buttons were, I starting looking at the room a bit better. I found no other side doors but did find two-floor doors. Both doors led to small rooms with little head room, one had what looked like the water pumping systems for the first room, and the remaining part of the desalt plant. The next room had some kind of life support equipment to include two diving suits that had some sort of breathing appratus that I had not seen before. This room had like a large locker that I just couldn't open. While working on trying to open it, I was stopped by ohs and ahs from above. I stopped and went up. On one of the small screens, it looked like a well-marked track that seemed to start at the cave's channel entrance leading to what looked like all the way to the blue hole. Jack said, while diving, he hadn't noticed any markers but there they were. None of us had seen the vehicle that we thought was down in the channel but all of us now thought the cave had been enlarged to permit the vehicle to enter the cave. When they started working the control panel, it was showing 21 red lights. At present 5 of those lights had changed from red to green. There was what we thought an engine panel that had three red lights. Looked like the engineers could start the engine but within seconds the green lights would turn back to red. The engineers took turns using the cot to rest. I must have worked to open that locked door that was a floor down below for 10 hours before my eyes just needed a break. We were in the Cave Room for 16 hours when I said we'd call it a day. Of the 21 lights we now had 8 in green. Heck we didn't know what might or could happen when we got all of them in green. We all went back to the house and ate a good meal. June had it all planned that she and I would get one of the hotel rooms. A hot salt water shower is what we got. My head was into opening that box. The next day we did it again, even with one of the engineers able to read and write Latin, we had only identified about half of the names on the panels. We were down there almost another full day and only got three more green lights. All of a sudden one of the engineers yelled and all but three turned green. They called out to me and said to look at the screen on the left. There it was an inside toggled camera of the inside of the vehicle. I then asked the engineer at the engine switches to switch onto green, when he did the three green lights stayed green and now all 21 lights were in the green. In front of the engineer's seat there were three toggle switches. The engineer sitting there slowly touched one of the toggle switches and we believed the vehicle moved. It seemed we were missing something. How to steer the vehicle without seeing where we were going? Then it hit me, years ago the navy had removed that I thought was some kind of sonar sphere. Ok I said, lock things down we're going back up. I didn't get any complaints.

When coming up out of the hole, again it was dark. We all went to the house where I started making calls. I wouldn't get called back until the next day. That sphere that Joe and I had opened for the Navy years ago, was somewhere in Navy storage. It would take until 2:00 p.m. the next day for someone in the Navy to locate it. The Navy said they'd have it here the next day at 11:00 a.m. This would be my third night with June. Her being almost 8 months pregnant and us only having salt water to bath in hadn't been the most romantic two nights. June said that this shouldn't count as her three days, I agreed. June didn't stay at the hotel during the day. I had told her not to walk along the beach as Lusca had been known to snatch pretty girls from the beach. I didn't think Lusca was still alive but then again we had no proof that Lusca wasn't still down there. Me telling June about Lusca was all she needed to hear to stay clear from the beach.

The next day the sphere arrived and the engineers and I checked on it and couldn't find anything missing. Our thoughts were that the sphere was down on the bottom waiting to be activated by the vehicle or the control room as we called it. From the first time I had seen this sphere my impression was that it was some kind of sonar device.

When we were ready the Navy dropped the sphere in about the same place they had found it. Our hope would be that once in the channel it could activate and send the vehicle the directions to the location of the cave entrance.

The engineers had taken photos of the controls so that they could keep working during our down time.

It being almost dark we decided to get an early start the next morning. I thought June might be hankering to get back to Nassau. I asked her if she wanted for Tommy to run her back to Nassau or even Miami. June said she wasn't going back to Miami until Christmas. June said she wasn't going to lose any opportunity to be with me.

The next morning our same group went back down to the cave room. To our grand surprise, the screen now showed a working sonar device with shadow images of the vehicle and the cave's entrance. At this point, our divers had removed the barrier they had placed in the cave to keep out any unwanted visitors, mainly Lusca.

The engineer at the controls looked at me for my approval, I said to see if it would slowly move forward. The feeling I got when the image started to move was unreal. It seemed that the sonar sphere was controlling the vehicle's direction as if it were pre-set for the cave. All of a sudden one engineer warned to shut it down, as she did, at least 5 or 6 lights started to flash. We shut down the engine and then everything. It was a fuel depleted warning that caused the lights to flash. We then recognized a fuel level gage and electrical use and storage gage. As we turned things on and off we got a good feel of what took the most power to run. Of course the propulsion system required the highest level of fuel and electrical use. We were concerned that while underway and before we even reached the cave, what if we depleted all power. If that happen we could end up with the vehicle just crashing back to the bottom and end up right where we were before finding the room. Well maybe not exactly but at least where bringing up the vehicle was concerned.

We knew that the sonar could be used to guide the vehicle while the sphere could find the vehicle and the cave entrance but what about once the vehicle entered the cave. We calculated and hoped that the dots that appeared on the computer screen were there to also guide the vehicle through the cave to the cave's door where we could stop it. We also thought about running out of power and not being able to open the vehicle's door. We figured that the door system would be much the same as the cave's using power to open the door, then to close it, pumping the water out, then opening the enter door. The reverse would be required to come back out. Should the power be lost during these steps anyone inside could get caught inside without enough oxygen to last until we figured a way out. The cave room showed a high amount of fuel and stored power.

Our thinking now turned to the rooms power source. From the first time we entered we carried a Giger counter. Thus far the radiation level was there but no different than everything else had that was left over from the original bomb some 37 years ago.

One of the engineers and I went back down into where the pumps were. I couldn't find any outside power source. From the water pump there was something that looked like cables that led to the systems panel, but we couldn't find the source.

It was getting late and this required some quite thinking time. We would all leave and go top side.

We all ate a good meal together and then Tim, June and I would leave for the hotel. My thinking time would have been a good hot freshwater shower with June. I settled for that hot salt water shower with June. There was something about not showering alone. June said she couldn't sleep good with the salt water drying on her. The salt water made me feel like the old days down at Elliot's Key Park with Rusty. This water smelled better, maybe it was June's perfume. It also could have been my Lagerfeld.

When I opened my eyes the next morning something had come to me. The pumps, the water moving thru the pipes was generating the power that was charging the power source. The water movement maybe generated more energy than it took to run the pumps. If this was the case, then maybe the movement of the vehicle could also do the same. If my theory was correct, we could activate the vehicle's pumps and see if this raised it's power level.

June had gotten up and made me coffee, she had stopped drinking it more than month ago.

We fetched Tim and on the way to the dock house I explained my simple theory. Back at the dock house the engineers thought it too simple. If this would work why hadn't someone used it before. That's just it I said, they did.

Sure enough we went back down there and worked on activating the pumps, pumping the water in and out of the vehicle while watching the power level rise. We did this for 4 hours until the gages were well into a normal looking range.

We were ready to attempt to move the vehicle.

CHAPTER VIII

MOVING THE VEHICLE

Ok, let's give it a go. To save power, there were several switches we didn't turn on. It looked like there now were two engines started. The toggle was moved forward and the vehicle's shadowy image on the screen began to move. Hell the more we looked the more we found, there must have been at least 20 indicator gages. There was a depth indicator that was showing that the vehicle was rising, we were not steering the vehicle, it had its own course. More throttle on the toggle switch meant more speed. We stayed at the lowest possible speed. It appeared that there was another power source that was either depleted or running on reserves. Looked like the vehicle was running on electric only. Maybe the slow speed that we were traveling at was all the vehicle could do at the moment. Any way the Vehicle was on its way to the cave's entrance.

All of a sudden there appeared an object on the sonar screen. The object seemed to be heading directly torward the vehicle. The speed in which the object was traveling looked as if it would overtake the vehicle. I don't know why but I just knew it was Lusca!

The engineer that knew Latin was struggling to find some kind of defense mechanism. I expressed that even if we found such a thing that if we used it we may lose propulsion. I said I thought we should start the water pump and attempt to outrun the object. The pump was restarted and the engineer at the throttle eased it forward. The vehicle jumped up in its forward motion and the energy alarm sounded, then went off by itself. Seemed the forward motion along with the pumps running were generating enough power to sustain the higher speed. The object was still gaining however it looked like we might make it to the cave.

The vehicle made it to the cave first and when entering it disappeared off the sonar screen. At the same time the vehicle dropped off the sonar screen, it appeared on the cave's screen. The object still coming also went into the cave. By now the engineer working with the defense mode thought he could use it. Now if the vehicle stopped it wasn't in a place where it could or would fall. The defense mode was turned on and a circle appeared on the screen showing the vehicle. The circle being 360 degrees, and then the dial was turned until it was pointing toward the cave's entrance, and with my order, he pressed the fire button. A light left the vehicle and headed toward the entrance. When reaching the object that was following the vehicle, the light did not stop. The light kept going but the object had stopped. Whatever was following was still there but not moving. The vehicle didn't even hiccup. We slowed it down as much as it would go. We were worried that it could hit the diver that was watching the outside cave door. We pulled back the throttle and the vehicle came to a stop at about 10 feet from the cave door entrance.

We had now been down there quite some time. None of us were tired, we all wanted to get inside the Vehicle. We worked to find how to open the outside door of the vehicle. We knew there wouldn't just be a button to open it from the outside.

The first thing was to restart the Vehicle's oxygen support system. It was found and turned on and within ten minutes the green light turned on giving us the thumbs up.

We did find what we thought was the door and once we were sure the Vehicle's first chamber was full of water, opened the door using the cave's controls. Two engineers would stay in the room while Tim, Jack, Mira and myself would put on our scuba gear and return to the cave. The diver that had been watching the door signaled me up the latter. He wanted to tell me that just after the Vehicle had arrived at the cave's door, the water had turned black. My take on this was that the black stuff was Ink from Lusca.

We went back down and found Tim and the others at the first door. There wasn't enough room for us all to enter so Jack and myself would go first. Once inside the vehicle we would rework the door to close. The process with the water and doors worked once the first sections water had been drained we opened the cabin door. Jack and I were surprised to see how small the interior was. I was 5'-11" while Jack was over 6 feet tall. We didn't rework the interior door because of the space. We could hardly move ourselves. One of the first things I found was a skeleton. From the bones it looked much like a human only much shorter and with a smaller bone thickness, by the size and head shape, I imagined that the skeleton was a match for the drawing on the panther skin that I had. I did not touch the skeleton, in fact both Jack and I had put on gloves. Jack mentioned that here, like the cave's room there were two control seats but only one skeleton. There was also what looked like two bunks. I found a booklet that looked like a design and repair manual. There were what Tim would have called floppy disks with each page. I told Jack to return and to send me in Mira. We would be short on time, but I needed her opinion on what I was about to do. Jack was to go up top and get us something that was water proof so I could remove the manual that I had found. Jack went out of the main cabin, shutting me in, then started the water intake process. When the outside cabin was filled, he and Mira would change places. Once Mira was inside, I showed her what I had found. It looked like a removable panel that could possibly contained most if not all the vehicle's systems. The only thing we weren't sure of was if we pulled it out, could we get out. We agreed to try. The panel was a sealed unit about 12" wide and 18" long and about 1" thick. It weighted about 10 pounds. I pulled it out and all but one screen went blank. I could feel the air movement stop indicating that the life support system had most likely shut down. Jack came back and without entering the main cabin, gave me a water proof case and then Mira stepped out with Jack and the door then again closed. With the removal of the what we thought was the control system the interior lighting had gone dim. Only a small light at the control seats was on.

For a good three minutes I was alone in the vehicle. I went to the skeleton and removed a chain that was placed around the Shelton's neck and a gold Bracelet on the right wrist bone. I had noticed the chain and bracelet at once but didn't know if Jack saw it. I placed the chain that had what looked like two separate metal credit card size plates and the bracelet in my waterproof gun pouch. The door reopened and Tim stepped in wanting a quick look. We then entered the middle space behind the door, it closed and refilled with water. Once out and in the cave I signaled for

Tim and Mira to go up the ladder and Jack to get the others out of the cave's room. Still carrying the control box, I then climbed up the ladder and was helped out of the hole.

It had been one heck of a couple of days. Once at the dock house, Tim got a look at the floppy disks and noted how similar they were to the technology that he was now using. I would ask Mira to switch rooms with the two male engineers and have them go to the Hotel for one night. Lee's bed room which he had loaned to Mira had the only safe in the house. Fernando was also quietly put on high alert. June was happy to get a hot fresh water shower before going to bed.

I would sleep on my thoughts and the next morning had Tommy fly the three engineers, June and Jack to Nassau. The three engineers and Jack would stay at the Hill Top House on Paradise Island. Cat was called and would make the house ready. Even though the three engineers had signed the contract that Roy had drawn up, there was always the possibility of one of them talking or making that call. Jack would go along to kind of baby sit, at least until I made contact with Washington. My guess was that it could be weeks before we would need the engineers to continue their work.

My plan was to go down one more time to see if the cards that I had taken from the skeleton could open the box in the basement below the cave's room. I hadn't got a good look at the outside of the vehicle, but my though also was that maybe one of those cards was used to open the vehicle door from the outside.

Lee said that he would be ready to break ground over the cave's tunnel in about one week. He said they would be ready for the vehicle in another two weeks after that. I knew I would need to return to the Philippines right before the elections. I told Lee that I needed to cut that time. I know I said you are pushing it now, but I'm running out of time. Lee said that I once told him that the possible is done at the moment and that the impossible is done but takes a little more time.

With the engineers gone Tim and I would enter the cave's room one more time. Once inside I went straight to the box that was located in one of the small rooms under the control room. There was a slot that looked good for the card, I slipped in one of the cards. I was not surprised the box opened. First there were two items what looked like some kind of weaponized laser guns, I was sure that's what they were. There were also two sets of what looked like fuel rods and one set of protective clothing. The two containers with the rods had a kind of sight glass which I could see the tubes and an indicator light that was well into the green. The tube had markings that I just knew were radiation warnings. I checked the outside of the containers for radiation but found none. There were what looked like tools and parts. Then I saw a familiar looking box. I was sure it was a spare to the control panel that I had taken from the vehicle. I took the control box, both weapons and backed out. I relocked the door and I was ready to go. Tim had found more floppy disk that resembled the others. The ones we had seemed to be copies. This time I had brought with me the water proof case. The control panel fit in but the weapons would not. We were in there no more than 30 minutes and we were finished. We got out of the room and once in the cave I tried to find some kind of slot on the outside of the vehicle for the card. Maybe the lighting wasn't enough but I couldn't find one. With only one tank of air, we were running out of time. I turned and signaled Tim to climb up the ladder. We were done here. By the time we reached the house I knew that Tommy should be back. I didn't shower I just gave the guns a fresh water wash and towel dried them. I got my stuff to include using Tim's small case to load the two control boxes. I had a .30-06 Springfield rifle with a scope in a case, but the shape and size of the laser gun wouldn't fit. I would rap both laser guns in towels and then a sheet. Fernando would take us to the airport with four of his best men. When we reached the airport Tommy was there waiting. Tim was ready to get back home, he now had two children and of course his beautiful wife. Tim was now operating two container business that played a major part of Sea Container's business.

Me, well, it hadn't been quite as long as I thought before I would see Lori again, but I was glad I would get to see her. I would keep one booklet with the disks, the two control boxes and the two laser weapons in my apartment safe.

Just as soon as I walked in my apartment, I opened the safe and once all was locked away, I called Lourdes and had her call the White House for the Secretary of State. She should tell him that I had made a break through and wanted to meet with him and the President. I also wanted Lourdes to locate Jena. Lourdes would call me back here and leave a message if I didn't answer. I then called Big Ted and left a message for him too. His message was that I wanted a guard at my apartment door.

I then jumped in the car and was headed for Chubby's. Once at Chubby's Lilly said that Lori was at the sailing club taking sailing lessons and Chubby was with the children at the Zoo. I was happy to drive to the sailing club. Once there I got to see Robert. Robert didn't know that I had a friend taking pram lessons but he was more than happy to take me out in the launch to see what he called the kids in their Prams. Lori didn't see me but I sure saw her. Lori was at the head of the pram pack looking like she was having the time of her life. As I looked at her, all I could see was her head and that red life jacket. I hoped she had more under that life jacket than the last time I had seen her wearing one. Robert and I only stayed for five minutes as he was working. Robert asked if she was mine or one of my friend's kid. I just smiled.

When I got back to the club I realized it was Saturday afternoon and the bar was open. I walked around the back door and asked the bar tender if he could sell me a beer. Paul turned and laughed as he saw me. He then came out and gave me a hug. I got news for you he said with a big smile! I got married he said. How great I said anybody I know? Yes, he said, I married Penny. Wow I said, now that's great! It did, it made me feel good. Two friends getting married. Paul went back in and I walked around to the bar. Once behind the bar, Paul started introducing everyone as nowadays I didn't know anyone. Sitting at the bar I faced the mirror and had a watchful eye out for the prams as they returned. I was wearing a flowered shirt and shorts, Paul said it reminded him how my uncle Bob and Carson used to come in. Paul looked good and said things hadn't changed. Paul was referring to my bulge under my left arm pit. Paul said the last he heard I was married. He looked at my finger and said he'd guessed it hadn't worked out. So Paul asked, how's the women in your life? I said I was quite busy. Paul looked around and asked whom had brought me down to the club today? I think it's the first time I've ever seen you without company Paul said. I glanced at the mirror and there she was. She was loading up her pram on one of the dollys. Paul saw me look and asked if she remind me of anyone? I looked at him strange and then thought of June. Paul then said if we were only that age again. Some of us never grow up I said. Paul said, that young and at your age her father would kill you.

I swung my bar stool around and looked at her. She's beautiful I said. I slipped off the stool and headed her way. I heard Paul say as I walked out the door. There goes trouble.

I walked half way across the lawn and whistled. Lori spun around and started running at me. When she reached me she almost knocked me down. What a sight we were. I then walked her to the pram and helped her put it away. I walked back to the bar's back door once more and introduced Lori to Paul. Paul said he should have known. I told Paul to give my regards to Penny, paid the tab and Lori and I were off.

When we reached the apartment there was a uniformed policeman at the door. He said he was sent by Ted until Ted could get someone else there. Ted was now a big shot detective on the metro police department.

It was to the shower, my first after diving the cave's room in the morning. From the shower I checked the phone messages. I would be expected at the White House first thing Monday morning just 8 days from Christmas. Lourdes's message said that Jena was in someone's Vineyard. I figured it was most likely Martha's Vineyard. There Jena would fit right in.

CHAPTER IX

PA'ME

There was a knock on the door. I looked at the camera and it was a beautiful young girl with a cane in her hand that I recognized. I opened the door and she stepped in. As the girl stepped in, I realized that she looked Filipino, the girl looked behind me and said hello in Filipino, she was talking to Lori. Lori answered her back in their language. I asked her in and shut the door behind her. Lori was right there chatting with her back and forth. Lori said that Mr. Montibelli had sent his cane for you to barrow. He also sent this message. I took the envelope and walked to the balcony, I opened the envelope and it said "Rasheed's yacht moored at the French Riviera with your friend aboard two days ago". I thought if I left now I might catch them, but maybe they'd be gone. No I would go to the White House and go from there. When I turned Lori was still talking to the girl and smiling. Lori said this is Pa'me she is also from the south part of the Pilippines. Lori asked Pa'me where she lived? Pa'me looked at me and stood and said she must go. Lori stood and looked at me as for me to stop her from leaving. I looked and said I was sure that Pa'me had a car waiting. Pa'me said yes I must go. Lori asked Pa'me how she could find her? Pa'me said you must not and went to the door. Pa'me waited at the door with her back to us until I came and opened the door. When Pa'me left Lori was confused and asked me why that had just happened? I thought about my words very carefully and then said that I thought Pa'me was not free. Not free Lori asked? Yes, I said, she may be working for a man that keeps close tabs on what she does. You mean she has a master Lori asked? I'm not sure I said? Can we help her Lori asked? What would you like me to do I asked?

She needs help Lori said. She was afraid, Lori said. Lori then looked at me and asked if I was her master. No I said, you are fee, you can do as you please. I am your lover, not your master; there is a big difference; I want what's best for you. You will one day be the master of your destiny. If you want me to help her, we can try. But where will she go, whom will look out for her? She can have my room at Chubby's Lori said, I will live with you. I will share with her what I have, everything except you she said. You don't know her I said. She's scared isn't that enough Lori asked? I went in and redressed, opened the safe and took out the magic box that Carson had given me, went to the door with his cane and said I be back in a few hours.

I drove my car to where I believed Mr. Montibelli lived. I located him by the guard at the door of the building. I told the guard at the door that Mr. Montibelli was expecting me. The outside guard removed my guns then tapped the door and handed my guns to the guard inside. The door was then opened, as I walked in I was frisked once more. The guard then pointed to the pool. As I walked toward the pool I could see Mr. Montibelli was in the pool with the Jewish girl. As Montibelli saw me he started out of the pool, Pa'me was there to dry him off. You must control your urges he said. For the girl you left yourself open. The girl I asked? Yes he said, Lori. She sent you he said.

You are here alone without your weapons, you are vulnerable. Most likely no one knows your even here he said. The girl I said I want to buy her freedom. Pa'me, Montibelli asked, are you unhappy here? No Sir she said, do you want to go with this man? No Sir she said. Why is he here Montibelli asked her? He is here because you sent me for him she said. I raised my eye brows and with my left hand pushed the button that was attached on just under my right jacket sleeve. At that moment, an explosion went off outside at the back of his building. Montibelli slowly looked that way and then said he might have missed judged me. Do I need the rest of the show I asked? That won't be necessary Montibelli said, I meant no harm. By now we could hear the sirens coming. I trust my people are alright he said. Well I said, noting that a little black coffee and two aspirin won't cure. Now what about the girl I asked? Pa'me he said, go up and pack your bag. Pa'me looked at him and he nodded his head. Your passport too I said. Sorry old friend no passport he said. The note, I asked, it was real? Oh yes he said quite real. Mr. Montibelli then said he was only going to invite me for a cocktail. I smiled and said to please not get another Philippine girl. Mr. Montibelli smiled. No more tricks on each other I asked? You have my word Montibelli said. Your cane I said. As I held it out to him, he looked at me slightly turning his head. It's not tainted I said.

Pa'me came down dress carrying a small bag. She went to Montibelli and thanked him. I put on a pair of latex gloves on and as we walked out I removed my guns from the man on the floor. When I open the door there was Ted. The guard that was at the door was propped up against the wall. Everything cool Ted asked? Yes I said, if you can please leave some one here to watch the place until he gets his guards back in working condition. I cleaned off my guns, removed the gloves then open my passengers side door for Pa'me. I then told Ted that I was having the elevator in the building blocked from my floor. I would provide him with the key just as soon as I had one.

On the way to the apartment Pa'me didn't say a word. We knocked on the apartment door and Lori opened it. We walked in and I said to Lori, remember, be careful what you ask for.

It was now after 10:00 p.m. we ordered pizza, Lori and Pa'me talked and talked. Pa'me took the small spare bedroom and Lori and I went to our bed room.

Lori asked what I was going to do with Pa'me? I asked about family and Lori said that Pa'me's parents had sold her at age 14. The men that bought Pa'me promised her mother she would be treated well. Pa'me said she was raped the first night by the very same men that had bought her. She said her mother must have known. Those men sold her to a prostitute house. The very next week a man came looking, Lori said that Pa'me said the house lined up the girls and the man picked her. That man paid the house and brought her to the states where she was sold to your friend.

What will you do with her Lori asked? The best thing we could do for her is to put her in a boarding school I said. Will she be safe there Lori asked? There the head master is responsible for her wellbeing. He would answer to me if any harm came to her. Can we visit her Lori asked? Yes of course I said, maybe she can spend some time with us during the summer I said. That would be nice Lori said. The next morning, I called Evette and asked Evette to come to Miami and stay with Pa'me while Lori and I went to Washington. I couldn't leave Lori alone with Pa'me and I couldn't leave Pa'me by herself. Leaving Pa'me at Chubby's was out of the question. I would send Tommy to get Evette from New Orleans. Lori lent Pa'me clothes as the little clothes that Pa'me had were to make her look older and sexier. The three of us went to breakfast then shopping at the Dadeland mall. The night before I had told Lori that she could go to Washington with me on Monday morning. We bought lots of clothes for both girls. When we got home I threw away almost everything that Pa'me had in the way of clothing. Evette showed up at about 5:00 p.m. and reclaimed her old room. Evette and Pa'me seemed to get along fine. Evette was with the orders not to leave the apartment until we returned and to stay out of trouble. The next morning Lori and I left the apartment before 5:00 a.m., me driving to Opa-locka. I took with me my normal carry on plus the case with one of the control boxes plus one of the weapons that was now boxed in a Astronomer's case.

Once in Washington we checked in at the hotel without question as Mr. and Mrs. We went up to the room and I asked Lori not to leave the room. I called and ordered her lunch to be delivered at noon, I would be back before dinner. Lori kissed me and thanked me again for helping with Pa'me.

I had a limo waiting at the Hotel's front door. This time, carrying what I was moving, I wasn't leaving my side arms at the hotel. When we pulled up at the White House gate I informed the guards hat I was armed and carrying top secret materials for the President. They asked the limo to pull over and I stepped out and they took both guns and opened my bag and both the case carrying the controller and the larger bag. I informed them that the bag nor case could leave my sight. I was held up at the gate until two secret service men showed up to check and carry in the bag and case. The three of us got in the limo and then it let us off at the front door of the White House. This was my third visit and I was no less nervous. The three of us were led to the waiting room where my good friend the Colonel was there waiting. The first thing the Colonel said was that he had his people sitting in Mandeville for almost two weeks. I looked at him and said that he shouldn't have sent them without clearing it through me first. The Colonel said, you don't return my calls. Just as I was about to say something I might have regretted, the Director walked in. Now, now gentlemen we are on the same side the Directir said. Colonel did you congratulate Jim for a job well done in the Philippines. Damn the Colonel said looking at me, I just wish you'd be more of a team player. The extra electronics, what's it for I asked? The Sandinistas might have received a few ground to air missiles he said. If they have them they most likely would use them close to where we are dropping supplies the Colonel said. The new electronics may pick the missiles up when they launch he said with a smile. We are also offering to supply you with anti-missiles technical support the Colonel said, but I suppose you don't want that either. My pilots are family men I said, they were promised by you Coronel, that they would not come under fire. And that airport that your building what do you plan on landing there I asked? The Colonel said the contras were in need of a tank or two. The tanks will keep the missiles out of range he said. The Colonel said besides, any missiles that are fired at our planes and miss would land in Costa Rica. Now your motive comes out I said.

We could have gone on and on but we were called into the Oval office. The secret service men said they would need to carry in the case and stay until the President asked them to leave. The Secretary of State was there and welcomed us all. Once we were all in, the President came in. The President first congratulated me on the fine work with the rebels. I trust your wounds have healed he said. Thank you, sir, and yes, Sir, I'll be ready to return for the elections. Good he said, I understand you want to report on some progress of my space ship he said. The President looking at the two Secret Service men asked what we had in the case and bag? It's a controller and a laser weapon I declared. The Vehicle, which I call it, is now parked in the cave almost directly under where the lab is being built. The vehicle is in good working condition, I said. As we were bringing her up a giant octopus was about to attack and we used the Vehicle's laser system to destroy it. Son, you mean that you moved this thing on its own power? Yes Sir, I said. That cave door that we talked about is actually a control room sir. The Colonel then jumped in and asked, Jim are you saying that this thing was moved by remote control. Yes Sir, that is what I'm saying, and it's more. Before most of you were involved, one of my companies built one of your first sonar devices that the Navy was using to tract the Soviet Subs coming and going from Cuba. I was then asked to build and design the next three such devices. Using one of the sonar devices that we supplied, the Navy found a small device that they couldn't open, my Dad is sort of a Black Smith Lock Smith. The Navy called me to open it. At the time I opened it for them, just as soon as I did the Navy men took over. The Director then cut in and asked what this had to do with the space ship. The Colonel said to let me finish. Well I said at the time I thought that the device was some kind of advanced sonar. The Navy found this device in the channel near the cave entrance, the vehicle was also spotted near by. Of course the Navy said nothing of the larger item their sonar had located. Last week I asked the Navy to loan me the device that they had found, I had this hunch. The Navy dropped the device back into the channel where they found it. The control room in the cave picked it up on its screen. The sonar device that the Navy dropped back into the channel had a pre-set destination for the Vehicle. Once under power, the Vehicle was guided into the cave. I believe, Mr. President you now have the technology to not only to knock down an incoming missile, but also the technology to guide a missile to a certain point and to change it's course while traveling. Oh yes, there is a skeleton aboard the vehicle that looks to match a being of the drawing on the panther skin that I showed the Director when I delivered him that medical laser, two years ago. Aboard the Vehicle there was also a laser weapon. The Laser is in the bag that your men are holding. The control room was meant to be in case of any emergency. I took the liberty of removing the control panel from the vehicle, this so that it can not be moved. The case I have here has the control board. The Colonel was quick to say that I had said it would be almost impossible to get into the door in the cave. No Sir, what I said was it would be impossible to do, from the caves entrance. We drilled a hole into the cave from top side. What security is on sight at this moment the Secretary asked? Well I said not much as the only way in would be thru the hole we drilled which is on the Navy base or through one of two of the cave's entrances. The lab should be ready to receive the vehicle within three weeks I said. I have put together a team of engineers that have worked with me so far. I suggest that you continue their employment as you go forward.

What about security of these people the Secretary asked? Well Sir all had been cleared by the state department. I believe we have one Israeli spy that you might or might not know about. I picked her because she's the best, she's being watched and will not contact her people until she has more information. You have a spy in your group the Colonel asked? Yes

Sir, she's worked at Nasa for over 20 years. The technology is here in this case, not in her hands, she nor anyone but myself has touched it. I will deliver the vehicle in three weeks as contracted. The President then asked to see the Laser weapon. As the bag was opened I warned not to remove it as I wasn't sure it was safe. All stood and looked at the Laser. I could see that all were impressed with what they were looking at. The bag was then shut and sealed, the President then gave a nod to his men, they placed the bag on the floor and they left the room. I now raised my hand to get permission to speak. Gentlemen I said, we haven't been paid for any of the services that we have provided to the Coronel. I'd like to get paid and then cancel that agreement.

The President then looked at the Colonel and the Director and thanked them for coming. They got up as did I, the President then said for me to stay seated.

Once the Colonel and Director had left the room, the President said I had contributed a great service and would be paid the agreed amounts. Son, the President said, we need your continued support. The Colonel, the President said, is a decorated American hero whose drive is to rid the communist of our hemisphere. The President then said it was his wish to free the world of communism. Son your skills are unique, we need you to be a bit more flexible with the Colonel and the Director. We need your birds to stay in the air and continue their support. We also would like to expand your service to your country. Your country needs you the President said.

We have a friend whom I've known since I was a young man in acting school, we would like you to meet with him and maybe do some business together. Mr. Crowbe has called your office but can't seem to reach you. I understand that you aren't very good about returning calls, the President said. I'd appreciate you getting together with Mr. Crowbe and listening to what he has to say. Can you do this son the President asked? I answered, yes Sir Mr. President. Now what can we do for you the Secretary asked? Well first of all, if my C-130s are going to be put in more danger, I'll need two crews that sign on for those dangers, what else he asked? I need a Visa for an illegal Filipino girl. I can get the visa I said, but it wouldn't be illegal. The Secretary and the President smiled and the Secretary asked that's it? That and pay my invoices I said. OK then we're all set the President said.

The Secretary said he'd have someone call my secretary about the visa. Jim keep up the good work the President said. The Secretary said he'd take care of the controller and the weapon and would add addition security on Andros. The Secretary said he keep in touch. I thanked them both and walked out the way I came in.

As I left the room, the Colonel was waiting for me. The Colonel asked, do we have the green light on the birds? Yes Sir I said, and we'll need that crew you had offered too. The Colonel then handed me an envelope and said I should now be paid in full. I apologized for not calling him back and said I'd do a better job of communicating. The Colonel said that we were on the same team, we then shook hands.

The limo was waiting and on the way out the guards returned my guns. I check both to see if they had been touched or tagged, they were fine.

I was happy to get back to the Hotel, Lori had lunch and said that a Mr. Crowbe's secretary had called. I sat and returned the call. It was still morning out there; I was calling San Francisco. I was put through to Mr. Crowbe and I apologized for not returning his call. Mr. Crowbe asked if I could come by his office tomorrow. I agreed and we set the time for 10:00 a.m. I was sitting on the side of the bed when I heard that whistle and the shower turn on. Oh that whistle I thought.

The shower was especially good. Afterwards I would make several calls. The first to Jerry, to ok the electrictronic work on the C-130s and informed him that we would be keeping our crew but they were off limits to any more Central America flights. I informed him that The Colonel's crew would be taking over those trips. I called Lourdes and said to call off the dogs on collecting the money, that the Conlonel had paid in full. We would deposit this money in the Caymans.

Lori and I would check out of the hotel and would take in some of the sights of Washington. Lori especially enjoyed passing by the White House, knowing I was just there visiting the President.

Lori looked good, she slowly but surely was becoming that fine looking lady I knew was in there. Lori hadn't quite reached the high heel thing yet, but her fancy black leather boots and Black leather jacket had her looking as good or better than if she was wearing high heel shoes. Today she didn't look 16, today she could pass for well maybe 20.

We finished up the tour with the Lincoln monument. Lori had no idea who Abraham Lincoln was. From there we made the airport where Tommy was there waiting to fly us to San Francisco.

We got into town early enough to visit China town, Lori and I had a good time. The next day I had plenty of time to make my 10:00 a.m. meeting. I decided to take Lori with me and we could go from the meeting to the airport. We had lots to do before Christmas. We would spend Christmas day in Miami and then fly all of us to Nassau for the week.

We were early to my meeting and while in the waiting room at the Maritime Building, I read how Mr. Crowbe's father had started his empire with a small row boat delivering supplies to the cargo ships anchored in the harbor. Lori was impressed. Presently Mr. Crowbe's was the third largest U.S. shipping company. This behind U.S. Lines and Sea Land.

At exactly 10:00 a.m. I was called and led into Mr. Crowbe's office. Lori would wait for me.

I was expecting a younger man but then his grandfather started the business in 1918. Funny it was the same year that my grandfather had started his business. I could see where Mr. Crowbe could have reached I'd say about 70? Anyway Mr. Crowbe came from around his large desk and shook my hand and sat with me. He ordered in coffee and we talked. Mr. Crowbe said he liked how I cleared the deck and made things ship shape in General Santos. He was bold with his questions, he asked what my investment in General Santos had been so far and what were my first quarter profits. Mr. Crowbe said that his shipping company was doing fine but that his larger competitors, the number one and two lines had been losing money for years. I'll be straight with you he said. I can't see how both of them will survive another year. I understand you took the McClean Terminal in New Orleans, by far the best facility in town. Your market for the tuna business is Japan is it not, he asked? Well Sir at present a large portion of my fish and shrimp, or prawns as they call them goes to Asia. I'm planning a third ship that will call the Gulf using the Rail Road to move our goods north. Mr. Crowbe then asked whom I was using to consult with on this new direction. I said no one sir, I just go with the opportunity that comes my way. Refrigerated fright on a Rail Road just doesn't appear overnight he said. I have somewhat of a mechanical back ground I said. We are now running 8 new generators in General Santos.

This has changed the amount of cargo I can ship and the quality of the product that reaches the customer's door. Using a Sea Container flat rack, we can mount generators with fuel tanks aboard rail flat beds. Each such flat rack could provide enough electric for 8 to 10 refrigerated containers.

I told him that I had made an agreement with the rebels in General Santos that will allow the U.S. Army Corp of Engineers to assist in the rebuilding of the bridge there in General Santos. Once the bridge is complete we will start using under slung generators on each chassis. This will open up more farms that at present are too far from the port.

Ok Mr. Crowbe said, I asked you here to discuss two things, first to make you an offer to buy your line, please hear me out. The President is concerned that the U.S. will lose the largest shipping line in the world. Looks like we may take over U.S. Lines or at least their ports of call, this within the next year or so. Yes he said, the minnow swallowing the whale. To offset their losses, I would need to buy your line and merge it into ours. Second the President says he needs you to be able to move freely around the world working some of his special projects. I also could use a man like you to travel to all our locations to make us a better line. What's the offer I asked? Ten Million he said without hesitation. No thanks I said, I know what ten million is I said, but we could make that much in the coming year alone. What then would be your magic number he asked? I'm not sure there a magic number Sir I said. I have 2,800 acers of farm land plus a Caning Tuna business that's all rapped into the shipping of that cargo.

No, if and when I sell it would need to be a package deal. I appreciate the offer but I'm not ready to sell. Mr. Crowbe said he understood and wanted to keep the line of commutations open between us. He said to remember that if his companies could assist with logistics for any of the Presidents work, that he was here to serve.

When I returned to the waiting room, there was a young man standing talking to Lori. Lori looked nervous, when she saw me she bolted into my arms. Here, here what's this about I asked? I looked at the young man as he came walking behind her. I'm sorry he said, I was just introducing myself to the young lady. I didn't mean to upset her. My name is Brian Crowbe he said, I'm Mr. Crowbe's grandson. That's ok I said she's just a little timid. Lori will be just fine. Lori the young man repeated, what a beautiful name. He then looked at me and said, you must be the man my grandfather was meeting with, my grandfather said that you have quite the reputation with the ladies. I should have known Lori was with you he said. Young Mr. Crowbe then said that with all the stories that he had heard, well he thought that I would be much older. Your great grandfather had a 48-year head start on me I said. I got started when I was 15. The past 20 years weren't without there rough spots but they have been good to me I said. Maybe we can meet again sometime and you could tell me a few of your famous fish stories Brian said. Maybe so I said. I looked at Lori and she then looked at young Brian and said it was a pleasure to meet him. Brian said the pleasure was all his.

Lori and I then went and caught a commercial flight for the French Riviera.

I knew we might be too late to se Martha, but if I didn't go now, I would have always thought, what if?

CHAPTER X

THE RIVIERA VISIT

On the flight Lori asked what Mr. Crowbe wanted? I told her that he wanted to buy the shipping company. She asked if I would sell? I explained that it was always my idea to sell when the time was right. I just hadn't figured an offer coming so soon. Will I ever go back to General Santos Lori asked? Well when you graduate high school I'll take you back for a visit. Would you ever leave me she asked? No mam I will not, if we ever separate it will be you that does the leaving. Lori took my arm and rested her head on my shoulder and went to sleep.

The next day, the 19th of December we were standing on the board walk of the Riviera. Now this was a rich kid's place. The women on the beach wore almost nothing. They were everywhere. We made our way to the dock master and inquired about Mr. Rasheed's yacht. The man in charge asked if Mr. Rasheed was expecting us. I'm the uncle of one of the girls on the boat and want to make sure she is ok I said, she's a US citizen. I gave the man my name and he called the Yacht's captain and relayed the message. The man then said that the girl was now one of Mr. Rasheed's wife's and that a boat would bring her to the pier. You mustn't touch her the man said, she could be punished. I didn't like the tone but understood that there was a hugh culture differance in that part of the world.

We waited until a small speed boat came alongside the pier. It was Martha alright. She was dressed in the standard Arabic women clothing with something that covered her head and most of her face. Without getting off the boat another woman said that Martha mustn't directly look at or speak to us. I asked if she was ok, Martha nodded she was. I asked the name of her Boston Whaler, Martha whispered into the women's ear. The "Tide Runner" the woman said. I knew that if she wasn't ok she give some other name. I said that her parents and I missed her and if at any time she wanted to come home to just send word. Martha nodded her head. The boat then pulled away. It was sad but I thought about it and said to Lori, it's all about the choices we make.

Ok I said, we're on the French Riviera! We first went shopping and got Lori a new bathing suit. She tried on several until I said that's it! I looked at her and said this was a onetime use suit. The bottom covered a small part in the front and nothing on the back side, and I do mean nothing. The top just covered what it was supposed to. Lori wasn't big chested so there wasn't that much to cover. Me I wore my American speedo. The beach sand was nothing compared to Harbor Island. Lori said there were too many pretty girls that walked by smiling and looking. Well enjoy it now because this is our first and last trip here. Lori asked where the men were? I told her maybe only the women came here. Lori got somewhat burned where what the sun hadn't seen before, but the rest of her body was just like I liked it, golden brown.

We stayed the night hitting the night life, now seeing more men, most with more than one women. Lori was wearing a long black satin dress with a thin golden belt about that small waist of hers. We had earlier stopped in a jewelry store that had to have charged double. I told Lori that the items were hers to keep on her 21st birthday. Until then they were on loan and would be kept in my apartment safe. She wore one-carat diamond earrings, pierced, of course, the piercing, a gift from the Cuban girls that worked in the Miami hair salon. A matching diamond neckless and wrist band. The kicker was this 3 carat diamond solitary.

Lori's waist looked as if one could put your hands around it and touch your fingers. The short sleeves and low cut neck line showed off her golden tan. She hadn't got a lot of lookers on the beach but tonight she was the one receiving all the smiles and stares.

After dinner we stopped at the casino, there was a young man at the tables that was gambling big money. Lori wanted to get close to see what was going on. We made our way to the table and Lori caught the man's eye. He saw me see him looking and acted as if it was no big deal. The man looked at Lori and, from across the table, asked if she'd wish him luck. Lori looked at him and said loudly that he should ask someone else. The man threw the dice and lost. He looked at me, I smiled and raised my shoulders. The man looked to be about the same age as me with a fare build and a three-day beard. Lori and I went and sat at the bar. I figured he'd come at us and warned Lori. I said that I'd do the rest of the talking. The man came as I thought he would and offered to buy our drinks. I stood and looked at him, thanked him for his kind gesture but said we would prefer to buy our own. I could see him start to steam. He then asked my name? My friends call me the King Fish I answered. A fisherman he asked? Something wrong with fishermen I asked? Yes, he said they smell like fish, then he smiled and looked at Lori. The man now had two of his men standing behind him. I said quite loudly said that Jesus had 12 disciples, 11 were fisherman. The other I said could have of been from Arab descent. His name was Judas I said. At the same time a third man walked and whispered into the ear of one of the man's men. Then the that same man tapped the young man on the shoulder and whispered into his ear. The young man then said maybe we'll meet again someday American. I looked at him and said, I'd bring my hook.

Lori and I finished our drink and waked back to our hotel. I apologized for ruining her night out. She dropped off all but the jewels and asked if she could wear them to bed. Right before she fell asleep Lori said she didn't know that Judas was an Arab. I apologized and said that I had got a bit carried away and I too had not heard that about Judas.

It was now just 5 days until Christmas, we would spend our last day at the beach and that night catch a flight back to Miami.

Once back at the Miami apartment I called Cat and said to get the message to Mary that we had seen Martha and she looked well. I told Cat that I would visit Mary and Tim the following week.

I had almost forgotten about Pa'me and Evette. Evette wanted me to know how smart Pa'me was, telling me that Pa'me could read and write and had been to etiquette school. Evette wanted to take Pa'me back to New Orleans with her. I knew Pa'me would soon be receiving a visa and most likely I would be signing as chaperone. Pa'me hanging out full time with Evette was out of the question, this because of Pa-me's age and Evette's behavior.

Christmas shopping would occupy two days, Lori helped me pick out new cars for Chubby, Lilly, Salinas and yes Evette too. I also purchased a new four door truck for Cat. Pa'me needed everything, clothes, shoes, belts, women stuff like perfume and even some moderate jewelry. The kids well they were growing like weeds and needed clothes and of course a pair of bikes. Samuel and Melody always talked about the dog they had left at General Santos. Lori, Pa'me, Evette and myself looked at 3 sets of puppies before I picked out a 6 week old German Sheppard. The male puppy was the pick of the litter whom had a barrel chest and big feet. I left the girls home and purchased a Hobie cat and Boston whaler for Lori.

June would get a diamond solitary that she could tell her father was an engagement ring. I had Jerry pick me out another German Sheppard puppy for Michelle, this time a female.

Lourdes was to pick up the car that I'd paid for in Miami for Salinas. Lourdes got what she wanted for Christmas, a divorce and full custody of her kids, a big fat bonus was also well received.

My Christmas Eve and day would be bright and tight. Tommy would not get that day off. I did Christmas Eve with Salinas and Michelle, then Christmas morning with Lori and the kids and then Christmas dinner with June and her family. Christmas evening Chubby, Lilly, Samuel, Melody, Pa'me, Lori and I would fly down to Nassau, hop on the "Salinas" and head out for Harbor Island. Yes, Lori had talked me into taking Pa'me with us to Nassau. Evette was going to spend Christmas with friends and I didn't want Pa'me out and about with Evette.

When arriving at Mandeville I was happy to see that the warehouse looked finished. Since it was Christmas eve there was of course no one working. I walked through the warehouse and the hanger. The only part left on the hanger was the a few touches of the office and the hanger doors. Jack would finally get some space by moving the Central American Cargo here to Mandeville.

During my short Salinas visit, Salinas said she had spoken with Cat over the phone and once the baby was born Salinas would move back to Nassau. Salinas was aware of June and now Lori. Salinas said that Cat and her thought that if all my children lived in Nassau, that I would spend more time there. Salinas was having another Girl while Cat would bear my first son. June would also be having a girl. Salinas said she would wait this time to have our next child and would keep on having children until she had a boy or I said to stop. Salinas said that Lourdes said that the hotel on Andros was now finished and that the engineers that were staying at the Hill Top beach house would soon be going back to Andros. Salinas said that I would soon tire of the girl from the Philippines and hopped I would return to her in Nassau.

Christmas morning with Samuel and Melody was great. It was their first such Christmas, as it was for Lori. I had parked the Hobie and Whaler in a Neighbor's yard and had them moved to Chubby's front lawn when I arrived that morning. The two cars for Chubby and his wife the same thing. Everybody was happy. I was planning on taking off the first week in January and Lori and I could learn about the hobie cat together. It was true that I once crewed on a hobie cat but Beverly had done the sailing. I had hoped that Lori wouldn't mind naming the hobie "Jamaica".

Bev's grandmother had since died and Bev and Nancy had both gotten married. Bev had named her first son Jim. I often thought of Bev and Nancy with the fondest of memories.

Ah the Christmas at June's house. June's house was a joyous day, here there was a complete family. The parents of both June's mother and father with Aunts and Uncles, Nieces and Nephews, brothers, sisters and grandchildren. June's father would mention the granddaughter that would be here shortly. June was happy with her ring and said how she was looking forward to living on the Island. Nassau was going to become quite busy.

The late evening flight to Nassau had our small group arriving to the "Salinas" at 8:00 p.m. Christmas evening. The kids loved the boat, yes we brought along the pup that they now called Saint. Saint wasn't allowed below deck. Cat had stocked the boat but she was not there to greet us. Cat was spending Christmas morning with Wendy Michelle and Johnny. She would spend the afternoon taking Lucy and her family for a sail on the Hunter. It would be Lucy's first outing since her latest recostructive surgery. Cat had left me two messages with Pete the dock master. I was to call Mr. Crowbe and Jerry.

I called Jerry first and he informed me that our C130 gun ship had return from its first trip piloted by the new crew. Jerry said the plane had come in on only three engines and lots of bullet holes. The 50 Calabria ammunition was short over 25,000 rounds. No one was hurt, only the

C-130. I told Jerry to be sure that the damaged C-130 was put in the hanger. Jerry said that he had done that when it came in and had given instructions of no on lookers or photos. I said that the second C-130 was off limits to the new crews and that to start repairs to the gun ship. Jerry said he had already ordered the same.

I then called Mr. Crowbe, he thanked me for calling and apologized for calling on Christmas. He said that he had spoken to his group and they had come up with an offer of $17,500,000.00 for the line the land the factory and my part of the tuna business. I didn't hesitate, I said that I had thought about selling and was now willing to negotiate a price for just the line. I mentioned that I would keep the Factory property and all of the origanal Santos farm which was one of the closest farms to town. The Santos farm ran along both sides of the river. I told him that I would offer The Fruit Company the remaining farms and my share of the Tuna business. The price, I noted was still much to low. Mr. Crowbe said he'd like to visit with me after the new year. My take was that Mr. Crowbe wouldn't have kept the land nor the tuna business but had planned as I did to sell it to the Fruit Company, lowering his investment into the line. I also figured that Mr. Crowbe also must have known that Marcos wasn't going to be around much longer. We wished each other a Merry Christmas and he said to call me when I came back from my trip.

We shoved off the dock well after dark and I would only last about two hours before anchoring. The space on the boat was perfect. Lori and I in the master, Chubby and Lilly in the other small bedroom, the kids and Pa'me out in the living room.

Once at anchor, Lilly and Pa'me would make dinner. Lori and I sat up top and I told Lori that one of my phone calls at the dock masters office was an offer for the line, most of the property and the Tuna business. I told her I hadn't taken the offer but soon all would be worth a great deal more than the present offer. I told her that I would save her old home which had been the factory and the old farm that had also belonged to the Santos Family before Marcos had taken most of it. As I recalled the present Santos farm had a total of 130 acers or so and a nice older house where Mrs. Santos still lived. We would collect rent on the factory and The fruit company would buy our fruit from the farm. Lori and I agreed that with that conversation we would not speak about any more business on the trip.

Dinner was great and we all bedded down for the night. At about 2:00 a.m. I got up to check the cabin door and found Pa'me out on the deck with Saint. Pa'me said she had heard Saint whining and didn't want him to wake the children. Pa'me asked if I also heard Saint whining. I told Pa'me that I had an alarm on the door that sounded as a beep when opened and or closed. Pa'me asked if she could take Saint back to bed with her? I said ok. I had the alarm system installed about a month ago. The cabin and the master also had small indictor position lights that had different colors that indicated the cabin hatch door, deck hatch and windows. Green was open, blue was shut and red was locked. If opened while locked, then a full alarm would sound.

Lilly was first up putting on coffee, that got me going. I pulled up anchor and got us heading east. The wind coming from the south east we were in the lee of the islands and the riding was smooth.

Once arriving at Harbor Island we docked as we always did at Valentine's and taxied on over to the Pink Sands. Mrs. King was happy to see us but not so about Saint. The rooms had tile floors and I managed to get Mrs. King to bend into letting Saint in as long he stayed away from the guest and the main house which was where the meals were served.

The kids, and all of us were enjoying the beach. Pa'me was the first that noticed the man watching us from the balcony of the patio bar. Pa'me quietly came to me and asked if I had noticed him. I told her that there were two of them and that they were with us. I thanked her for noticing and letting me know. The point of having extra help was that there were just too many of us for me to watch. I realized that if someone wanted to get to us that my men might not be able to stop them but at least they should get a warning shot off. I wasn't expecting any problems but felt better about having those extra eyes having the kids with me.

Pa'me was doing great with the children, her attention for them and Saint didn't stop. Looked like the kids and Saint had a new big sister.

We stayed another two days, the kids couldn't have taken any more sun, or fun for that matter. The only ones that weren't worn out were Pa'me and Saint.

Lori and I had spent a lot of time walking the Island with us exploring the beach homes that for the most part were empty. We looked in windows and sat up on decks of several vacant homes. One had caught our eyes as it was vacant and run down. The house looked as no one had been there in years. In walking around the house we couldn't even find the road coming up to the house, for that matter not even electrical wires. The house and property got my attention and I would come back another time and check into it.

We were ready to return to Nassau, we spent that night on the boat. Lori and I would get up early the next morning and we pulled out from Valentine's dock before the sun came up. I was up on the bridge when Lori brought up my first cup of coffee.

We reached Nassau by 1:00 p.m. on the 30th. I just had to take the kids out for a sail before we left.

My Nassau wedding anniversary didn't mean much to me but I had planned to be with Salinas tomorrow night. We would all take out the "Cat" for the rest of the afternoon. Of course the kids and Pa'me loved the sailboat. I could tell Chubby and Lilly were ready to get home for some rest.

By 7:00 p.m. that night we were on our way home with Tommy. The trip was a huge success. The kids were home and tucked in by 9:00 p.m., they still had another week off from school. I wanted to drop off Pa'me at Chubby's with the kids but Chubby nor Lilly offered so I took her back with Lori and I to the apartment.

Fortunately for me Evette was there at the apartment when we arrived. It was getting late but Lori and I could still get that hot shower and make it to Joe's on the beach. Lori was happy with the children's and her Christmas. She had a great time on the trip and was looking forward to getting the hobie cat into the water. I reminded her to work with her studies and the planned activities. She asked about Pa'me staying but I told her that I wasn't going to ask Chubby and Lilly to take on the added responsibility. Lori said she understood. Lori asked when she'd see me again and I said that I hadn't planned any long distance trips until next month. Maybe I could be back within a week or two.

The next morning after breakfast I took Lori to Chubby's and I would leave for Mandeville. Evette and Pa'me would leave with me to Mandeville. Evette still wanted Pa'me to stay with her but I thought it best to ask Lourdes to house Pa'me until I got her that visa. Pa'me could be a big help with Lourdes's children.

I spent New Year's Eve with Salinas having an early dinner in the Big Easy. Salinas had seen Evette coming in with Pa'me and asked if Pa'me was business or pleasure? I said business. We had a good dinner and then we called it a night. We were home and in bed before midnight. The next morning, we were in the pool with Michelle, Salinas said Michelle would swim before she walked. The puppy would be named Christy after my first dog. Presently Christy slept at the foot of Michelle's bed. The new baby was going to be a girl and Salinas had picked out the name Kelly. Kelly's room was ready to receive her.

Tommy would be off for the next two weeks and his co-pilot would be taking Tommy's place. We hadn't planned anything but moving the Engineers back to Andros.

The C-130 that was still flying had left two days before Christmas and taken Fernando and his new bunch of recruits to General Santos to change out our men that had now been there several months. Before they had left I didn't know about the new offer but even that wouldn't have postponed or changed the exchange of personnel. I wanted to get the original group of Haitians home in time to spend part of the holiday with Family.

Before flying off to Eleuthera I inspected the C-130 that had been damaged. There must have been one hell of a gun fight. The cargo that they were to deliver was still in the hold.

Me I had Buddy drop me off on Eleuthera, then him to go Nassau and pick up Jack and the Engineer group and deliver them back to Andros. Lee said the room to house the Vehicle would be ready early this week. The Director and the Navy had decided to have our people present while their people did the actually work, I also would be there.

Ok, here I was on Eleuthera, I was there to find out all I could about that vacant house. I would stop by my old friends Charles and Madilyn's. It had been a year since I had seen them but it seemed much longer. We talked about the house I found and we all got in Charles's boat and crossed the small bay to Harbor Island. I didn't want anyone to know I was looking so we got a taxi to the Pink Sands and walked from there on the beach. The walk was less than 15 minutes and I had brought a few tools in my tourist pouch. Once at the house I opened the locked door and we got a good look at the house. The house was a two bed room two bath that had poured concrete walls that were 12 inches' thick. The damaged roof that must have survived at least one hurricane had large wood beams. The entire house had Spanish tile floors. The kitchen and both bath rooms would have to be redone. The house sat on a small bluff that at one time must have had one hell of a deck. At present just like the road that once must have been there, the walkway and stairs to the beach just weren't there anymore. I told Charles that I wanted to buy the house and all the adjoining properties. I asked him to take care of all the details to include supervision of the rebuilding. Charles said they would gladly do this for me. We made our way back to the Pink Sands and sat at the bar overlooking the beach. I got them caught up with what was going on with my life. Charles thought it hilarious that I had three girls pregnant at the same time. Madilyn didn't think it funny at all. Charles asked if Rusty knew? I just shook my head and said that I hadn't spoken to Rusty in months maybe more.

I did tell them that I was working a large construction site on Andros and would be there off and on for the next couple weeks, then being in the Philippines for the Presidential elections. I didn't and couldn't tell them about the discoveries on Andros nor the upcoming removal of Marcos.

We were sitting in the bar when we had two unexpected visitors, it was the hotel owners, Mrs. and Mr. King. I had not met Mr. King but it seemed that Mr. King and Charles had become flying buddies. Both men had planes that were kept at the Eleuthera airport. Charles often flew into Miami with Mr. King when picking up supplies for the hotel. Charles would do his shopping for Madilyn.

Mr. King had lots of story's as he had worked with actors such John Wayne and Errol Flynn, the stories were nonstop and I didn't want him to stop. Charles said that I too had been a swashbuckler so to speak. Mrs. King said that I would win the contest for visiting the hotel with the most women. With that Charles couldn't help telling them about my three pregnant women. Mrs. King said she had met all three of the girls and the next two in line. I told them about the story behind Pa'me and Madilyn said I would always be looking out for that stray cat. Mr. and Mrs. King had heard of the Michelle Charity Work in Nassau but hadn't connected that to me or any of the companies. Charles mentioned that I was doing work over on Andros and Mr. King noted and asked about the no fly zone over the center part of Andros. Mr. King said that on his last flight just two days ago he had been escorted out of that area, first buzzed by two fighter jets and then a helicopter. I replied, and it was true that this was the first I'd heard of such. I could tell that Mr. King didn't like the inconvenience of having to fly around the sight nor having fighter jets buzzing him. Mr. king still in good shape had to have been in his late 70s or so.

Well I was pretty sure we had drank all the available rum punch that the bar had, it was time to head back. We were lucky that what we were traveling in a boat and not an air plane or car. Madilyn was smart enough to call me a taxi. Buddy flew me over to Andros where, when I got there was informed that the Navy had sent divers down the later to see the control room and what they called the space ship. What I always heard was loose lips sink ships. I didn't think they could even open either doors and I believed it would stir talk. For me the less personal that were involved the less chit chat.

Just as I thought it wasn't long before a jeep arrived at the Dock house with one of the Navy divers looking for some kind of instructions on how to open the cave door. I asked if he or they had the control board and he said that it was back at the base. I asked if it was under guard and he didn't like the question and I didn't like the answer.

I informed him that we were under contract to deliver the Vehicle into the lab and that we would not go back down there until the lab was ready. I also noted that they may be putting the entire project in jeopardy by attempting to open the door without the proper knowledge. I warned that there could easily be some kind of electrical charge that could be released to fend off intruders. The Navy officer was pissed and they drove off mad. I went to the telex machine and sent off a warning to everyone involved. I explained what was going on with the Navy divers as well as the control board. I didn't mention any thing about the cave room or the vehicle but my words were that should such an electrical charge occur and all the stored power lost, it wouldn't be days before we got started, but possibly months or more. I referenced, a cars dead battery and the only way to open the hood was with the cars battery. Catch 22, if there wasn't enough battery to open the hood, then you couldn't jump or charge the battery.

From there I wanted to visit the hotel and see how far we had come on its remodeling. The main house at the hotel on Andros had completely changed. The room where Cat and I had originally stayed was also completed. It was a complete rebuild with a new roof, windows, and floor;

the bathroom now had hot and cold fresh water. The fresh water would come from a hugh cistern that captured all the rain water from all four building's roofs. The hotel had street power but now also had a backup generator. As I looked at the beach I thought that with Lusca gone and more visitors that would be coming in and out of the base, this would be a good business for Lucy's family.

The two men jailed in Nassau for the Lucy case had been tried and convicted. Both were serving long sentences. The other two had been let go by the Navy due to lack of evidence. The Navy sighted Lucy's parent's refusal to bring Lucy back to the island to testify. Both men had left the Island on separate Navy vessels. Jerry was in charge of keeping track of them as we were not going to just let this go. We weren't going to take punishment into our own hands but one day we'd have them brought before a Bahamian Judge. One of their open charges was murder and here time was on our side.

It was Friday afternoon, the lab would not be ready until Tuesday afternoon or Wednesday morning. Other than the Lab not being ready we were all set to proceed in moving the vehicle.

I headed back to the airport and would return to Miami to surprise Lori. It was after dark when we arrived and by the time I got to Chubby's only Saint was there. Somehow I couldn't find my set of house keys and I couldn't even get into the back yard to pet Saint. I left a massage on the door to call my new cell phone that Lourdes had sent me. Ok I hadn't used my original cell phone because it was big and bulky. This cell was much smaller but still too big to fit in one's pocket. It must have weighed 3 pounds. Anyway I wasn't going to the apartment I was headed to my old stomping ground the 1800 club.

At the club, I sat in my old seat and ordered my regular drink. It was strange as when the pay phone rang I would automatically think it was for me. In the old days it would have been. I had many good times here, in fact every time I came here was a good time. I thought of several of the girls that Joe and I used to take home when the bar closed and wondered where they were at this time. Joe had gotten remarried to a Charleston girl. His wife didn't like me too much because she said I was a bad influence on him. Joe chewed tobacco, I remember the first time he got me to try some.

Joe was driving us to the Sea Container office, he told me not to swallow any of the juice but I must have. When he parked the car and I got out my head started spinning. I spit the stuff out and called him a SOB. I was still dizzy when we rode up the elevator. I remember so many things like Joe and I flipping quarters on whom would take home which girl from the club. My cell phone rang and it was back to reality.

The phone was of course Lori. They had just got back from going out to dinner and a show. She wanted me to come get her. She said that she knew I wasn't at the apartment because I couldn't get in. Why because the elevator wouldn't stop at my floor without the new Key. Lori said that Miami safe, following my directions had dropped the keys off at Chubby's.

I paid the tab and was off for Lori. Once at the house I asked what was planned for tomorrow. I asked Chubby's if he could tow the Hobie Cat and we'd put her in the water just past the first Rickenbacker bridge.

Lori and I went to the apartment and for the first time, we used the elavator key to stop at our floor. When we walked in I checked my messages, of course there was one from the Colonel and two from Lourdes. It was late but I called Lourdes with Pa'me answering the phone. Lori got to briefly say hello to Pa'me before Lourdes came to the phone. I could hear Lourdes ask Pa'me to leave the room, then Lourdes said that the Colonel, the state department and Mr. Crowbe had called. Lourdes said that the state department said that Pa'me and myself would need to visit the Philippine embassy in New York to pick up her visa and then visit the US Department of Immigration. There was a list of paper work that I was to bring with me to the Immigration Department to include a Doctors certificate of health, where Pa'me would be living, with whom and what school she would be attending. I asked Lourdes if she had found Jena and got her a key to the elevator. Lourdes said that Jena was in Paris and that Jena said to just shove it under the door at her Starr Island home.

I then called The Colonel also wakeing him up. The Colonel wanted to inform me on what had happen to the C-130 and asked that the cargo be transferred to the other bird and sent back to Nicaragua. I wasn't too happy with his request nor attitude. I just told him that the other bird as he called it was on a mission and I'd like to meet with him before sending the other bird. I said his crew wasn't going to tear up one bird, then just come back and use the other. I asked if he was available for dinner Monday night in New York or Washington. He said Washington at 9:00 p.m.

I called back Lourdes and again got her up and said to make arrangements to have Pa'me, Jerry and myself in New York early Monday morning to do the immigration thing and then in Washington Monday night to meet with the Colonel. Lourdes asked how many rooms for Monday night? I of course said two.

Lori was of course listening and asked if she could go along. I said that she had already missed more of her studies than she should have. We got our shower and went to bed. The next morning my coffee was ready and we would get an early start. When we got to the house Chubby had the hobie trailer all hooked up and ready to go. The kids would also go.

It was easy to get the boat in the water and set up. Lori and I would try it out first with Lori getting the hang of it almost immediately. We were the first hobie out there but within an hour there were several others. After Lori and I went, it was Lori herself then it was the four of us. The kids had a blast. We had a small ice chest that would hold maybe a six pack and ice. At noon Chubby left with the kids and Lori and I stayed with the boat. The hobie hadn't come with and anchor, I had purchased an anchor that had been dipped in some kind of rubber that wouldn't cut into the canvas. This was the first anchor that I saw that came in a canvas case. The agreement was that if Chubby hadn't heard from us he'd pick us up at 6:00 p.m.

Lori and I sailed on over to the Marina on Key Biscayne. We tied the hobie to a buoy that wasn't being used and swam on in to eat lunch at Sundays. Lori loved the hobie! She wanted to get back on and sail all night. We ate a good meal and I called Chubby. Lilly answered and I told her to please have Chubby pick us up at about 11:00 a.m. the next morning. We had two cokes left in the ice box with enough ice until tomorrow. I bought four more cokes. The canned cokes were put in a plastic bag and we were off in the water swimming back to the hobie. We unhooked the buoy and raised the sail and jib and were off. The hobie was fast, we sailed south to the keys. It was January and 80 degrees. We anchored off of Elliot's Key and swam until almost dark. From there we claimed aboard and pulled up anchor and sailed another mile west. We anchored and would spend the night. If it rained, we would use the sail to cover us. We used our two life jackets for pillows. The only thing we had to keep us warm was each other. We counted falling stars until we fell asleep. The next morning, we got up and would sail back to Sundays where we would catch their Sunday morning brunch. Most of the people at Sundays were dressed for church, people looked at us funny as we were bare footed in our bathing suits and wet. After eating a good brunch, we were off to meet Chubby. I thought how fun it would have been to have had Lori along that first trip to Nassau. Rusty would have enjoyed Lori. Of course Lori hadn't even been born yet. We got the boat on the trailer and went to Chubby's house. Once there we washed down the boat and sails then we all jumped into the pool. I was that much more tanned and Lori was that much more golden brown. The afternoon went by and I took Lori with me promising Lilly I'd have Lori back before her Tudor got there at 8:00 a.m.

We got back to the apartment and showered and took a nap. We awoke at about 9:00 p.m., dressed and went to the 1800 club. Lori had a low cut dress up top that showed off her great shoulder tan, and those legs, wow. She didn't over dress, no makeup or jewelry. For some reason she had lost that 15-year-old look. We had only been at the club a short while when I went to look for Jan. Jan was happy to see me again. Jan spotted Lori and said for me to take a look. From where Jan and I stood Lori looked in her early twenties. Jan made the comment that five years ago that I would have never walked past that. I smiled and said she was 100% right about that. I then whistled and Lori jumped out of her seat and came over to us. Jan this is Lori, Lori Jan. Jan looked at Lori from head to toe then looked at me. Jan said she should have guessed it by the tan. Jan asked Lori if she knew Karen. Lori said no but that she had seen photos of Karen and that she was beautiful. Jan said that Karen had been in the week before Christmas with the million-dollar man. Jan looked at me, my face must have shown that I didn't know she had been here. Years ago on any given Friday night, the club hosted the Jim, Joe and Karen show. Jan said we all had lots of fun. Those were the days Jan said.

The next morning, I had Lori at Chubby's by 7:00 a.m. and myself at Opa-Locka by 7:30 a.m. With Pa'me and Jerry already aboard we took off for New York. It was 11:30 a.m. when we walked into the Philippines Embassy. Pa'me was photo'd and her passport was ready within 30 minutes. I paid some small amount and we were off to the Department of Immigration.

Jerry stayed in the first floor lobby while Pa'me and myself took the elevator to the 9th floor. I was asked if we had an appointment and I said no that the state department had said everything was ready. I had all the papers that Lourdes said to bring plus Pa'me's new passport. First they would interview me while Pa'me waited on the other side of a big glass windo. The person doing the interview didn't look happy. The older women first asked why and how did Pa'me get into the country and where were her parents? I looked at Pa'me through the glass and stood and sat two times. The women said that they would need to keep Pa'me there under their custody until they investigated the circumstances in which Pa'me came into the US. The women said that just because some big shot State Department person tried to railroad this visa through didn't mean that she was going to give custody of a 15-year-old girl to a 35-year-old single man. The women then picked up the phone and ordered child services to take Pa'me into custody. Mam I said, would you let me explain I asked? No Sir, she said we won't be needing you anymore today. Thank you. Before I left the room the phone rang. It was whomever the women had sent for Pa'me. The women looked though the window and Pa'me was gone. The women said I must sit right there and not move. A police officer was called and I was asked where Pa'me was. I then said that I had come in and left Pa'me in the care of, well the immigration services. Don't tell me you've lost her I asked? Seemed that the camera had caught Pa'me going into the lady's room and not coming out. Pa'me had vanished into thin air. The immigration woman wanted me held but the police asked on what charges? The women said they would put an all-points bulletin on Pa'me and would have her back before dark. The police asked for me to come down to the station with them of which I gladly did. At the station I called Lourdes and within two hours they let me go.

By 5:00 p.m. an envelope was delivered to my hotel room with Pa'me's passport with a newly stamped visa. I called Lourdes to give Jerry the news that everything had been cleared and that I now had Pa'me's passport and visa.

Jerry had warned me that the Immigration Services may give me a hard time. When I first brought Pa'me home I had paid to do some handy work for Pa'me to have at least a passport. The handy man took Lori's passport and made an identical one with Pa'me's photo on it.

Pa'me had taken a small bag with us to the immigration office and when I gave her the signal she used the bathroom to change clothes and added a wig. Pa'me went into the bathroom and someone else came out. Jerry was waiting for her on the bottom floor with the instructions if things didn't go as planned he was to take her to see the Statue of Liberty and call Lourdes when they finished, and then again every hour until he had the all clear or other instructions.

Jerry showed up with Pa'me and Pa'me was excited to finally feel secure that she couldn't be taken away and or sent back.

I would make my 9:00 p.m. meeting with the Colonel. The Colonel said that the plan to land on the strip that they had just finished was spoiled by the Sandinista's waiting for them. There was a fire fight with contra's verses the Sandinista's on the ground and his men returning fire from the air. The Colonel said that the starboard outside engine was hit and caught fire before they could land, the mission was aborted. The Colonel said the contras badly needed the troop carrier, tank and supplies that were in the C-130. The Colonel said that the Sandinista's had pulled back for now and weren't expecting a second plane. The Colonel said his contra's were depending on the supplies. For me it was only a matter of money. The Colonel said he had sent 12 men from a nearby base to assist my mechanics to restore the damaged C-130. He said they should have the gun ship ready within a week. I went to the pay phone and called Lourdes and told her to get the C-130 that was working on Andros back to Mandeville ASAP, tonight if at all possible. I told her to send Fernando and 5 men with the plane. I then called Jerry and informed of my decision and asked him to take Pa'me and the Leer and get back to Mandeville. He was to start at once to unload the damaged gunship. The other C-130 was on the way to Mandeville with Fernando and 5 of his men. I wanted the good C-130 to leave Mandeville loaded with the cargo from the damaged C-130 by 2:00 p.m. the next day. I called Lourdes again and informed her what was going on and that I would catch a flight to Miami. Once the leer had Jerry in Mandeville it was to go pick me up in Miami and deliver me to Andros.

I went back and told the Colonel that he could take the second C-130. It should be returning from Andros by early morning. The Colonel knew where the bird was as he had supplied four reserve paratroopers for our men's training on Andros. I reminded him that I expected my plane back in the same condition he took it. It was the first time I saw the Colonel smile. The Colonel then asked what my plans were for the Haitian army that I was training? The Colonel said he could use those men in Nicaragua, 70 so far he asked? I reminded him that I had lost three of them in General Santos. The Colonel said he'd pay $1,000.00 per man per month and drop them in the fight in Nicaragua to help his people. He showed me a few photos of what he called the contras. Most looked like farmers, some looked like children, some were women. I thought that the Sandinista's would think twice if they ran into my men. The Colonel asked me to think about it. I told him that I had a bad taste in my mouth how the US treated the brave Cubans of the Brigade of 1,400. The Colonel was quick to say that it was Kennedy and he had paid the price. The maître d came to the table and said I had a phone call. It was Jerry saying that Pa'me had locked herself into the bathroom saying she wasn't leaving with him. I told Jerry to leave her and I'd deal with it when I got back to the hotel.

Dinner lasted more than three hours. The Colonel talked about his wife and children. I could tell that he would do anything to stop the spread of communism.

When I returned to the hotel I had the front desk get me two airline tickets on the first flight to Miami. When I got to my room Pa'me was asleep in my bed. I checked under the sheets and of course she had no clothes on. I then got a pillow and blanket from the closet and would sleep on the couch. The red light appeared on the room phone and I picked it up, our flight would leave at 9:45 a.m. I asked for a wakeup call for 6:00 a.m. Needless to say I didn't sleep good, I kept sitting up at looking toward the bed. Finally, the 6:00 a.m. wakeup call came.

We both got up with the ring, I told Pa'me to either get her shower or get dressed. Pa'me said she would like to bath me. I looked at her standing naked and told her that the first time we had sex before she was 18, I would put her in a boarding house, one that she would be force to stay in. You don't want me she asked? I want you to become the best you can be. I want you study hard and learn how to be a business person. How to manage people and money. I need you to be my friend not my lover. She looked at me and said, until I am 18 and then what she asked? At 18 we'll talk I said. You will promise not to marry before then she asked? You promise to do what I ask until then and respect the relation I have with Lori and keep this agreement between us I asked? Sealed with a kiss she asked? No with a hand shake I answered. She stuck out her hand and we shook on it.

Pa'me and I made our plane, I would make some arrangements for Pa'me in Miami. I only wanted to be there a short time as Lee would be ready today with the lab. I didn't want to impose on Chubby or Lori. I would drop Pa'me off at the apartment and go talk first to Lori and then Chubby.

When speaking to Lori, I was straight with her. For the first time I told her how I felt about her and that if she agreed I wanted her to take and treat Pa'me like a sister. If she couldn't I'd send Pa'me back to Lourdes. Lori said she understood and wanted Pa'me to live with her and the children. I then talked to Chubby and Lilly. Lilly was suspicious of my motives and said so. I told her that I understood her concerns and would be careful not to cross the line. It was agreed that Pa'me would move in with Chubby and Lilly.

I would go and get Pa'me and tell her that she was to stay with Lori and the family and was not to make anyone uncomfortable especially Lori. I dropped Pa'me at Chubby's and was off to Opa-Locka.

Lee and the engineers were on Andros at the lab sight testing the lift and the top side sea doors. We didn't know if we were going to be able to or if we wanted to risk moving the vehicle into the lab under its own power. We decided that we would drop the lifting device down into the cave and then move the vehicle under its power onto the device. Once on the device, which was much like a large net, then the vehicle would be lifted up into the lab. We did a trial run and decided we were ready to try it first thing in the morning.

I would be staying at the Lucy's family hotel. The room was now much different than when Cat and I first stayed here. I remembered those nights with Cat. I dreamed of that girl on the French Beach. I don't know whom I reached for in my sleep but it was that same problem, there was no one there. I thought, how could a man have so much and yet sleep alone?

CHAPTER XI

DELIVERY OF THE VEHICLE

The next morning accompanied by a Navy engineer, four of us would open the cave door and then open the vehicle door. Two of us would enter to install the control panel into the Vehicle. Everything went smooth. With the control panel installed it took the rest of the day before we found a way to communicate from the control room in the cave, to the vehicle and vice versa. It took us the next day to understand how the radar of the vehicle worked and was used, the vehicle didn't have windows, it worked strictly using radar and sensors.

Thursday we would attempt to move the vehicle. The cave had sensors that had guided the vehicle to the cave control room. We would use the same sensors plus we used a 3 inch steel pipe and fittings to form a stand that we hoped the vehicle's radar would pick up and stop as it got to where the pipe was. The pipe was located so that where the Vehicle should stop was just below the lab's door. The vehicle was unmanned at the time with our engineer at the controls from the control room. Moving the vehicle ever so slow, the vehicle's radar did pick up the pipe. The cave at the lab sight was well lit and Lee and others were standing on the lab's edge waiting for the Vehicle to reach the marked spot under the lab. The vehicle stopped within inches of the pipe. The vehicle was now in place. We in the control room shut down the power. We got into our scuba gear and went top side. When we reached the lab Lee gave the ok to begin to lift the vehicle, the vehiclel that was now sitting on the net, slowly came up until Lee motioned to close the sea door that was now under the Vehicle. The Vehicle was then set down on a rubber pad, the Vehical's small flat bottom holding it in place. This was the first time that we had really gotten a 360 degree look at the vehicle. Everyone was elated. It almost seemed like a dream, however with the touch of my hand I was sure it was not.

The Navy base commander was there and mentioned that they would take it from here on. I wasn't surprised and asked the Commander to please notify the State Department that as far as he was concerned, I had completed my delivery. The Commander acknowledge that he would send the communication.

That same afternoon myself and the engineers would fly to Nassau to await any further request. I didn't think that the Navy would have any issues except the fact that they might want to keep eyes on my engineers.

My arrival in Nassau wasn't planned, it was early evening when we got into Nassau. The engineers still accompanied by Jack would return to the Hill Top beach house. Me I went right to find Cat. I hadn't seen Cat in almost a month. I was anxious to see that big belly. I no longer had keys to the apartment over Angee's restaurant. I knocked and Cat came to the door. Cat cried when she saw me saying she didn't want me to see her with such a big belly and being so ugly. We laughed about it all the way to the shower. In the shower we laughed even more. Cat only had three months to go before our son was to be born. Cat said that Jacob was being a jerk over the whole thing. Cat had applied for a divorce but Jacob was dragging his feet and the Judge whom was Jacob's father wasn't going to sign any papers without Jacob signing first. Cat said, all that wasn't going to stop her from registering me as the father. Cat said that Mary and Tim offered their house which had belonged to Deanna but Cat said she had found and purchased a small beach house on the east side of the island. Cat said that she wasn't sure that June would come but that if she did, she would be welcomed. Cat said she had been busy as she finally had got an insurance company to come and inspect the gold and treasures we had in the banks. Cat knew that I wasn't counting dollars but she smiled when she said that the gold bars were now worth over $30,000.000.00 and the newest treasure another $50,000,000.00 to $70,000,000. She asked if that wasn't enough?

Cat and I were asleep when the phone rang. It was Lourdes saying that the Director was urgently looking for me. I called the Director and he said that my C-130 had been damaged on the runway in Nicaragua and that the Colonel and the Contras were surrounded. The Director said that the

Colonel went along as he said he felt obligated to bring back my plane. The Director said the President had asked him to call me. The Director asked how fast I could get some help to them? I told him I would call right back. I then called Jerry, Jerry said the gun ship could be ready within 24 hours. I said to get everyone up and working. I told him that the gun ship would leave ready or not in 6 hours or less. Tommy was now back from vacation and staying at the boarding house. I called and told him I'd be at the airport in 20 minutes. I called Fernando, I wanted every man we had, I would be in Andros in 40 minutes to pick up the 6 men there and then fly to Haiti and pick up the men he had there. I called the Director back and said that if he had any volunteers to get them to Mandeville ASAP. I asked him to have someone draw up two sets of plans to get in and out. My plan was to drop as many as I could on the south side of the airstrip having my men clear the southern side and then attack from the strip northward. The Director said he would gather up some volunteers and get them to me just as soon as he could. When I hung up the phone and turned, there was Cat standing with tears rolling down her eyes. You're not going to let your son be born without a father here on this earth are you she asked? Not planning on it I said. I kissed her and told her I loved her and got dressed. Cat drove me to the airport where she said to make sure I was around for the birth.

We left Nassau, our first stop was Andros where we picked up 6 men. We then flew to Paix, where we picked up 22 more. From Paix we flew to Mandeville. At Mandeville Jerry was putting on the gunship's last fishing touches. I spoke with our flight crew and all volunteered to go. We had a crew of 4, myself. Fernando and 46 men. Of the 46 only 15 had previously jumped out of an airplane before, all volunteered to do so. We only had 40 parachutes. By the time we were ready to take off not one of the Director's men had shown. Of the 12 men the Colonel had sent to help get the C-130 back in service 5 volunteered to go. One such man, Ryan said he was obligated as he was the only one that knew how to operate the new Gatling Gun that he had just installed on the port side. The Gun he said had the capability, that once our new radar system picked up an activated air defense system it could atomically fire at its direction. The 20 mm canon could fire 6,000 rounds per minute and was capable of taking out the Sandinista's defenses.

I had sent someone to the house to bring Salinas and Michelle. Bubba would stay and watch them and the house. Salinas didn't panic, she noted that her Haitians would protect me. I kissed them both and boarded the plane.

We took off from Mandeville heading to Barrios Guatemala. There we would refuel. I didn't like this but since we were no longer welcomed in Limon, Barrios it was. I was worried about the information leakage to the Sandinistas that we were coming.

CHAPTER XII
THE LOSS OF OUR FIRST C-130

We would fly in low from 50 miles out and stay that way until we rose to parachute altitude. Just as soon as we did, our special radar picked up the activation of a Sandinista missile sight. We dropped 30 paratroopers and then dropped down below the radar. The way we had looked at it, the Sandinista's wouldn't fire at us as if they missed their missiles would land somewhere in Costa Rica. Our paratroopers would be landing on tree tops due to the thick jungle below. The C-130 was now headed west, we then made a 180 degree turn and headed toward the missile sight. Still passing just over the tree line Ryan engaged the port side gun and we raised altitude a bit and bang, all hell broke loose with that cannon. As we flew east we could see one then two then three and four big explosions on the ground. We radioed the Colonel and said to bring what forces he had back onto the strip zone as we were going to take a few passes with the cannon. We warned not to engage our men coming in from the south. Our men on the ground were to wait until we cleared the south side of the strip with the cannon before they came within 100 yards of the strip. Our men would engage whomever was between them and the strip.

We did another 180 and fired along the south edge of the strip, then did another 180 and fired along the north side of the strip. The following 180 turn we would bring her down and land on the strip. We could see our C-130 on the ground was charred to rubble, it still was smoldering. We hit the ground and as we slowed we lowered the ramp and our remaining men exited and scattered to the north. We did a 180 on the field, and the bird was ready to take off. I could hear fighting on both sides of the strip. The

Colonel was to fortify the south side but was to be careful not to engage our men coming his way. The fighting to the south was coming our way while the fighting to the north was moving north. Fernando whom had parachuted in with his men, made contract asking for permission to bring his men in. Fernando said the little resistance they had was terminated without him losing a man. All 30 of our men had made it down without a single injury. So far we had three wounded. The Colonel asked what had taken me so long and then smiled. We now had 6 scouts out and the rest of our men back at the strip. The Colonel had lost half of his Contras and asked us if we had any volunteers to stay. I asked for a huddle without the Colonel. Fernando said he would stay with 16 men, do what they could and then cross the river into Costa Rica. Fernando said we were to pick them up in Limon in 30 days from now. I gave Fernando a pouch of money to use where necessary. I hugged him and all the men. We had more that wanted to stay but Fernando promised them there would soon be another time for them. The Colonel, his wounded and flight crew would come out with us. We unloaded what supplies we had and we loaded up and were on our way out down the runway. Once in the air, we were heading east and stayed low until we got over the ocean. We had made it in and out with no loose of life with 5 wounded. Limon denied us permission to land but we did any way. Limon had this big beautiful international airport with only one small piper club parked in the grass. Our flight from the Nicaragua border to Limon was only about ten minutes. We had called via ship to shore for a pair of ambulances to meet us at the airport. We landed and were there only five minutes when the first ambulance arrived. That ambulance took the two most seriously wounded men. I went with them to insure their care. We agreed that the C-130 would leave once the second ambulance arrived and took the last three wounded men. Once at the hospital the doctors and staff were great, no questions were asked about where the men had received such wounds. I had given blood once while in the Air Force and was requested to do for the second time. While on the table giving blood I had two visitors. An American name Richard and an English man name Ian. Both also offered blood. While the three of us were introducing each other another two more men appeared. These men, neither in uniform, were officials, one the Limon Chief of Police and the other the head of the Limon Immigration. All four men knew each other well. The two Ticos as people called Costa Ricans, spoke almost perfect English. I had my passport as well as did my men. I told the story that we were on a mission and had run into some bad weather. Richard took me in the hall way and asked if I had some grease money. I remembered grease money from my Africa visit. I asked how much and Richard said he thought that $100.00 each for each immigration stamp and a total of $100.00 for the chief. With that, Richard said everything would be fine. I did as Richard suggested and each man said they appreciated my contribution. The immigration man took our passports and said he would return with them stamped in as tourist. The police chief asked whose airplane we came on? I told him it was one of my cargo planes. The policeman's name was Linearis, he carried a 38 model 36 tucked in behind his belt on the right side of his back. I knew this because he took his out and handed it to me and asked to see mine. I had left my berretta on the C-130 but still had on my Walter at my left ankle. I didn't take his but did hand him mine. He looked at it and said it was a nice weapon. He asked if maybe one day on my next visit I could bring him one like mine. I told him he could count on it.

One of our men needed to be transported to the San Jose Hospital for better treatment. Petti as we called him would be fine, he'd go via ambulance and I thought I would rent a car and follow on my own. I asked where I could rent a car? Richard and Ian thought that was funny, both laughed. There was no renta car in Limon, just the buss.

Ian said he would keep an eye on the other four while I went to San Jose. Richard said he would drive me to San Jose. I got to a phone and Called Lourdes and said for her to let the girls know I was fine. I told Lourdes to call the Director's office and tell him that the Coronel was ok and should be home soon. Lourdes said that The Admiral had called and asked for the return of Jack and the engineers, seemed that one of their bright Naval Engineers had shut the cave inside control door and spun the wheel. Now the original master lock had been re-engaged and they couldn't get back in. I told Lourdes to send Jack and the engineers but I didn't know if Jack could open the door or not. Jack was with me when I had opened that door two times and could have picked up on what I was doing to open it. The Navy had not yet even opened the Vehicle's door to get in.

Richard, the American whom had a car would ride me to San Jose that night. Traveling at night, I didn't get to see much except that the fog was so bad I didn't see how Richard could see the road. Going up the mountains and looking out my window I could see what looked like a straight drop off just inches from our car's tires. I felt safer in the C-130 when the Nicaraguan's were shooting at us.

The ambulance left before we did, Richard had to stop by his house and advise his wife. We arrived about two hours behind the ambulance. By the time we got there Petti was under the knife. Richard dropped me off at the hospital while he went to some all-night bar. Richard said I should meet him there when I left the hospital. Richard said the bars name was Key Largo.

Petti would be fine and was resting, I got a taxi and went to meet Richard at the bar. The bar as Richard called it was a Cat house. This place was three stories tall with bars and rooms everywhere. It took me another hour to find Richard and another hour to drag him out. Richard couldn't remember where his car was so we walked to a popular hotel and got two rooms. After a few hours of sleep, I revisited the hospital and saw that Petti was doing ok. Petti had lost a kidney and his spleen. The doctor said Petti would need to be there two or three days more. Petti's wife would be here by tomorrow morning. One of the other men that had a shoulder wound would be here this afternoon via bus from Limon. Once Angelo was here I would go back to Limon.

That night Richard was at it again, the Key Largo opened at 11:00 p.m. Richard was waiting at the door. While waiting outside with Richard I noticed that I had caught the attention of a girl about 30 feet away. I walked to her and asked her name. Her name was Silvia she was dressed well, kind of like she was looking to make some money. I asked if she worked inside. Silvia said that one had to be 18 to work there, Silvia said she was only 16 but needed money to support her sick mother. I hadn't heard that story before but thought it a good line if you wanted sympathy. I said I like to visit her mother. She said that she couldn't at that moment as her family thought she worked in the sewing factory. I asked what time she got off from the factory? She smiled and said she would have to be home by 7:30 a.m. to cook for her brothers and sisters. I thought Silva thought that I was picking her up. I asked if she was hungry and she said yes, we walked back to the hotel and she ate while I talked. Once Silvia had eaten she told me her life story, supporting her family of six. None of the children were hers, she had none. At 7:00 a.m. we got in a taxi and headed to her home. The house was small and in the center of a row of connected homes. Everything she had said looked true. The cupboards were bear with hardly anything in the house. Silvia and the children were living with their grandmother and mother whom really was sick. With my poor Spanish I wasn't sure I was understanding this all but it looked like her mother was in the last stages of breast cancer. As we walked down the row of houses we passed a store where Silvia said she purchased most of their food. The 12-year-old sister was awake and I gave her $40.00 to go to that store and buy breakfast. I knew I would have to be leaving but wanted to have some way of contacting Silvia. Silvia wrote down the numbers of the pay phones at the corner, she gave me all three numbers, she said the three phones were quite busy as they were the only phones around. She also gave me the address. Before going I gave her $1,000.00 in cash and told her that one day I would return possibly offering her a job. Silvia thanked me and kissed me good bye.

That same day I would drive Richard's car with Richard opening one eye every once and a while giving directions. We were on our way back to Limon.

Once in Limon I got a room at the Park Hotel. The hotel which only had two rooms with AC, was on the ocean with waves breaking over the 8 foot high sea wall. The water from the breaking waves reached the hotels second story windows. The hotel must have been 100 years old made with the same stones as the sea wall. It was rustic but cool.

I revisited the hospital and visited with the men, they were concerned about Petti. I assured them he would be alright. Limon was Costa Rica's main sea port.

Long ago, Jamaicans' were brought here for labor, building the train from Limon to San Jose, this over 100 years ago. Chinese were the first laborers brought here but within the first year it was said that 70% of them died off from the heat. Limon has a large Jamaican and Chinese population. Due to the large number of Jamaicans, there were many people here that spoke the Queen's English.

Our men in the hospital felt right at home, them being able to talk with most of the hospital staff.

When I got back to the hotel, there was an urgent message to call Lourdes, there was also a call from Cat that said to call her first. I called Cat and she asked me to be calm and not to blow up but Lori had gotten on a commercial flight for Costa Rica and should be in the country by now. Cat said that Lori had called her and asked where I was and she had told her. Cat said, and she agreed that Lori wanted to make sure I wasn't lying about my health and I wasn't down here lying in some hospital. Cat said besides that Lori promised to get you back here before little Jim was born. My only concern was Lori coming alone.

I then called Lourdes and got the second hand information, but did get the flight number. I checked at the hotel desk and they made the airport call noting that Lori's flight had come in late last night. The girl at the hotel desk said that Lori could have taken one of the early morning buses and be here in Limon before mid-day. As I walked out of the hotel to go check the bus station, guess who I ran into. Yes, it was Lori, I wanted to give her a good spanking but that didn't happen. Lori said she had first checked the San Jose hospital to insure I wasn't there.

We were all in Limon for another three days. There weren't to many sights to see besides beaches and pretty girls. Lori had already seen the prettiest beaches in the world. Me, after seeing Harbor Island's beach well, nothing compared to it's pink sands.

Lori and I had made good friends with Richard and although his wife Eleanor didn't speak a word of English Lori got on good with her too. Lori didn't meet Ian, seemed Ian attended almost all the cargo ships, selling them everything from fuel to food. Richard said he had been living down here for almost six years, Ian too. I timed this to the start of the Nicaragua problem. With these and other pieces I made the conclusion that Richard most likely worked for Langley and Ian for some group out of London. I had also noticed that there was an East German here in Limon that was pushing little too hard to be friendly. I noticed that Richard didn't like him too much.

I had made a privet agreement with the immigration man, that we could again start revisiting Limon's airport for as long as San Jose didn't again step in. Of course there was a price attached that would be spread among several men within the local political power.

Tommy had flown in with the leer to take us all home. Petti and his wife had bussed on down to Limon, the others were now at the Park Hotel. We said our goodbyes to all our new friends with me making a head note that the next time I came down here should be for pleasure and I should come alone. The girls here were almost as good looking as the ones I had at home. Lori noted that my eyes were working overtime.

We finally flew out and would make our first stop Paix and then Miami.

The first thing I did once in Miami was to check on June. June said she had her small bag packed and was just waiting for the moment. Lourdes was calling her twice a day keeping her informed of my whereabouts. I told her I could come by and pick her up and take her to the apartment, but June said she was comfortable at her mom's, but it would be nice to see me. I would drop off Lori at Chubby's and head on over to June's. I didn't spend the night but stayed too late to go by Chubby's. The next morning I was at Chubby's checking on Lori, the children and Pa'me. All the children would have their classes lined up for the day. June would call telling me she was on the way to the hospital, within 4 hours, June had delivered our 7.2 pound baby girl. We named her Kayla. Both mom and baby were doing great.

I felt bad and got lots of bad looks from June's mom and father when I brought June and Kayla home from the hospital. June's father didn't even talk to me, I told June's mom that I had to be in Manilla within the week and didn't know how long I would be there. June's mom asked where I was living? That was a good question that I couldn't answer.

CHAPTER XIII

THE REMOVAL OF MARCOS

Within the week, I had Tommy fly me to Chicago, where I would catch a flight to Manila for the elections that would start within 48 hours.

I arrived in Manila on the day of elections. It was February 7th 1986. There were many people in the streets. I checked into the Hilton in down town Manila. That same night Bob whom I hadn't talked with in some time called to let me know that Baby Doc was no longer President of Haiti. Baby Doc, his wife and his mother Pilar were taken to France on a US Air Force plane. Bob was only giving me heads up that Pilar would soon be calling me. I asked Bob about their share of the shipping money and Bob answered that it would most likely be shifted to whomever was left in power.

The next day Marcos was declared the vote winner by some 56%. The opposition declared fraud and there were people amassing in the streets. The opposition claimed that Marcos was declared the winner even before the votes were counted. Seemed this was true as several key election officials had walked out of the election center resigning under protest.

I wondered what Ninong was thinking, this and where he was? By the next day, Lourdes had called and said that the Director had asked I find Ninong and bring him into Clark Air Force base. I few to General Santos. It was the first time I had been there since the night that I had met with Ninong and been shot. I went to the Tuna Factory which was now almost in operation. My trip was not to bring Ninong out, but to tell him to stay put. I was worried that our side may have had a change of plans.

With a small group of my men we crossed the river that night to look for Ninong. The fisherman at the village said that they had not seen Ninong since I was wounded. The family that had taken such good care of me had moved into the city. I had made sure they were rewarded for their kindness. They and several of the fisherman now had newer and bigger fishing boats.

While there at the small fishing village, I went to the wooden dock where when wounded that night, I had pulled myself on shore. I re-located my pouch that still held my stainless 9 mm. I had left the pouch in the water attached to the dock post. Besides my Walther the pouch was full of river sand. Standing there at the river bank brought back quite some memories.

With no Ninong we returned across the river and I used my apartment to sleep the rest of the night. The next morning, I greeted all of our people and answered all their many questions. There were rumors that I had sold the line and that The Fruit Company had purchased the land and the tuna business. I said that that so far that I hadn't made the disision to sell. I was asked by some of the men especially some from the guard force, that if I did sell, could they stay. Some of the men as I had, found women and either wanted to bring them back with them or stay there in General Santos. I assured them that either way we would assist.

I met with Mr. Partridge, spending most of the morning with him and a few of his staff. Afterward I had lunch with Nilo and his wife telling them how well Lori and the kids were doing in general especially with their education. I let Nilo know that if I did sell, I would still own the Factory and the Santos farm. Nilo said that he'd like to quit The Fruit company and manage the farm. I offered him a full time job.

I mentioned the story about Pa'me and asked Nilo to visit Davao and find Pa'me's family and let them know she was alright. I wanted Nino to see about Pa'me's siblings to make sure they were alright too, them not receiving the same type of treatment from their mother as did Pa'me.

It was getting that time of day so Nilo took me to the airport to start my journey back to Manila.

There was a helicopter waiting for me at the National airport that took me 83 miles to Clark Air Force Base. At Clark I was briefed about Marcos's pending departure. Marcos was unaware that he would be leaving. Marcos was now using one of his three dialysis machines on a daily basis.

It wasn't until more than a week later that the votes had been verified that Marcos had indeed won the election. The problem had been that Marcos hadn't been in any hurry to count the votes because he had planned to be the winner no matter what the count. Unfortunately for him, the ball had begun to roll and Marcos couldn't have stopped it no matter what. We had already met with Enrile and Ramos. The problem was that this had to look like it was a people thing and we would just go by what the people wanted.

It started on the 23rd of February with several defections including Enrile and Ramos. The people's movement wasn't without problems, some 76 people lost their lives. The US played a small part of keeping down the violence. We had used unmarked helicopters to bring down snippers that Marcos and General Ven had sent to pick off the People's leaders during people power protests. Marcos had put a price on the heads of Enrile, Ramos and others.

For two days we watched the tide turn against Marcos. Marcos was furious that the US wouldn't assist him. At one time Marcos declared that if we didn't help him he would close our military bases there.

On the afternoon of February 25th we Landed several helicopters inside the Palace walls. At first Marcos thought we had finally come to our senses. That was until he saw me.

It was Marcos that had given the order to kill me the night I was shot in General Santos. Once he saw me he knew I had come back for him. We loaded up Marcos, the family, a few family servants and took them to Clark. From Clark we flew them to Guam. It was my third Guam visit in the last several months. Guam was as far I would go with Marcos, by the afternoon of the 26th Marcos had arrived at Hickam Air Force Base in Hawaii and was officially exiled there. Corazon Aquino was now the President of the Philippines.

I wanted to fly back and look for Ninong but I decided to call it a trip. I had been gone now for 18 days.

I hitched a ride from Guam to San Francisco where I would call on Mr. Crowbe and Standard Fruit. I was warmly welcomed by both parites. I visited Mr. Bozzni first. We would agree on them buying my share of the

Tuna business not to include the factory nor the property that stretched from the plant, north to the river. The Fruit company would purchase all the farms with the exceptions of the property that I had given to the farmers, and all property that Marcos had taken from the Santos farm. These 165 acers ran along the north side of the river across from the Santos farm. It was said that just before he died, that General Santos had sold these 165 acers to Marcos. Mrs. Santos said that Marcos had stolen them. My intention was to return the 165 acers to the Santos Family, me then buying the intire farm having Mrs. Santos live out her days on the farm as her home.

I was in San Francisco for two days before all agreements were signed and I got paid. During my time negotiating with Standard, I had met several times with Mr. Crowbe. I was running out of time but before I left San Francisco Mr. Crowbe and I had come to terms. The agreement wasn't as black and white as the Land and my Tuna shares and could take weeks before the contracts were signed. In the end we both signed letters of intent.

Home, it sounded funny. I wasn't so sure exactly where or what that was. I was ready to just go and relax somewhere.

While in San Francisco I had lots of contact with Lourdes, Cat, June, Salinas and of course Lori. The only contact that I got that I wasn't expecting was young Mr. Crowbe. Young Crowbe paid me a visit at my hotel asking about Lori. Seemed Lori's short encounter had left an impression on young Mr. Crowbe. I smiled when he asked about her as I knew where he was coming from. I told him that she had just started high school and was doing just fine. Young Mr. Crowbe asked If I would mind him keeping in touch, kind of keeping track of her progress. I told him she was living with her God Parents, a Sister and Brother. He could call or write me any time and I'd keep him up to date. Either he didn't understand or didn't care that Lori was my girl.

When and where was I going first? It had now been almost 30 days since June gave birth to our Kayla. Within a short time period I would have a second daughter from Salinas and a son from Cat.

Fernando and his small group had made it to Limon and to the Park Hotel. Tommy hadn't picked them up as yet as the men were, as Fernando put it on holiday. The men had never seen anything quite so much like home and having it all paid for. Fernando's group raised hell on the Sandinista's, the Colonel said that while monitoring Managua's radio, it spoke of an international group of special forces that used hit and run tactics. Destroying ammunition depots and knocking out electric. The Colonel said Fernando had done a good job of training our group. Fernando too said he was proud of all the men.

I would go to Miami first and spend time with June. I picked both her and Kayla up and took them to the apartment. June said she would now stay there until she would take Kayla to Nassau. From there I would travel to Mandeville to see Salinas, Michelle and of course Christy. Michelle took her first steps and Christy had knocked her down. Betty now getting up there in age had her hands full. Betty had lots of help but as always she wanted to do things herself. Betty still gave me the same hard time whether Salinas was present or not. Salinas's second pregnancy gave her little or no problems. She said she was happy it was almost over and this time would listen about not having another until I was ready. Salinas said that once she had this child, she would be ready to travel with me where and whenever I wanted her to go.

The Mandeville airport now had a new look, no, not just the finished Hanger and Warehouse. Seems that part of my payment of the Andros Vehicle delivery was made in a Newer C-130 gun ship. Plus, the Colonel had replaced the C-130 we had lost on the Nicaragan airstrip. And then there were three.

Jerry greeted me with petition from the Manderville neighbors, they claimed my expansions needed to be approved by the Airport managers as well as the local residents. The letter said I was militarizing the airport. Jerry said he'd deal with it.

I visited the Terminal in New Orleans, we now called it the Jack and Jody show. Evette said that Jody had learned it all and there was no need for her to stay. Jack was happy to have the extra warehouse space as for almost two months the Central America cargo was being shipped to and received in Mandeville. Jack said he was receiving new clients all the time and sometimes didn't even know where the business was coming from.

Jack, his wife Marge, Jody, Evette, Lourdes, Salinas and I all dinned at Salinas's favorite restaurant, K-Paul's Kitchen. Chef Paul loved to come and speak French with Salinas. Paul was not French as Salinas thought.

Paul was born here in South Louisiana, one of 13 children whom learn his basic cooking skills and French from his Cajun mother.

I stayed in Mandeville for 5 days. Just long enough to receive the men back from Limon. Fernando looked rested and was anxious to get back to training. Fernando said we were lucky as the Sandinista's were not well trained nor organized.

The Mandeville house that still served as a Consular for Haiti and the Terminal in New Orleans would now get their guards back. With the change of government in Haiti, we didn't know what changes would take place and even if we would keep the Consular status.

Salinas knew my next stop would either be Miami or Nassau and asked that I stay close by to be there for the birth of of Michelle's new little sister. Salinas said that she would be ready to spend some time at the beach house as she knew it was now empty. I told her that if she was in Nassau that didn't mean I be spending my time at the house. Salinas said she understood but said she was going to do her best to get close to Cat once again. Salinas said she wanted to be friends.

If I went to Miami, I would run into trouble with space. June was at the apartment and Lori would also want to be with me. Sooooo I went to Nassau. Cat was now living at the small beach house that she had just purchased. She had hired a woman who would help with the house and baby. For now, I would stay with Cat, Salinas was scheduled to have her baby first and at any time I would be heading that way. It was great to once again share that shower and bed with Cat, even if she had that big, huge belly.

CHAPTER XIV

AND THEN THERE WERE FOUR

That call did come and I was gone within minutes. Salinas was already at the hospital when Tommy dropped me off at the New Orleans airport. Salinas said she was holding back until I arrived. The baby came just 30 minutes after my arrival. Kelly was a healthy 7.8 pounds at birth. Mom and baby were doing just great.

Seven days and it was finally Cat's turn. I was lying next to her when her water broke. Once the baby was born you could never imagen how many people came to the hospital. The flowers filled the room and lined the halls. Finally, Mr. Johnson said, one of his daughters had giving me a son. He was of course implying Deanna, Janie and now Cat. Mr. and Mrs. Johnson now had 5 grandchildren. Me, I had my first boy and three daughters, all within about one year.

Work was the furthest thing from my mind. At the moment it was going to be getting to know the girls again and the children.

June showed up the next week and June not thinking Cat had enough room and thinking she'd see more of me, wanted to move into the apartment. Salinas hearing the news that June was there in Nassau made the quick change back to her Paradise Island home.

All of a sudden I was encircled. If I spent more time with one than the other someone's feelings would be hurt. Besides, that baby stuff was getting on my nerves. Everyone wanted me to learn to change dippers. Before I knew it I was ready to sleep on one of the boats. It was Cat that made the first move. She came aboard one night and cast us off. She did all the work while I watched. The next morning, we were on what she said was a second honeymoon. We were on our way to Harbor Island.

Jack had gotten the cave control door open, it had taken him three days of trying. Presently the vehicle was on deck at the lab with engineers all over it. I was told by Jack that the Navy said that it would be years before they could reproduce the laser in the vehicle but that the hand held weapon would be much sooner.

Meanwhile Jack and our engineers had reconnected with the sonar device from the cave control room. The sonar picked up what they thought was a Soviet sub that had passed thought the channel several times until just settling in, listening. Jack had informed the Navy as he was concerned that the soviets may want to destroy the sonar device. It was my opinion that we should at once pull the sonar device up.

The next day Cat and I arrived at Valentine's on Harbor Island. I had purchased the house on the southernmost tip of the east side of the Island. Charles might even be there today supervising the repairs. Once Cat and I arrived at the Pink Sands Hotel, we got a Rum punch at the bar and started walking south on the beach. My plan was to surprise her with the house. During our walk, Cat asked how much money she had of her own? She said that she was thinking of offering Jacob a cash sum for her divorce. Before I could answer, Cat said she was also missing the children and they her. I told her that she should get Jacob out of the beach house where he was now, maybe trading houses with him. Cat said she was afraid of what he may do? Do, like what I asked? When I was pregnant she said he had made several unwanted advances. Now that I'm not she was sure it would get worse. Cat said she was afraid that Jacob would want to trade time with the children for time with him. I stopped in my tracks and looked at her. Of all the things that I have taught you I said. How could you even think of being black mailed by that SOB. If we can't buy him off I will have to do something about him myself. I was pissed, I turned and started walking back to the hotel. I wanted to go back to Nassau and confront him. Cat was crying pulling on my arm trying to get me to stop. Cat said if I did anything to Jacob she wouldn't love me anymore. She couldn't she said. Cat stopped and yelled, Jim you stop right now. I stopped and slowly turned. Cat pointed to the water and said for me to walk in there and cool off. I asked her if she loved me? She said yes. I asked her if under any circumstances she'd let that SOB put a hand on her? She said no. You won't go back to him no matter what I asked? Cat said, no I will not. Cat then asked if I loved her? I said yes, she again pointed to the water and said you get your butt in there and when you come out I want us to be right where we were before I asked you about the money. I took her hand and pulled her in with me.

Cat wasn't in perfect shape but the shape she had was good enough.

When we left the water we again started walking south. Cat said she wouldn't mind a nice air-conditioned room with a hot water shower and a soft bed. She stopped and pulled me back toword the hotel. I said there was something that I wanted her to see. Just as soon as I said it, she knew what it was. A house she said and started running south. It wasn't far and yes Charles was there supervising the crew. There must have been twenty people working there. Cat didn't even stop to say hello to Charles, she ran right past him. I was standing in the sand at the end of the new porch when Cat came running out of the house diving into my arms. It's beautiful she said. Promise me she said this will only be for us! Charles looked at me as he knew that would be a tough sell.

Charles later said that the Island most likely would have several more houses added to it.

Charles had made lots of progress but the house still had months to go before it would be ready. At the front of the house there were piles of large chunks of coral rock plus small rocks and sand to make cement. Charles said that he had decided that a chain link fence would ruin the looks of the place. Set back on each side, there were two more structures being built. Charles said each unit was called a mother in-law house. Charles then laughed. He then said one was for the help and the other for guests such as Madelyn and himself when they had too many cocktails to make it home.

Needless to say Cat was happy with the house. We headed on back to the Hotel and got a late lunch and then found that hot shower and bed that Cat was talking about. We stayed on the Island for another two days.

Not surprisingly Jerry and Fernando had come to Nassau for a visit. Jerry said he had met with the Mandeville airport managers and agreed that we would only have two C-130s at the airport as the original agreement yent stated. Jerry said that he and Fernando wanted the other, the newer one, to be stationed on Andros. I figured that we better get that permission before

I had my little visit with Jacob. Jacob's father was now a national judge, not just a Nassau judge.

Salinas was now at the beach house and had, to my surprise visited June while I was gone with Cat. June said that the apartment was too far from the beach and asked if I minded that she move to the house with Salinas. I couldn't imagen this working and told June that if it was for the beach then I would arrange something. June said she just couldn't go back to her parent's house. I met with June and Cat whom I had stayed with the two of them before. I couldn't see June keeping busy enough to stay in Nassau unless she had a friend. Cat was the one that could do anything. The next day Cat invited both Salinas and June for a sail. Boy was I glad to see them off together. I hoped Cat wouldn't lose them both overboard.

It was the perfect time for me to go see Jacob. Jacob's law office was empty, not even a secretary. I then caught a taxi out to Deanna's old beach house. Jacob was there and not happy to see me. I got right down to business. What would a devoice cost? Jacob said he wasn't interested. I said I'd pay him $1,000,000.00 to fee Cat up. $2,000,000.00 he replied. I said $2,000,000.00 with Wendy Michelle. Jacob was cocky, he then said $3,000,000.00. I said my final offer was $3,000,000.00 and he moved to Miami, with Johnny if he wanted. Johnny would spend the summer months, June, July and August plus one week every three months plus the week after Christmas with Cat. He was not to contact Cat directly. Jacob was thinking about it. I said that his Father was not to know until the agreement was signed and he was in Miami. There would be no restrictions on Wendy. $3,000,000.00 he asked? I said that once he signed the papers, he would receive $2,000,000.00. The papers would be filed in Nassau as well as Miami. $1,000,000.000 would be held in trust until the first anniversary of the agreement, as long as everything went as agreed he would receive the last $1,000,000.00. Jacob asked where he would receive the money? Where ever you want it I said. Jacob asked when he could have part of the money. I said I'd have Tommy fly him to Miami and have Roy draw the paper work. Jacob said that he agreed and would go today. Jacob stood and then said that he would be taking little Johnny with him to Miami. Jacob didn't say it, but he was thinking he'd be safer traveling with Johnny. Jacob asked to have a taxi pick him up at noon. Jacob said he'd drop Wendy off at her grandmother Johnson's house on the way to the airport.

There was to be no foul play, Jacob, whether he liked it or not, would live up to the agreement.

Cat wouldn't like the agreement because she didn't get Johnny. I figured that Jacob would get lost in the money and send Johnny back to her. $2,000,000.00 in Miami wouldn't last Jacob very long. With Cat not being in the house, Jacob and the house already was a mess and smelled like booze.

I went from the beach house to the city dock bar where Jerry and Fernando were waiting. I had already called Lourdes and asked her to arrange an appointment with General Namphy, the new leader in Haiti. Our meeting was set for tomorrow at the Palace.

I knew that the Haitian General had no money and already, many people were challenging his authority. He needed money to buy the support from the army and police. I would ask for three things. One, the status quo on the Haiti embassy on Andros and the consul in Mandeville. Two, permission to use and expand the airport in Paix. And three to pick out another 37 recruits to include 5 with with some form of medical degree.

I was at the bar with Willy when Cat and the girls returned from their sail. All came and kissed me, all smiling like they had something planned. I told Salinas that we were headed tomorrow morning to Haiti to meet the new President. I had already sent a boy to let the shop owner know to come by the house tonight and do Salinas's nails and hair. Salinas gave me another kiss and asked if I be coming home tonight. I said I'd pick her up at 7:00 a.m. I then looked at Cat and said that she should probably go and pick up Wendy Michelle at her mom's house. She looked at me and asked where Johnny and Jacob were? I said that they had gone to look for a house in Miami. Don't worry I said everything will be fine. Cat then kissed me and she was off. June then looked at me and said and me? Well, I said I had in mine dinner at my favorite restaurant and then, we'll see I said. I Kissed her and then swatted her on the butt. Go get ready I said, I'll be by at 8:00 p.m. sharp. Whatever the girls were cooking up, June would tell me after a bottle of champagne. I had called Lee and would send Tommy by for Jack and the other two original divers to accompany me to Haiti.

Tommy was gone taking Jacob to Miami and would on the way back, stop by Andros and pick up the three men.

Jerry would fly back on a commercial flight while Fernando wanted to stay and talk about when he could go and pick up his men from the Philippines. Fernando also wanted to build a bigger better training and barracks facility on our property on Andros. Should things go as we planned in Haiti tomorrow there was reasons to believe that we could soon have a 100-man force. Fernando asked for another two trainers, both retired Rangers.

While at the city bar our fishing boats came rolling in, still by far the biggest thing in the Bahama fishing industry. We now had two more boats, both concentrating on the west side of Andros. After all these years, we still sold 95% of our catch to Deanna's uncle. He was getting up there in age but still came to the dock everyday but Sunday. Mark whom was now known as Captain Mark, now was stationed in Nassau only going out every once and a while. Peter was still the Boss, he'd been working with me from the beginning, almost 20 years. Peter's men ran two tourist boats, the fishing trip at night and a diving trip in the day. The diving trip wasn't to the wrecks, we would take tourist from the cruise ships, anchor and let them skin dive and hand feed the fish.

Carlos the Cuban in the shop now had a full machine shop. The only one in all of the Bahamas, they could build or repair almost anything.

Otis would be a father sometime within the next two weeks. Yes, it was said to be a boy, Ms. Agree would finally get her grandson. Between the bunch of us we'd have a dozen kids that we hoped would one day keep this all going.

My dinner with June was interrupted by Cat. She had put the children to bed and just had to know how it was that she had Wendy Michelle and where and what was going to happen to Johnny. I stood to go to walk outside but Cat said we could talk in front of June. Cat said that Salinas, June and herself had made a pack that they were now family and would stick together. I only used the words settlement and agreement but told them the basics of the agreement. Cat gave me a hard kick under the table as she wasn't happy not having Johnny. I said that with Jacob's drinking, we'd have one of Jerry's men keep an eye on both Jacob and Johnny. I said that somehow we get Johnny back. Tears came from Cat's eyes but she knew that it was the best we could manage at the moment. Cat reminded me that I had promised to keep my hands off Jacob. Cat came to me and kissed me saying she loved me and hugged June and was off.

June asked what I had to pay for that to have happened? I told her that I had made an offer that he couldn't resist. Like in the movie The Godfather she asked? No I said. He could have said no, but he couldn't resist the offer.

The next morning, I picked up Salinas as planned. I hadn't planned on her looking so good. It was hard for me to believe that she was that beautiful after having the two children. She was irresistible, kind of like my offer to Jacob. Salinas and I would be late to meet Tommy.

We arrived in Haiti's Port of Prince and we had one of only three limos on the Island waiting. Jacks men were there at the airport waiting, they were not happy with what they saw going on in the streets. We made our way without any troubles except Mack having to fire a few warning shots. A few meaning almost a full clip from an M-16. At the sound of gunfire, the crowd ran every which way.

I had not notified my contacts nor the US Embassy that we were coming. I wanted it to be a privet meeting. I was carrying a bag with $500.000.00 in US cash.

We were well received, of course being a military man the General didn't make us wait as his predisessor would have. The General had gotten some intel of why we were there and knew he needed us just as much or more than we needed him. The talk was straight forward him requesting more money than I would give him. Part of the agreement was that we would come in force if he was in need. The General said he was an Honest man and wanted what was best for his people. He was happy to see that I had chosen a Hattian girl as my wife as he had the impression that most Americans thought his people below them. I said that beauty came in all colors. It was the heart that was important. He knew of my Haitian force and I assured him they were a match for any adversary. I never open the bag, I just left it where we had been sitting. The General assured us that we would have his full support leaving the two out of country locations status quo and adding the additional men. The General gave permission to expand the runway at Paix as use in conjunction of training our force.

The meeting only lasted an hour, we could hear gunfire from outside the Place. On the way out I turned and asked if he needed any reinforcement at the Place. The General said that we had already helped.

Salinas asked to stop by and visit her mother, we did not. We flew directly back to Nassau. The situation in Haiti could change at any time. Besides I hadn't forgotten that it was Sharron whom talked Salinas into leaving me.

We arrived back in Nassau in the late afternoon. I would meet with Peter's wife Ida and we would visit Deanna's beach house. As I walked through I remembered my first visit here with my first girlfriend, Kelly. Things had changed a lot since then. Jacob had left a mess, Ida said she'd have the place cleaned and repainted within a week.

It was time for me to visit Lori, we dropped Fernando off on Andros and we went on to Miami. I gave no warning to Lori that I was coming. Once in Miami I drove straight to Roy's office.

Roy said I was just too much trouble to keep as a client. Roy first represented me when I was 17 years old. 18 years later he said I was still more trouble than I was worth. He said that I knew that Jacob wasn't going to honor his part of the agreement and that would just make more work for him later.

By the time I went by Chubby's, he, Lori and Pa'me were on the key with the hobie cat. I stopped in and saw the children and asked a favor of Lilly. I asked Lilly to pack a small bag for Lori. I was going to take Lori away for a few days. With the bag in hand I drove to Winn Dixie and purchased groceries and then stopped by the sailing club. Robert was there and had an old ice chest that he put the things in that needed refrigeration. Robert would take care of all the rest.

I then drove on over to Key Biscyne and parked next to Chubby's car. As I drove up I noticed a familial car, it was Evette's BMW, the Louisiana tag insured my hunch. Chubby was sitting in his car using binoculars to watch the girls. He saw me coming in the rear view mirror and held the binoculars out to me as I walked up. I counted one, two then three, I looked good and the third girl was Evette. Before I saw her BMW I had forgotten that Evette was back in Miami. I thought for sure she'd be staying at the apartment. Lori must have spotted my car as they headed back toward the beach passing by yelling for me to come on in. I opened my trunk and moved things around until I found a pair of shorts. I changed and walked up to Chubby that was still in his car. Chubby looked at me and said that this one was no child. Chubby was speaking of Evette. The girls came in closer and I walked in and then dove on in the water. As they came in closer Lori headed the hobie into the wind just enough time for me to climb up. Lori was at the tiller and once I was aboard she steered the hobie to catch the wind and we were off. Lori was showing off her new skills, Evette crawled over to me and kissed me then Pa'me. Both kisses were a little too friendly. The girls were wearing next to nothing, all three. Pa'me then took the tiller and Lori came crawling over and latched on. Lori kissed me and said that this was her best gift ever, she loved sailing. We sailed another hour and then headed in. We beached the hobie and took the sails down remove the rigging, then put the hobie on the trailer. Lori asked if I'd take all three girls out to dinner, they all wanted to dress up and go out. I wasn't looking for that kind of night but I said yes.

Evette went straight to the apartment while I took the girls to Chubby's where I washed the boat and gear. The girls went in and would get their clothes, they would get ready at the apartment. Pa'me would spend the night in the spare room.

The children were happy to help with washing the boat. Both Melody and Sam were now taking their own pram lessons at the sailing club. How cool was this.

Once at the apartment there were several messages on the recorder. Pa'me entered into the spare room while Lori entered mine. I checked the messages and then made a few follow up calls. Nilo had called and left a strange message. I called Jerry to have him do a follow up. Jerry also had news that one of his men had located one of the two Navy men in Lucy's case that we were looking for. My instructions were to stay back but not to lose him.

The Colonel called and I called back and got his recording. I left a message where he could find me during the next 12 hours, after that I would be out of contact unless it was an emergency. This I said would take a helicopter to find me.

Lori was waiting for me for our shower, it was great! We then started dressing, Lori asked to use her jewelry and asked for somethings for Pa'me and Evette. I opened the closet door then the vault and left the vault door open. I told Lori to get hers which was in a separate box and said she was to pick out something for each girl. Lori came back with several items and curiously asked what was in there that required so much security. I noted the question as strange and didn't answer waiting to see if she would ask a second time. She did not. I asked if she had what she wanted and closed and relocked the vault and closet door.

For the first time I saw Lori sit in front of the mirror and put on makeup. I asked where she learned to put on that stuff and she said that Pa-me was teaching her. The makeup didn't make her prettier, just older. It wasn't a bad thing but it didn't sit well with me.

There was a knock on the bed room door, when I opened the door it was Pa'me looking like I had not seen her before. She had a short black dress that would catch every man's eye no matter where we went. Pa-me had come to ask Lori if she need any help with the makeup. Lori said she was fine. The door was still opened when Evette caught my eye, Evette too was dressed to kill. I would be taking out three of the most beautiful girls in town. We were headed for the studio. This was Bob's favorite restraunt. From there the plan was to visit the Alley in the grove. To get in the Alley one had to be 21 years old. We would soon see if we were to get in the door.

One day this month it would be Lori's birthday, I picked out something that we both could enjoy and had planned to present it to her tonight after dinner. Seemed that plan might not work out. We took both cars.

The Studio was packed, Lourdes had made reservations for two, now we were looking for a table for 4. We sat at the bar for almost an hour. We were finally seated an ordered champagne and then dinner.

From Dinner we went by the Alley only to have them ask all three girls for ID. If it would have been just Lori and I, we would have gotten in. None were 21, Pa'me and Lori being only 15. I wasn't going to push it. Lori was down and didn't want to go home so we went to the 1800 club. I asked Evette to take Pa'me home as I said that Lori and I were going to take a walk on the beach. Evette and Pa-me left at about 2:00 a.m. Lori and I headed toward the sailing club. When getting to club I open my trunk and got out her small bag. The sailing club was empty, but the dock wasn't. As we walked down the dock Lori looked and then started running, we were facing a large sail boat. The stern which was facing us had 4 big letters that spelled LORI. Lori left her high heels on the dock and jumped aboard, ran forward to the bow and then back to the stern. Is it really ours she asked? It is, I said. She then jumped into the cockpit. She was standing in the cockpit when I threw her the cabin door keys and her bag. I walked up the dock to the bow of the boat and untied the bow line and threw it aboard. I then walked to the stern and with the stern line in hand got aboard. I started the engine and put her in reverse and then forward. As the boat moved forward I switched on the running lights and headed out. Lori was down there until we got into the channel, when she came up she was wearing a one-piece silk bed wear. The wear was held on by two strings on the shoulders and stopped about 12 inches higher than her knees. I thought there was no way that Lilly put that in Lori's bag. Lori came up into my arms and said to please stop this boat and throw out the anchor. I said we needed to get a little farther out but she didn't wait.

When I purchased the boat I had made a list of items that must be delivered with the boat, Lori had been down there checking things out to include taking the silk sheets out of the package and putting them on the master bed. She had done the pillows too. Lilly didn't put the bed wear in Lori's bag, Lori had planned to drop her dress once at home and just have that on.

CHAPTER XV

THE "LORI"

The boat was a 38 foot Morgan, she had a 50 horse power diesel and a draft of 4'- 6". It was more draft than I wanted but we could still sail both through the keys and the Bahamas.

The next morning, we would be headed for Key West. It looked like Lori's bed wear was going to be her dress of the day. She asked if I liked it. I said that I liked whatever she was wearing and that she didn't need to be putting on any make up on unless she was with me and she got the ok beforehand. Lori said that both Evette and Pa-me said that men like sexy things and girls with makeup. Evette, I said is looking for a man, unfortunately Pa-me was taught that she had to please a man to survive I said. Are you looking for a man I asked? No Lori said I have my man. Do you want to impress me I asked? Yes, Lori said, I want you to love me more. Haven't we already talked about this I asked? I will not leave you I said. Accomplish the things we talked about, be the best you can be. I'm sorry Lori said but it's hard knowing you spend time with the other women. Don't let Pa-me or Evette put things in your head. Stay the course, follow the path. Now I said go and put on a bathing suit top and some shorts. Lori kissed me and said she was sorry, then went below and changed.

When she returned she said that she had left her high heels on the dock. I smiled and though about Robert coming to work this morning and seeing the boat gone and the high heels there on the dock. Yes, it brought a rather big smile. Lori asked that I not be upset with Pa-me and Evette. We get along very good she said and Pa-me helps past the time when you're gone. Lori then said that the teacher always says how fast Pa-me learns. I believe that she too is in love with you Lori said. She never stops asking about you Lori added.

We were now on the east side of Key Largo heading south. The wind was brisk and the sails full. I had Lori behind the wheel as much as I could. Once in a while I'd have her come about and work the lines all by herself. Lori was getting good at this. Night fall came and we kept right on sailing. We agreed we wouldn't stop until we arrived at Key West. We took two hour shifts, just like the first trip with the Hunter when delivering it to Nassau. The Morgan was much easier to handle by a single person. I wanted Lori to be able to master this boat. The next day at about noon we were coming around the end of Key West's southernmost tip. We lowered the sails and started the engine. We motored past the Navy yard and then pulled into the city docks. We had used the ship to shore to secure a birth at the dock. Once there we docked and signed in with the dock master and then set up a wind catcher that would push the air it caught down into the master bed room. Lori and I would sleep until just after dark. We dressed, as one in Key West would dress and were headed to find some food. We ate and did a little bar hopping to include some of the spots that I had visited some 15 years ago almost to the day. At that time, I had sailed the "Princess" down here with the intentions of drowning myself in alcohol. Yes, it was just after I had returned from active duty and learned that Deanna had been unfaithful and was pregnant and June had gotten married. It was during that time that I took that infamous Donzi ride. Lori got to hear the entire story. That night after we went to bed it seemed that in my dreams I relieved all those years again. Seeing Michelle for the first time at Bob's, coming down that spiral stair case in that Red satin dress. Rusty and I were diving with Johnny, seeing that big all-white teeth smile of Johnny's. I looked at Lori sleeping and saw Deanna there in that second story boarding house bed. Looking at her I had to touch her to see if she was real. As I put my hand on her back side the smooth curved body rolled over and my dream came to an end. It was Lori and not Deanna. A few tears rolled down my face, sad that Johnny, Deanna and Michelle were no longer there but happy that I was here with Lori.

I couldn't go back to sleep. I stood up and found a light in the galley and looked for a coffee maker. There it was right where it should be. My coffee and filters too. I said to myself that I loved it when a plan comes together. While the coffee brewed I found the phone. Yes, this boat even had a phone connection.

I called Lourdes and got that, good morning boss! I gave her instructions, she repeated them, I said she had gotten it all correctly and to have a good day. We were docked on the west side of the Key, the Island would block the sunrise. I got Lori up and told her to put on some clothes. Lori asked what time is it? It's time for a walk on the beach. We got some clothes on walked to the beginning of the dock and tapped on the window of a sleeping taxi driver. He jumped up, we got in and headed to the beach on the Island's east side.

Lori and I walked some on the beach and then I picked a spot. As we sat, Lori with her head on my shoulder the sun began to appear. It was a beautiful sight. All Lori said was that it was all worth it. Looking at the sun rise I mentioned that she hadn't taken off the diamond solitary ring. Lori said she was going to asked if she could keep it on. If the answer was yes, she said she wanted to refit it to fit a little tighter so not to easily come off. I pulled her back to the sand and kissed her.

We weren't the only ones on that beach, seemed lots of people were there to enjoy the sun rise. There were lots of joggers too. We then walked a short distance and found coffee and breakfast. At breakfast looking at her looking down at the ring, she looked at me and asked if she could keep it on? I said she could keep it but once she started high school I wanted her to leave it at home. No need to tell all those young boys your already taken I said. No she said, if it's truly mine I will not take it off.

When we got back to the boat Lori had a surprise, her two best buddies were sitting in the cockpit. Just as soon as Lori saw them she started running. The girls yelled to me and said the phone had been ringing since they had stepped aboard. I greeted the girls on my way down to answer the phone. It was Lourdes, she said that the Colonel wanted to know where to send the helicopter as he needed me at a lunch at Joe's at noon. Lourdes said he said it had some urgency. I told her that Tommy should still be here on the ground and to first call Tommy then the Colonel and tell him I'd be there. Lourdes also said Jerry and a Mr. Cord had also called, both men said it was urgent. While talking to Lourdes she said she was receiving a call from Jack, Lourdes spoke with Jack and connected us both to the same line. Jack said that something had gone wrong within the vehicle and

I better come and see for myself. The only thing is that that leer's radar and directional devises may not work. I said I'd be there sometime today. I then informed Lourdes that I would need to leave in order to make it to Miami on time. I said I would return the other calls from the leer. Lori already knew it was bad news, she hugged me and said she'd be right there waiting. I looked at Evette and said that they could go out and have fun but no drinking. Lori asked if they could go dancing and I said yes but not to be out past 1:00 a.m. I grabbed my clothes from the other night and headed for a taxi.

My early morning call to Lourdes had been to get Evette and Pa-me up and to Opa-Locka. Lourdes saw to it to call Tommy to bring them both here to Key West.

When I got on the leer I made my first call to Jerry. Jerry said that he was sure that Pa-me was a CIA plant. Nilo whom I sent to Davao found no such family living there. With the help of a few new government friends and using Pa-me's new passport photo, Nilo found a police record where Pa-me known as Christina had been arrested several times for prostitution, Christina was 20 years old and somehow got a US passport through the US Embassy. Jerry said he figured the CIA. Jerry said that even I had said that Lori and Pa-me had looked alike. I told Jerry he had done a good job and to keep it under wraps. Somehow I wasn't surprised, it was just too easy that day at Montibelli's house.

I then called Mr. Cord, I had known Cord years back in the container business. Cord was the owner of one of the largest stevedoreing companies in Miami. I called the number and it was him. Cord's voice was crackly, what I understood was that his son was flying a helicopter from Haiti to Miami when they lost contact with him. Cord said his son's last call said it was impossible but they were lost and out of fuel. Cord said he had heard that I knew the area and now had a few planes of my own. Cord said he had called everyone to help and was asking the same from me. I said I would do whatever I could. I then called Jerry and said to somehow get everything we could in the air to search for the downed helicopter. I warned Jerry of the possibility of the GPS and navigation systems not working. Jerry said the C-130 on Andros was grounded because of bad weather. I said to be careful but to get it up there. Jerry said they'd do what they could.

Before I had changed my clothes we were in Miami. I told Tommy to refuel and also assist in the search. I warned him of what Jack had said about the Navigation and GPS system being jammed. Don't trust the system I said, don't get lost.

I caught a taxi to Joe's Stone Crab and arrived just before noon. The Colonel was sitting with Montibelli and another rough looking man. As I walked up to the table only the Colonel got up to receive me. The third man was introduced as the General and, President of Panama. I wasn't as impressed as he thought I should be and the same man commented in Spanish, something like Pendejo, which meant stupid. The Panamanian General looked like he been drinking most of the morning. I took a quick look around and noticed at least two Latin body guards and three girls talking Spanish much too loud at the bar. I figured that those five were with him. I picked out a least one Israeli that should be with Montibelli. The Israeli looked seasoned and was most likely in Montibelli's house that day I took Pa-me standing by as a backup.

The Colonel noticed that I was uncomfortable and ordered me a Chivas on the rocks. I looked at him and asked what he need that was so urgent. The General again used the word Pendejo. I didn't speak much Spanish but I knew several curse words. I could have called him a dick face but thought I would first hear what they wanted. Hell I thought that name fit him so well. A new round of drinks came and the Colonel made a toast, to friends of freedom he said. I downed my Chivas and hit the glass on the table. The Panamanian General was annoyed. I thought that would get his attention. The Colonel then started saying that he needed transport from Panama to Iran, he said one trip per week. The Colonel said the Air force would refuel the C-130s while in the air. I looked at the Colonel and asked, if that was it. No he said, we have information that the Soviets had already or were sending a man to stay in Limon. The Colonel said that he needed someone to keep track of this man. He then passed me a photo of the man. The Colonel said that the man was fluent in Spanish, German and of course Russian. His mission was to strengthen the south east side of Nicaragua which to this point was under the Contra's control. The Russian was to stop any outside assistance that was coming from Costa Rica, supplied by the US. The Soviets knew that we had used the Limon airport to supply the contras.

It was almost perfect timing that our waiter came and said I had a phone call. The call was from Jack, Mira had found a switch on the Vehical control panel that one of the Navy engineers had switch on by error, Mira said she thought this had somehow effected navigation for maybe up to a 100 mile radius. Jack said that he didn't think the Navy even noticed or had put two and two together. I told him that there had been at least one airborne that I believed was down, maybe due to this problem. I called Lourdes to contact Tommy and get him back for me. I'd be at Opa-Locka in an hour and then on to Andros.

I went back to the table and one of the Latin women was now sitting in the general's lap kissing on him. I looked at Montibelli and said in Pilipino, "must be your friend" When I said this Montibelli's smile disappeared and the Panamaian General looked upset. I hadn't sat down as yet and stated that the transport could start at any time and that I'd take care of the Russian in Costa Rica. I looked at the Panamaian General and said don't bother to get up, I see there's a lady present. The waiter had brought me another drink and my stone crabs but instead of sitting, I thanked the Colonel for the drink and was on my way.

I taxied to Opa-Locka, Tommy was there waiting and we were off to Andros. While in the air we could hear chit chat from pilots in the air searching for the downed Helicopter. We had even spotted three different planes and what turned out to be another helicopter but not the one we were looking for.

Once on Andros Lee picked me up and now said that the Navy had made the connection that the interference with the navigation had come from the vehicle. The Navy didn't know how but knew most likely it was the vehicle that caused the problem. Mira had followed the connection and found that there was a small device within the control panel that somehow messed with the magnetic pole. Mira had asked Jack's permission to remove the transmitter as she called it but Jack had said to wait for me.

By now the Navy engineers were all over the Vehicle looking for the cause. Not only did I think the vehicle twas possible of blocking the magnetic pole, I believed it was at one time the technology used for part of its defense. If the device or the transmitter was located in the control panel, then I had one in my apartment's safe.

I would move from Andros back to Miami. I would return to the apartment and check on my safe, I didn't think it was possible that someone especially Pa-me could get into my safe but I would go check anyway.

Once at home in the apartment I first notice that my bed room door lock had been breached. I always slipped a small clear gel pack in the key hole. Even I couldn't open the door without breaking the tiny gel pack. I put on a pair of latex gloves and started to check. The gel pack was already broken. I unlocked the door and went in. I open the closet door and then stepped back. No it hadn't been opened or touched. I then started to look and found a small camera that's purpose was to film me opening the vault. She was good I thought but, not good enough. I removed the camera and checked if it was transmitting. It was not, I then put the camera in my underwear draw.

I opened the vault and checked its contents. Everything seemed to be in order. It didn't seem real that I could have so much and not have somewhere else that I thought would be safer. I thought that the explosion that it would take to open the vault might take down the entire building. I locked it back and would be checking the remainder of the apartment. The whole place including the phones were bugged. The jewels that both girls barrowed were here and placed in one of Evette's draws. Nothing was missing.

Tommy got me back to Key West just after dark. The news of my friend's son wasn't good because there was no news. If he was out there alive, he would be spending the night. The weather could have played a great part as the seas all around the posible crash area were about 10 feet.

When I arrived at the boat in Key West there was no one home. I got a drink and sat in the cockpit and waited. I could hear them coming from some distance, talking and laughing, lots of laughing. I stood and looked, it was hard to believe that Pa-me wasn't having the time of her life. All three looked to fill that spot. When Lori saw me she came a running. Lori said they had a blast and had found just the place to go dancing tonight. Since I had missed lunch I asked about a restaurant? They said that they had picked that out too.

We all got ready and had a great night out. It was the first time that Lori and I had danced. Seemed that Pa-me had thaught her a few moves. The girls didn't let me sit down not even once.

The next morning while the girls were still asleep, I paid the dock bill, picked up a few bags of ice, untied the boat and pulled on out of the harbor. I motored until well out of the channel and then while still under power raised the sails. I then cut off the motor and took a northerly heading toward Miami.

Pa-me was the first to come up. She came and hugged me. I asked if the hug was from Christina or Pa-me? She said it was from someone she'd like to be. She said that she wished she had met me years ago. She apologized for the deceit but said at the time that she was recruited it looked like the thing to do. I told her that she owed me nothing but that Lori was a different story. Lori I said looks at you like a sister, she trusts and looks up to you. I don't know what the next step here is except that you need to come clean with Lori and Evette too. Pa-me said she had opened my bed room door and place a camera in the room to see how I opened the vault. She said the apartment was also bugged, but by others. She said that the CIA was worried about what I would and wouldn't do. I said that I had found the camera and all the bugs.

It was my sleepy head's turn to stick her head up from the cabin. Is it too late for coffee she asked? I'd love a cup I said. What will you do with me Pa-me asked? Do, I asked? You can go as you please I said, I can't keep you and staying with Lori is out of the question. She then walked along the deck to the bow and took a seat on the deck. Soon Lori came up with coffee and asked about Pa-me. I told Lori that Pa-me wasn't her real name and she was still working for Montibelli. It was strange but Lori didn't seem surprised. Lori asked what would happen to her? I said that on my part she was free to go. Lori said that Pa-me had kept saying how lucky she and the children were. Lori asked if I was mad with her for asking me to help Pa-me? I said we helped because we thought it was the right thing to do. I said not to worry that we didn't get hurt, only our feelings. Lori sat with me a while and then asked if Pa-me or Christina could quit her job. Of course she can I said, they most likely would deport her, but yes she could quit. Lori then stood and walk up to the bow.

The two girls would stay up there for more than an hour. Evette came up and asked what the pow-wow was about. I said that they were just having a heart to heart and to leave it. Evette looked at me and said I looked like I needed a drink. I'll take another coffee if you don't mind I said. I got my coffee and asked Evette to sit and talk. Evette asked, I still got a job right? I asked her to take the wheel. I then asked her what her plans were? Plans she asked, I have to have a plan? I guess, I one day will find another man, but I'm not looking for one like you think. You tell everyone that I'm looking she said. Besides except when you left me in the Philippines, I've had a blast working for you. Seems we lost our friend Karen but I found Lori and Pa-me. Keep your eyes on that compass but always check your surrounds I said. As I looked forward Pa-me and Lori were coming to the stern. Evette looked at them and asked, so what's the big pow wow about or is it a secret? Well, I said looking at Pa-me? My real name is Christina I'm 20 years old and I work for the CIA, Pa'me said. Well blow me down Evette said, then Evette said, "you little bitch". Evette then looked at me and asked if we were going to feed her to the sharks? Then Evette smiled, well sort of. Lori said she'd still like to keep Christian with us. Lori said if I'd check the camera that was placed, it had been tampered with and would not, could not take any photos. Evette said that Christina could work with her at the depot, there's nothing secret there she said. I looked at Christina and asked what she wanted to do? Go home or start a new life somewhere? Christiana said she like to stay with the family, meaning the family she had now. Besides the apartment she said there's nothing else they've asked of me. Maybe not but they will ask for more I said. I then said that I'd go and talk with Montibelli and see what we could do. In the meantime, your name is Pa-me and you're on probation.

We sailed up to the Ocean Reef Yacht Club, arriving the next day at sun up. Pa'me had spent most of the night up with me sailing. We talked a lot and I tried my best to look at it from her side. The only thing she was doing was her job, I was the one that allowed her to mix with the family. Wow I thought family, I now had quite a few young children. It almost made me want to change the heading of the boat and go east. Pa'me would help with the docking. Everyone besides us were sleeping even the dock master. The boat was secured and I went up front and snuggled in with Lori.

We spent the morning at the club, the girls ate breakfast while I made phone calls. We got back under way at about 1:00 p.m. We went through Caesars Creek and being almost low tide we sailed by Billy's Point as the cove would be too shallow for our draft. We anchored about a half mile north of the Elliot's Key Park. Here we all could go for a swim using the boats top deck as a diving platform. Not that we were anchored at a location that I could have done some diving for fish or crawfish but also we had no diving gear on board. The girls did however cook a good dinner.

The next morning, we sailed back to Miami and I dropped Evette off at the sailing club to get my BMW and drive it on over to the Gables Water Way where Lourdes had gotten the Morgan a berth. Lourdes had called the women that had rented me my first slip there but that slip was taken. The woman, Mrs. Mergan did however, call Lourdes with the name of another slip owner's phone number. Anyway we had a slip there. Evette of course beat us there and was waiting at the pool. We all loaded up my car and were off to the apartment. Lori would spend the night and then tomorrow go back to Chubby's to restart her training and or classes. It sure was a joy to have her around. Pa'me or Christina would not be going back to Chubby's not even for one night. She would stay close to me until I figured out what I was going to do with her. I tried to reach Montibelli but with no luck. I called Jerry to see what was going on with the Central American Flights and talked about The Panama-Iran flights. Jerry said that the Panama flights could start just as soon as we had another set of Pilots. Jerry said that one of our C-130s had just returned with our people from the Philippines. That C-130 had stopped there in Mandeville then Miami and now was in Haiti's Paix. Once they returned with the C-130, we would again start dropping supplies into the Central America. Jerry said that Fernando was waiting for Tommy to pick him up and take him to Paix to start the new process of selecting men for our group.

Jena had left a message that she was back in town staying at her Starr Island house and had invited myself and whatever wife I was on out for dinner one night soon. I figured that I should take her on over to Nassau to meet the children. Boy would she get a kick out of that. Anyway I would need to wait to call her hopefully to get things settled with Pa'me first. It wasn't two minutes after we hung up the phone, Jerry called me back.

CHAPTER XV

CAPTURE OF LUCY'S THIRD ATTACKER

The Navy man we were watching that was wanted for the Lucy situation was on his way to visit New Orleans, the man, Jeffery Stuart, would only be there for two days and one night. Jerry said if we wanted him, now would be a good time. I thought for about 30 seconds and said for Jerry to keep his man on Jeffery's tail. I hung up and asked Evette and Pa-me if they were ready for a little work related trip. Both said yes. The Idea was to get both girls in front of Jeffery and close the trap on him. The girls would leave for Mandeville at once. The clothes and jewelry that they had on for our night out at the Studio would do just fine. Whatever else the girls needed once in New Orleans they could get Jerry to buy for them. The girls would be the bait and the leer jet the trap. The girls would be accompanied by two of Fernando's trusted men. Once Jeffery was on the jet, his next stop would be a Nassau jail. I warned both girls that at no time were they to be separated, not even to go to the bathroom; both girls said they understood. The girls soon departed and that left Lori and I alone for the night.

The next morning, I took Lori back to Chubby's to keep her studies going. The children were happy to have Lori back. Lori told them about the new boat and our trip to Key West. The children wanted to see the boat, Lori looked at me and said maybe on the weekend. There would only be 3 more months for Lori to get ready for 10th grade. I had spoken with every one of Lori's teachers and all said she was progressing just fine. Lori knew the plan would be for me to stay in Miami during the next few days and that I'd see her tonight. Lori would be 16 on June 18ᵗʰ. As I drove back to the apartment I remembered the day that Deanna had turned 16. Deanna had made a big deal that at 16 she was then not my girlfriend, but my woman. Deanna's mom had gotten married at 16 and then shortly there after had Deanna's sister Wendy that same year. Deanna and I had three great years before I had gone into the Air Force. Lori was living in a much better environment than Deanna had and I felt comfortable about her making it through these times.

When I got back to the apartment I called Bob, it had been a while since we had talked, right off the bat he started off on how long it was taking to unload his cargo at our new terminal in Mandeville. I invited him to lunch to talk. We would meet at Joe's at noon.

I would then go and visit Tim at our Miami terminal. Tim was there with his wife Joan; Joan was now pregnant with their third child. I wondered why she would be working; I knew or at least hoped it wasn't because of the money. Besides, I had seen some of Joan's paintings and they could have made a living off of her art work. Tim said that Joan didn't want to stay home all day with the rug rats.

Tim had started our own leasing company that he named BlueWater Leasing. Tim said that Bob's shipping company was his first customer. Tim would buy Sea Container's older and or damaged containers and rework them and paint them with the Lines color and logo. Tim showed me the numbers and they were quite good. I asked Tim if he would be interested in buying my half of both the Miami and New Jersey businesses. Omni was worth at least two million and Terminal 51 as he called it had started out with a boom. Part of Mr. Crowbe's agreement was that he would still use our facilities for his drop offs of damaged equipment and use Terminal 51 for at least some of the repair work that would be generated by his Petty Island Port. Tim and I would come to an agreement that he would pay me $1,000,000.00 in payments plus 50 percent of the leasing companies profits for 5 years. If they needed any financing I would assist. I was happy for him as he and his wife had worked hard to build the business. Evette of course would stay with me.

From there I would meet with Bob for lunch. We would meet at Joe's of course and for the first time I saw the two of them together. It was Bob, my best buddy and partner sitting there with his big unlit Cuban cigar and Montibelli. At first my head was spinning and I didn't know what to think of the relation. The only misgiven thing that Montibelli had done that I knew of was to add Pa'me into my life and her attempting to be able to get into my safe. Seemed the General as Bob called him had been a friend of Bob's for some time. Montibelli had a boyish smile that looked like he wanted to be friends. Bob had not brought Montibelli along to talk business but to see if I could help with a situation that Montibelli was in. Seemed that Mr. Montibelli was being deported for being an international arms dealer. Bob wanted to know if I could keep him at one of my houses outside of the US. I then could see that this wasn't Bob's Idea but Montibelli's. Montibelli staying at one of my homes would be like a vacation for him. Montibelli was most likely thinking of Nassau or Paradise Island. My first thinking was NO way. But my mouth opened and I started on them both. Bob I asked? Did you know about Pa'me? Bob asked who's Pa'me? You didn't know that Mr. Montibelli here set me up and sent a spy into my house to steal from me I asked? Bob said no. It was the first time I had ever seen Bob's face get a little red. Both Bob and I then looked at Montibelli. Montibelli said it was true but that it was from directions from the CIA Director. Pa'me works for The CIA not me Montibelli said. Montibelli said the action was not meant to hurt me but to watch me and report back. Montibelli said that when the Director knew of my safe he wanted in, not to steal anything but to see what was in there, the CIA was worried that I had something on them. Something like the Kennedy Assassination, Montibelli said. Montibelli said that the CIA knew that Carson and I had collaborated on a Kennedy investigation and wanted to see what we had. Montibelli also said that they all wanted to know where my money was coming from and where and how much it was. Montibelli said they wanted to be able to use some kind of pressure to insure my cooperation. Montibelli said they had threatened him with deportation and confiscation of his funds. I looked at him and asked, so how did that work out for you?

Montibelli then said, we do enjoy some of the same things and we do have businesses that could help one another. Besides, that you like young women, what other things do you have that we might mix I asked? Montibelli said he would still be moving a lot of freight, you sell transportation. I have a lot of contacts around the world that will help you get around he said. Together we would make a good match for any group he said. I looked at Bob and said the man's crazy. Bob smiled and then said maybe that's why we're all sitting here and started in with that terrible laugh of his. Montibelli said I don't need much just three rooms. Then we all started laughing. I said, for now he could go to Paix and stay at the château, he'd have to put up with Salinas's mother but then I said, she is a good looking woman. I said he could have one room and whatever help he had would stay outside of the house. I also told them both that Fernando was in charge of the compound and they'd have to abide by his rules. Montibelli put his hand across the table and tried to put his hand on mine. Thank you friend he said.

Well Bob said how about lunch. I then said not so fast. We still had Pa'me to talk about. I asked Montibelli if he had Pa'me's original passport, he said he did. I asked them both if she, Christina, could resign from the company. Both answered yes, but would they let her Bob asked? They would hold deportation over her head like they did Montibelli Bob said. What if I was to marry her I asked? Bob then almost choked and then started that laugh and asked how many wives did I already have? Legally not one I replied. Montibelli said that marrying her could solve two things, she couldn't be force to testify against you he said. Bob still laughing asked what about the other three or four wives? Bob looked at me and said he had forgotten to congratulate me on my three newborns. What was it four children in less than one year Bob asked? Bob was now getting a lot of attention from the other tables as he just couldn't stop laughing. I then looked at Montibelli and asked what about the other thing. They couldn't deport her Montibelli said.

We didn't talk much more on the subject. I asked Montibelli how much time he had to leave the country and he said midnight tomorrow. I said that Tommy was busy delivering a package but should be free sometime tomorrow. The stone crabs were as they always were, delicious.

Bob said he'd be sending something to the Island for the kids and he hoped to see me soon. Maybe at the wedding he said as he laughed.

From there I went to see Roy again, the visit was twofold. One was the control box and weapon, the other Pa'me. Roy had set up a US company that owned part of the technology of the mechanical arm but G.D. hadn't wanted the small laser. I told Roy of the GPS jamming ability and that

I was sure that the control box possessed the ability to guide a missile to anywhere that satellite coverage was available. The weapon, I told him I hadn't even tried but knew that it was way beyond anything that our military had. Roy said he thought any new agreement should have control over how and where the weapon was used. Roy also said that since the Navy had the same equipment that we should move at once toward G.D. so they could start working on a paten.

So far Roy hadn't complained about the work, here he was 10% owner of the holding company and although we hadn't received any money as yet from the mechanical arm, what we now had was much different.

The complaining came when I told him the story with Pa'me. Why don't you just settle down and live a quiet life on one of those Islands that you love so much Roy asked? All this running around messing with advisories and all these women is only going to get you killed he said. Now you want to marry a CIA operative? No I don't want to marry her; I just want it to look like I'm married to her. What Roy asked? Another marriage to someone with a false passport? No marriage I said, I want Pa'me's, Christina's passport to show my last name. You can have her sign a pre-marriage agreement, and the divorce papers at the same time I said. Then I said, I don't know, you figure it out. I'm going to start working on an operation where it needs to appear that Christina is my wife. This plus, we need to get Christina out of the CIA's hands. Roy didn't want the details, of what I was going to do, he just repeated what he said about getting myself killed.

Roy let me use one of his small offices. I called Lourdes and she informed me that Tommy now had the package and was headed to Nassau. Lourdes said that Evette and Pa'me would be staying overnight in Nassau to see all the kids. I told her to have Tommy come and pick me up and take me to Nassau and Montibelli to Paix.

Cat was now back living at Michelle's beach house; Jacob had been misbehaving and got into trouble in Miami. The divorce papers and separation agreements had been signed and Jacob had his first payment. Jacob was in jail for an at-fault DUI accident, leaving the scene of that accident and assaulting an officer while resisting arrest. Mr.& Mrs. Johnson, Cats father and step mother, Johnny's grandparents had to fly into Miami and pick up little Johnny from a juvenile facility.

Jacob had made bail but since then, couldn't be located. If he showed up in Nassau even his father couldn't help him as the Miami police had taken Jacob's passport and he now had a warrant of arrest for jumping bail. I was always told that money could ruin a good man. In Jacob's case the money was a sure thing, the good man part I always doubted.

No I hadn't set Jacob up, contrary to what Jacob's father would think, Jacob had done this all on his own.

Little Johnny was now with Cat and his sister Wendy Michelle and brother Jimmy at the beach house. I would visit there first.

When Evette and Pa'me arrived in Nassau, Mr. Stewart whom didn't know where he was, was picked up by the Nassau police and delivered to strait to jail. Three down one to go.

Tommy picked up Montibelli and me at Opa-Locka and dropped me off at Nassau. Tommy would then fly Montibelli to Paxi. Montibelli was accompanied by his Israeli body guard and girlfriend. Both Fernando and Sharron had been notified that there were visitors on the way. I got a taxi and went straight to see Cat and the children. Cat was calling our baby boy Jimmy.

Cat wasn't as happy to see me as I thought she would be; she was concerned about Jacob. It just didn't seem like it should. I didn't get that hot shower that I was so looking forward too. The kids were put to bed and it looked like I was going to call a taxi when Cat came and took my hand and led me into her bed room.

The next morning Cat took me down to the fisherman's wharf. We held hands as we walked the docks and said our hello's and saw our boats off. We had always talked of one day having children that would grow up on the Island's beaches and learn to fish and dive. Seemed almost like a dream that here we were with a little Jimmy, Johnny and Wendy Michelle. Cat asked when we would be taking the children to the house on Harbor Island. I said that I would fly over tomorrow and see how the work was coming along. Cat asked if I would take Salinas or June with me? I said no.

Pa'me and Evet had seen Tommy at the boarding house and Evette had told Pa'me that I 'd most likely pass by the wharf that morning. As Cat and I were walking off the docks we ran into Pa'me. I congratulated Pa'me on a job well done, Cat also thanking her for assisting in bringing

Mr. Stewart to justice. Cat and I were heading to Angee's for breakfast and Cat asked Pa'me to join us. During our good as usual breakfast we heard all the news from Angee. Cat offered me a ride to my next stop. I thanked her and said I'd see her before I went back to Miami. Pa'me asked Cat if she and Evette could come by later to see the children. Cat said yes of course.

I walked Pa'me back to the boarding house and while walking Pa'me asked if I had made up my mind what I was going to do with her, I told her that I was still thinking on it.

June was at the hill top beach house with Salinas their kids. Cat now had three children to care for and her job. I got a taxi and headed to see Salinas, June and the children.

I thought it was going to be awkward but June got to me first and then Salinas. Both girls looked like a million. Both greetings were warm, and all three kids were awake, with Michelle now walking, well, almost running around. It was Salinas that made the first move. She got me in her room and shut and locked the door. Salinas said that she liked June but was not going to share the same bed with her in it. June had told her that when Cat and her were pregnant that I had slept with both of them in the same bed. This was worse than when I got to Cat's. I just didn't feel comfortable.

When I left Salinas's room I walked out and took June by the hand and walked out and we almost reached one of the cars. I asked her if she could spend the night out and she said no that she would have to care for the baby. June asked me to please come back in and that the next time she promised to be at her own place. It didn't make me feel any better but I did go in. In the middle of the night while in June's room there was a knock on the door, I got up it was Salinas. I open the door and in she came, she stopped before getting to bed and said she was sorry that she had made me feel uncomfortable. She loved me and wanted me always to come whenever and whoever was here. Salinas pulled back the covers and got under the sheet.

The next morning, I was gone early, I met Tommy at the airport, seemed that Pa'me was keeping close tabs on me and Tommy as she was also at the airport. Seeing her I asked if she was ready for a day trip. She of course said yes. Tommy flew us on over to Eleuthera, we taxied to Charles and Madelyn's house only to find Madilyn there but Charles was in Miami with Mr. King. I introduced Pa'me as Christina, it just came out that way. Madilyn looked at me with suspicion. Madilyn knew that I had three newborns in Nassau. Pa'me and I didn't stay long, having our taxi wait. Pa'me and I then left for the eastern wharf for the boat ride to Harbor Island. The boat ride was only 15 or 20 minutes and we were shortly standing on the Harbor Island dock. This was the first time that I could actually take a taxi to the new house, the taxi driver knew exactly where it was. The Taxi driver said his father had the only big tuck on the Island and he had made many trips with supplies to the house. Pa'me hadn't said a word during the trip over. It wasn't until we stopped at the wrought iron gate. I got out and opened a visitor's door and signaled for Pa'me to come in and the driver to wait. As Pa'me stepped in, that's when she said her first words. It's so beautiful. She was so right. The house had changed quite a bit. There was building supplies everywhere but I could tell things were headed in the right direction. The roof had been completely replaced and the fireplace had been reworked to where now the same chimney was used for the fireplace in the living room and a new fireplace in the master bed room. I walked out on the balcony and looked toward the ocean. With the balcony rebuilt the ocean seemed even closer than before; it was still the most beautiful beach I had ever seen. The salty air was calling me in.

I took off my shirt, shoes and socks and started walking toward the water. I place my Beretta on the sand just 6 feet from the water. I looked back and Pa'me was standing there looking like she wanted to join me but was waiting for the invite. I waved her on and kept walking. When I got waist deep I again turned and saw her standing there at the water's edge. Pa'me hadn't packed for the occasion, she was standing there in bikini underwear and a brazier that only covered, well it didn't cover much. I held out my hand and said come on, there will be no boarding house and no sending you back. The water was warm with almost no waves. The reef that was less than a half mile out took care of the waves. Most of the waters movement was a slow rising and lowering motion. I tried not to look at her to much but it was uncontrollable. I asked her what she wanted to do with her life. She didn't hesitate and said that she most wanted to stay with me and Lori. I said that if she agreed I was going to put her to work. Close by you she asked with a smile? Yes, I answered. I'm asking you to continue to lead two very separate lives. The first as Pa'me the 15-year best friend of Lori, and the second you will start traveling with me playing the part of my 20-year-old wife. If Lori finds this out and no doubt she will, then she is to be convinced as it will be that our, yours and my relation is strictly business. Do you think that you can accomplish this I asked? First of all, Pa'me said, yesterday Pa'me was 16 and Christina 21. Would I still be working for the CIA she asked? No I said I have arranged for our marriage to seem perfectly legal. Your Christian passport will now show my last name with us being married sometime next week. You will be asked to sign several papers that will be explained at that time. One of these papers will be your irrevocable resignation from the CIA and you will not have any more contact with them. There mustn't be any pregnancies as you will be working as we travel. Evette will also be working with us and will take you to a Doctor James tomorrow or the next day.

You will be asked to follow my directions as our lives may depend on it. What about Cat she asked? You will need to turn it on and off as I will make it clear, if you can't then we'll have to go our separate ways, you may leave anytime you wish. I have enough problems with all these girls as it is I said.

So when I'm with you alone or traveling I'll be Christina your wife and when we're with Lori, Cat, June or Salinas we're friendly but I work for you. Yes, I said. I think it would be best if you leave me out of Nassau altogether she said, but if you can ever bring me here, well that would be different. As we walked out of the water, me walking behind her, I was looking at what I thought was the best body I'd ever seen. I didn't touch, just looked. I asked if she wanted to walk down the beach to dry off some. We walked, and as we walked. I said that once they had visited Doctor James and Roy, that she and Evette would be going down to Costa Rica and looking up an acquaintance that I hoped would join our group.

We walked back to the house and got dressed and taxied back to the dock and then ferried back to Eleuthera. Tommy was there waiting at the airport and once in Nassau I revisited all three girls and then by 8:00 p.m. would fly out with Evet and Pa'me.

We landed in Opa-Locka at about 9:00 p.m. I drove by and picked up Lori on the way to my apartment. Lori was happy to see me and the girls. Once home Lori and I went in and closed our door. It would be morning before the girls would talk again. I got up early to start he coffee and turned the door handle on both girl's rooms, of course, neither door was locked.

Evette and Pa'me would go off early, they would make the planned stops and both do some shopping. Lori had a full day planned and I would drop her off at Chubby's and pick her up in the late afternoon. Montibelli had given me Christina's passport, and I had passed it to Jerry. Jerry would fly to Philadelphia and then contact the Philippine consul and pay to have the changes made to Christina's passport. When Jerry returned Christina's passport would show her new name as being the same last name as mine. The Philippine Consul also would provide a marriage certificate showing Christina and I as married.

Evette and Pa'me had a very busy day with Pa'me saying she wanted to rest that night, her deciding not to go out for dinner. The girls hadn't got to do much shopping and would try again tomorrow. Lori worried about Pa'me also didn't want to go out. Evette told me in privet that Pa'me had a rough day, Roy's office had her for 4 hours and that made them late to the Doctor James appointment. They then had to wait there two hours. Pa'me said both Roy and Doctor James gave her a hard time. Roy, not being very diplomatic and Doctor James because she had only just turned 16. For Doctor James, Pa'me was Pa'me and not Christina. In both cases Evette was left out of both meetings.

That same night Jerry called and said he was ready with Christina's passport. Evette and Pa'me would need to do their shopping and then the four of us, Evette, Pa'me, Jerry and myself would meet back at the apartment to discuss their trip and our plans.

I would again drop Lori off at Chubby's for her planned activities.

During my free time after dropping off Lori, I would go and purchase some jewelry for Pa'me to include a diamond satire and matching wedding band. Pa'me would need them for her trip. Only Evette, Pa'me and Jerry would be going to Costa Rica.

At 1:00 p.m. Evette, Pa'me, Jerry and myself met at the apartment. Evette was told that Pa'me would now be playing the part of my wife while in Costa Rica. The idea of this trip was to make contact with Silva and if possible get Silva permission for a Stateside visit to Miami. I had sent word to the Secretary of State requesting assistance with a passport and visitors visa for Silva. Silva was going to be the bait for the Russian. Evette was the only one of us that was fluent in Spanish so she was in charge of translations. We now had a full packet on the Russian. The Russian's name was Peter. He was a good looking man of 26 years. His father was a colonel with the Kremlin. Peter was a first lieutenant and this was his first assignment. Peter had just rented a house in Limon and we were in a hurry to get Silvia in place.

The three of them would take off for San Jose at 7:00 p.m. this evening, before they did I called Pa'me into my bed room and handed her the rings that I had purchased. She didn't take them asking me to put them on for luck she said. I did and she kissed me. She then turned and walked out. I followed also giving Evette a kiss and a pat on the butt.

This might be my last night with Lori for a while and I was going to take her out to dinner for her Birthday. What Lori wanted instead was a night's sail coming back sometime the next day. Lori would get what she wanted. Once out in the Morgan, Lori just wanted to just keep sailing. She said she loved the boat and wanted to master it. Lori did most all the sailing, working hard even dropping and pulling up the anchor. That next morning, I called via ship to shore. Lourdes said that she hadn't heard from Jerry and the girls. I was good for time so while sailing back we anchored just off of Key Biscayne and swam in to visit the light house. Of course Lori got to hear me tell all the stories about when I was a boy and my Dad telling us all the stories about the light house Keeper and the Seminole Indians. Lori seemed to love hearing all of my old stories. I didn't take Lori home that night, we slept at the apartment and had one of the best hot water showers we ever had anywhere. I really didn't know how I could wait until Lori graduated high school before I made this being together permanent.

That night I heard from Evette and Jerry, they all, all four would be here tomorrow after 4:00 p.m. Jerry said just as soon as he arrived he needed to get back to Mandeville. Things weren't moving fast enough for anyone. Cargo was beginning to pile up.

Jack had called and said his divers that were on hold wanted to return to start diving the wreck again. Jack didn't think that was a good idea. Jack had taken on other rolls that included assisting getting the newest C-130 serviced after each run too Panama then Iran then back to Andros. Bob had secured another year for the treasure site, this since Nassau's largest hall ever was their share of the gold found in the Andros cave. We were on Nassau's good list. Of course, us just delivering Mr. Stewart to them to stand trial for the Lucy and Carla case also helped.

Jack's three divers had collected large sums of money and each had taken long vacations and come back for more. Jack said they were just restless.

That night before we went to bed I called Lourdes and told her to send messages to Mr. Crowbe, Mr. Bozzni of Standard, Chiquita and Delmonte and let them know that I would be spending time in Limon Costa Rica and if there was anything that I could assist with. I was sure we would at least hear from Crowbe but wasn't sure about the others.

The next morning, I took Lori back to Chubby's to restart her regular schedule, it was the first time that she hung on me not wanting me to go. I too didn't want to leave her but I knew it was the right thing to do. Lilly, Chubby's wife stopped me in the driveway and said that she'd still kept the children if I took and kept Lori. I told her that I was going to be doing a few things that could get me into trouble and that I had to get them out of my system. Lilly was originally from Cuba and had come to the US as a refugee. She also hated Castro. She reached in through the window and said God bless you Jim. Please she said come back safe, we will all be waiting for you.

Today I was having lunch with and old friend, yes it was Jena. We would meet at Joe's; the years had been good to Jena. I was 21 when I met her in that New York bar. That was 14 years ago. At one time we had even talked about marriage. Jena's father was once the top Mafia boss on the east coast. Nothing happened without his approval first. If there was going to be a hit, it had to be sanctioned by Benny. Jena was a certified Bitch. She had caused Benny and myself many of headaches. I was still trustee of her inheritance, Jena was still worth a fortune. Jena had since been married twice and said that if I hadn't had her money she would have been broke long ago. Her grandmother's house, which she also inherited, back then was worth about $2,000,000.00 now that same place was worth $7,000,000.00. The taxes and up keep were a small fortune. We laughed about old times. She laughed the hardest when I told her about my four children. She was happy to hear that Cat didn't get me as Cat thought she would. Jena knew that I loved Cat back then and even now still did. We talked and talked. She said that a key was delivered to the house and that recently another key was left. The first was to

let the elevator stop at our floor and the new key was to not let the elevator open when locked while upstairs. She asked how to override that key? I said there was none. Only a phone call to her or me could open the door. This as she said was serious. Yes, I said, so don't use it unless you're in some kind of danger. Being Jena she understood. After Jena had a few under her belt she popped the question. Jena wanted to become pregnant, she hadn't known about my newborns but said she still was asking. She said her father Benny would have wanted it this way. I told Jena that she wasn't ready for a child and may never be. Jena said she was serious. She said that she could change. Stop smoking and drinking for six months and we'll talk about it I said. No I want your word she said, then I'll stop smoking or whatever else you want. You couldn't raise a child I said, you couldn't sit still long enough I said. Yes, she said just like you, why should you be able to have four kids and have someone else take care of them? I thought about it and agreed, you stop smoking for six months and we'll set up some parameters and if you meet those parameters then and only then we'll do this. I gave Jena the name of June's Doctor here as I kind of liked him. Jena said she would call for an appointment tomorrow. We were at Joe's until we were asked to leave, we had been there 4 and a half hours. Jena invited me to her house to finish up the talk but I said I had to go. I told Jena that I was going to buy a house in Costa Rica and for her to come visit. Jena said she would but would first go visit Cat in Nassau. Jena said she promised not to mention our agreement. We walked out and the valet brought Jena's Mercedes convertible around first, she kissed me like she used to long ago and thanked me, she said she'd keep her end of the agreement. As she pulled off I wandered just how I got myself into so much trouble.

I went back to the apartment and got a shower and would fall asleep on the couch. The next thing I knew there was that knock on the door. Of course it was the girls that had just arrived in from Costa Rica. As I opened the door Pa'me whom was now Christina came and gave me a hug and kiss. Evette and Silvia also gave me a kiss.

Silvia looked like she had put on a few pounds, it looked good on her. Evette showed Silvia her room and Christian took her bag right into mine.

Silvia went right for phone and wanted to call her family whom wasn't to know where she was. Evette helped with the call and after at least 4 or 5 try's a neighbor of Silvia's answered the pay phone on the other end. Silvia waited as the neighbor went and fetched Silvia's little sister. Silvia told the sister she was in Limon working and she would be back in a few days. It was now almost 11:00 p.m. and we would start classes tomorrow. I would go to my room and turn on the news watching it while in bed. Christina took her shower and came out in one of those night wears that was next to nothing. She came to the beds side and said that she heard from Lori that I didn't allow clothes in my bed. I said she should wear whatever was comfortable for her. Christina walked to the television and turned it off then came back to the bed side, dropped of the night wear and turned off the light and got in bed.

The next morning Christina had coffee ready and was in the kitchen cooking breakfast. I had seen Christina slip out of bed and put on one of my matching cotton red, white and blue robes. I soon got up and followed her. Silvia was in the kitchen helping. When I walked into the kitchen I received a good morning hug and kiss from Christina that gave me a feeling that I hadn't had before. Maybe it was the way that she had her body so close to mine. Anyway it was nice and had me smiling with my right hand on her butt.

Evette was a sleepy head and only got up when breakfast was ready and set on the table.

CHAPTER XVII

SETTING THE TRAP
FOR THE RUSSIAN

Once breakfast and clean-up were made, everyone changed clothes and would sit in the living room. We spent most of the day talking about how Silvia and Peter would accidently meet. With how easily Montibelli had gotten Christina into my house, our Costa Rica plan would be that Silvia was to have a bicycle accident in front of Peter's house. Silvia did have an aunt that lived in Limon and Silvia would be there visiting. As I put myself in Peter's shoes, if Silvia while riding a bike, ran into the back of my parked car I would have at least offered her some assistance. If it were me, I would have wanted to get to know her better. Peter was spending a lot of time in a place called the American bar. Richard and Ian would meet and drink beer there every day except Sunday. Peter had tried to sit with them and talk English but Richard and Ian wouldn't have it. The bar was also home to as many as 30 working girls. Peter always had one or two girls sitting with him but didn't look too interested. Christina and I would stay at the Park hotel until we found a house to buy or rent. Evette would play the part of a friend of Christina's and come and go either staying at the Park hotel or at our house. Silvia was to get close to Peter and get invited to move in with him. Once that happen, we will start slowly but surely getting into Peter's business. Peter's house was in a strategic place, high on the top of a hill. There was an antenna on his roof that we were sure could assist in broadcasting and receiving information from Nicaragua.

The girls would take Silvia shopping to insure she wore clothes that would attract Peter. Silvia's mom would be moved into a better neighborhood and be given $500.00 a month to live on while we would put another $500.00 a month in an account for Silvia.

Lourdes had called me back saying that all four companies working in Limon responded favorably to us supplying container related work in Limon. Each gave a name and location in Costa Rica for me to contact when I got there.

That night we all went out to Joe's for dinner then stopping at the 1800 club. The next morning all four of us would fly to San Jose via Delta airline. Once there in San Jose, Silva would head to Limon via Bus while Christina, Evette and myself would rent a car and make the two-and-a-half-hour drive. Traveling downhill to Limon was a lot easier than driving up from Limon. San Jose was about 3,800 feet high while Limon was at sea level.

Once in Limon, Christina, Evette and myself checked into the Park hotel. From there after checked in, I walked to the American Bar. It was now almost 5:00 p.m. and the place was wall to sailors and working girls. First I spotted Richard sitting with Ian and what I thought was one of the working girls. I walked over and when Richard saw me he stood and offered me a chair at their table. The girl at the table was name Susan whom was the girlfriend of Ian. Ian and Richard were stacking up empty beer cans on the table. All three of them were feeling no pain. I then noticed Peter whom was sitting with a pretty girl that looked like she surely had his attention. Peter hadn't spotted me as yet but his girl did. Peter looked to where she was looking and had the girl change seats so that her back was facing me. I was asked what I was drinking and I chose a local beer called Imperial. Richard said I should order a canned beer so to add to the pile that he and Ian had going. My Imperial was a bottled long neck. It wasn't long before Peter's girl got up and walked out across the street to a park bench, she then came back with another girl. Peter's girl walked the new girl over to our table and introduced me to herself and the other girl. I looked over at Peter and saw he was getting upset. I stood and walked over to him and explained that I didn't mean to bother what he had going on. Peter gave me a smirk and invited me to sit down. I thanked him and said that I wasn't looking for any female company. Peter told both girls, in Spanish to leave and then looked at me and said to please sit a while. I sat and the girls looking pissed went and sat at another table. Peter introduced himself and I the same. Peter seemed friendly, said he was Swedish and was down there looking for the good life, puro vida he said. I told him that I was tired of the states and would open up a small shop here working with the shipping lines and the banana companies. Peter told me the girls here were great but he was getting tired of the same old working girls looking for money. I told Peter that I was married to a Philippine girl that I had brought with me. Peter was also pounding down the beer, he drank two to my one. I drank 4, he had 8 or more. Peter seemed to have lots of money, I ask him about the town and he said there was not one good restaurant. After my 4 beers I said it was good meeting him and was sure to see him again soon. From there I stopped back by Richard's table and then walked back to the hotel.

The women behind the desk at the hotel told me that my wife was sitting on the seawall with her friend. I walked to the window and it looked like neither girl was wearing very much of anything. I walked out there and over to them asking what they were doing? Evette said that they were just watching the waves. Maybe it was just where I had come from but it didn't look good, especially out the hotel window. Both came down from the sea wall, Christina asked what was the matter. I took the towel and rapped it around her and led her back to the hotel. Our two rooms were both on the second floor. We climbed up the stairs and Christina opened our door; I told Evette we'd meet her downstairs in 30 minutes for dinner.

Once we got in the room Christina asked why I was upset. I told her I was not upset but didn't like her showing so much skin. Christina was quick to say that I let Lori wear a string bikini bathing suit showing much more. I said that Lori was only 15 at the time and that maybe if we were at the French Riviera she could do the same. You don't want people to see my body she asked? I answered that I wanted to her to wear a one-piece bathing suit and that it should cover both the top and bottom. You want my body only for you she asked? I said yes. When you ask me she said, I'll say yes, but you haven't as yet. I opened my brief case and pulled out our Philippine marriage certificate and asked her to sign using her new name. Christina held the paper and read it. This paper is real she asked? It is as real as the divorce papers you signed I said. But when I sign this we are married she asked? I looked at her and said yes. A pen please she said. Christina signed the paper and promised to make me happy for as long as

I wanted her. I looked at her and said three things for now. A one-piece bathing suit, a kiss and a cold shower. The last two I can do now she said as she kissed me. We had that shower and went to dinner with Evette. That night before we went to sleep Christina told me she loved me.

The next day the three of us found a house that was for rent. The house was owned by the richest woman in town. Mrs. Alcon, a widow, owned a hotel, a restaurant, a disco, several houses and a banana plantation. Her late husband had built this house for their 50th anniversary but he died before they moved in. When Mrs. Alcon found out that Christina and I had just gotten married, she wanted us to move in. The house was three bed rooms, four baths on a bluff right on the ocean. There was a large swimming pool, and the coolest diving board that stretched 10 feet over the Atlantic Ocean. This house was located next to one of the nicest tourist hotels, just blocks from from a beach called, Playa Bonita. That same day we move into the hotel next to the house. The hotel, The Malibu Caribe had air-condition rooms an outside bar and a nice pool. The house we rented was 100% unfurnished. It would most likely be two weeks before furnishing could be picked out and delivered. I visited the American bar that afternoon after 5:00 p.m. Richard was there alone, Ian was said to be working a ship and Peter was a no show. I had a beer with Richard and then walked back to the Park hotel checking messages. One message for Evette was in Spanish saying "We've hooked a big, good looking fish". I was happy to hear that, hopefully meaning Silvia was in Peter's house. Lourdes had called leaving the message for me to call her back. Lourdes said that June would be bringing our daughter, her nurse and the house keeper for a visit to Miami and wanted to know where I wanted her to stay. And of course I was to call Roy tonight at his house as he had made an appointment with G.D. in two days. I told Lourdes to contact Jena and get her ok to put June in her apartment next to mine. Then if Jena said ok, and I knew she would. Lourdes was to call June and tell her the good news. June was to fly Delta, Lourdes could get Big Ted to pick them up and open Jena's apartment. I called Roy, we had an appointment with G.D. at 10:00 a.m. in two days. We discussed his travel plans, I called Lourdes back telling her to get Tommy to pick us up here in Limon tomorrow morning at 9:00 a.m. and to find Fernando and Jack and have them call me at the new hotel. When I left the Park hotel's desk I said to tell anyone that called that we were now staying at the Malibu Caribe. The women at the desk said that soon there would be a new hotel owner and that he was going to start remodeling their hotel.

The Malibu Caribe had a fair restraunt, I didn't like the 3 inch Scorpion that was crawling on the table that night, but the food was ok. Our room was nice but the pool and pool bar were the best part. Evette wore her show all bathing suit while Christina wore her same bathing suit with one of my shirts over it.

I received calls from both Fernando and Jack, Jack would have some work for his crew, Fernando too.

It would only be my fourth night sleeping with Christina. Every time I looked at her and touched her was nicer that the time before.

The next morning Salvia was there waiting to speak with Evette. Seemed that Peter took Silva in just as we planned. Silvia said that Peter had left the house at 4:00 a.m. this morning and said he'd be back in a few days. Silva said she thought he was headed into Nicaragua. Silvia said that Peter had a locked room where she was sure there was a radio. Silvia said Peter had given her money to go and get her things from her grandmother's house and bring it to his house. Silvia said this with a big smile. I told Evette to tell Silvia that she had done well and that we'd be back in a few days.

We taxied to the airport where Tommy was there waiting. I had told Christina the news about June, she didn't say a word but I could tell she wasn't pleased.

Evette and Christina would have a lot of shopping to do, the new house needed everything especially a VCR player as Limon had no cable or TV channel for that matter. We would also need some kind of four-wheel drive vehicle. We arrived at Opa-Locka at just after 1:00 p.m. We caught a taxi and headed to the apartment.

I told the girls that I was going to be traveling the next day and Christina said she wanted to go too. I told her that it may get tricky and that I didn't want her involved. Christina said I wouldn't be able to stop her.

Big Ted was informed, as I would be making a delivery to Roy's home. From the time of that delivery until Roy,s returned from Fairbanks, he wouldn't know it but his home and including himself, would have a heavy shadow presents of security.

We did go pick out a car, a land rover 4 by 4. It would be shipped to Limon. We then went to Sears where we picked out a washer, drier, stove, refrigerator, and air conditioners. Christina tried on bathing suits but none looked just right. It took taking girls to Burdines to get the right bathing suit, funny though, she still looked to damn good. To damn good.

We went to eat at the 1800 as Joe's was closed, Joe's closed three months a year. I wondered how Montibelli was making out with Salinas's mom at the Château in Paxi. I'd have to try and call him tonight. We were using Evette's BMW to get around in. She wanted to send the BMW to Limon, but I ruled that out.

CHAPTER XVIII

MOVING THE CONTROLLER

Christina and I would be going to Fairbanks, Connecticut, tomorrow morning. Christina showed me what she'd like to where, I went into the safe and brought out a fine looking leather jacket and said that whatever she would be wearing this jacket would be worn over it. The jacket was designed and built for a day like tomorrow, it was lined with a supper thin but effective kevlar. I too would be wearing my kevlar vest.

I didn't call Paix that night as I figured it too late and Montibelli would be asleep.

Early the next morning Evette drove Christina and myself to Opa-Locka. Our flight took about three and a half hours, putting us in Fairbanks by 9:00 a.m. Christina and I were each carrying a brief case. I was armed with my Beretta. Before we started to travel through the small airport I told Christina that nothing in the cases were worth getting hurt over. If they come for the cases, let them have them I said. I asked her if she understood, she said she did.

As we walked through the terminal, I noticed three men walking behind us and now I saw two more walking our way. There were only a few people in the terminal and as the two passed us, one crabbed at my brief case and the other Christina's. I let mine go but Christina fought. The man that was with Christina pulled a knife and was going to cut Christina's hand. My Beretta was already out and even before I realized it, I had shot the man twice. First in the arm that held the knife and then the left inside thy. My next move was to spin around checking our backs. By then all three of the other men plus the one that took my case were on the ground. Jack was standing there holding my brief case. Christina was fine, we would have been a lot better off if she hadn't fought and I hadn't shot the man but, it was what it was. Airport security were soon there as were several police. The man I shot needed to get quickly to the hospital as the thy shot had hit an artery. Carson had taught me that the artery was always my second shot and sometimes my second and third. Carson said the first was the head and the next two the right and left inside thighs. Carson said if the head shot didn't kill them right away that the two thigh wounds would bleed them out before reaching help. My first shot was the arm with the knife, I wasn't shooting to kill but, I said the shooting just seemed to come naturally. Jack had one of the other four men off the floor and assisting the injured man. We had collected all their IDs and got their information and then threw the IDs on the floor.

It looked like Christina and I were going to be late for our meeting as we were all going down to police headquarters. None of our group were put in cuffs but we were disarmed. I had called Lourdes to notify Roy and tell him to make the meeting and let G.D. know I'd be there just as soon as possible.

The police wanted to know what was in the cases that was so important. I told them that my wife and I were on our way to meet with G.D. and those men must have though there was something of high value in the cases. The detective had all our IDs in hand including Christina's old Central Intelligent Agency credentials. Christina was questioned in a room by herself. All of us carrying weapons were doing so legally, each brief case had $9,999.00 in cash, plus several magazines.

The detective said it was unusual that I wasn't inquiring about our assailants. He asked why? You will find nothing on those men I said, they most likely have a master that sent them to retrieve the cases, it wasn't personal until that one man pulled out his knife and I was able to get off two lucky shots. The detective said my record only showed a short Air Force duty during the war and asked if I had seen any fighting. I told him the last time I had gotten into a fight was in high school, with what had afterwards become a good friend. The detective also asked why some lawyer hadn't shown up as yet. I said because we hadn't done anything wrong, we didn't have records and that as I said, my lawyer was waiting for us at G.D. for a meeting.

It took four hours down at the police station, we didn't press any charges on the five men.

Christina and I were 4 hours late to our meeting, the G.D. folks understood. Christina hadn't beforehand asked what was in or supposed to be in the cases. Once at G.D., Christina would wait in the waiting room.

I was first taken into what looked like some testing facility. The weapon was there, and they asked if I wanted to see its capability. I said that they could skip the show and just tell me what range it had. The technicians smiled and said they could only estimate that the range through our atmosphere was at least a mile depending what it's intentions were. It can cut steel like butter at that range. In space however was a different result. In space we think the range could be hundreds or thousands of miles. Could it take out a satellite or a missile I asked? With ease, if you could hit it, the technician replied. Ok I said what about the control box I asked? The control box as you call it the technician said has several functional systems, as you mentioned it may have the capability to disrupt satellite GPS signal and the surrounding magnetic north as we know it. We don't know its range but estimate that in our atmosphere, that 100-mile radius you mentioned. Everyone then stopped talking. I then asked if both the system and weapon were placed in a satellite, if they could be used to target items in outer space and or here on earth? The technician then paused and said we were a long way off, but yes he thought so.

What about my water pump I asked? Well sir the technician said, we reproduced one according to your specifications and it does what you claimed. It produces more electrical power than it takes to run the pump. It is truly a remarkable item. The technician said the control box and the laser could change the balance of world power, but this pump can change our entire planet's ecosystem. This makes using the most abundant thing we have on earth, water, to produce clean electric power. Here the only thing missing is a battery that can store the unused energy. So far we have not built the battery you have patented, however there are batteries out there that could somewhat do the job.

The technicians asked if I had any more questions? I told them that I owned three C-130s that from time to time few into a zone that had ground-to-air missile systems. The C-130s have the technology to pick up the missiles when activated, what would it take to disrupt the ground missiles tracking device and or have a laser capable of downing such a missile if fired at the C-130? Well the technician said if the missile was heat seeking we would need to see what we could come up with. If the missile was satellite guided, then by all means the missile could be launched but would not receive any directional assistance. Can you work on such a device for my planes I asked? I'll talk to our project manager and see what we can provide the technician said.

I thanked the men and women for their show and was then led into what looked like a board room. Myself and Roy then met with the chairman and several members of the board. They said that they agreed on our terms and said that all 23 of my patens were completely Legal and would be respected. The chairman asked how much of this did the military have. I didn't hesitate, they have a working model of the vehicle in which all this technology is found. They have possession but the vehicle and what they have except the sonar device is registered as my personal property. When we moved the vehicle I claimed it as a ship in distress and claimed salvage rights. Yes, we see the registration but you don't really think the Navy will return such property do you. No sir I don't, but what I'm sure they will do is turn the work over to you people with the agreement that the military items be used to build the Star Wars System that the President has promised. It will take a massive amount of money to make this work I said. I say we make Uncle Sam the partner with the money. The other items such as the electric they will not touch. This will stay with G.D. Are you asking a price for our 49 percent the Chairman asked? No sir I'm not. The patents are ours and you may use them for as long as we receive 51 percent of the profits.

Well the chairman said, the board has approved your plan and will start at once on our part. I mentioned that I had requested a special device from their technicians. Please approve my request and if you need any funding for this project please let Roy know in advance. The chairman said he'd look into it at once and the meeting was adjourned.

As we walked out Roy said asked what security was provided him carrying the control box here. You had the best money could buy I said. Roy wasn't happy and said in the future he would not be carrying even a briefcase for me anywhere. Roy also said he would now need to hire at least one more attorney to keep track of all this. Of course he looked at me and asked if I knew what I was doing bringing Christina into this. Roy said this in front of Christina. I reached into my coat pocket and handed Roy an envelope. Please, I said, get this resignation letter out to Christina's ex-employer. Roy knew about the airport incident and asked Christina if she was alright. Christina said she was fine and that it wasn't anything that a good hot shower wouldn't take care of. I loved hearing that. Roy would fly home the same way he came, he though traveling with me could somehow shorten his days here on this earth. Roy asked that I stop by the office in a few days to sign some paperwork.

The trip back to Miami seemed long. While thinking back I thought about Carson. His son Malcolm and even Carson's friend Debbie had slipped my mind. I called Lourdes and told her to contact them both. I also hadn't heard from Diane and Marco and to contact then too. From the time we left Fairbanks, Christina stuck to me like glue. We arrived in Miami and drove home. It was now almost 10:00 p.m. and Evette was there wanting to go out. Christina said she would have a good shower and hit the sack early. Evette was ready and said she would pass by the Alley and see what she could find. Christina would get that hot shower she had mentioned to Roy. Christina said she was sorry for causing so much trouble and that the next time she would listen better. She once again said that she loved me, this time crying as she said it. The shower made it all worth it.

Morning came and Christina was up early cooking breakfast. The smell of coffee filled the apartment. Evette had a do not disturb sign on her door. Christina and I both knew that I was going to see Lori today and this would be awkward for Christina. I checked my messages and found that Montibelli had called along with Lourdes calling twice plus the Director, the Colonel and the Secretary of State. This time I was hankering to speak with Montibelli so I called him first. A house girl answered and went to get Montibelli whom was out on the porch having his morning coffee. Montibelli seemed happy to hear from me. He said that if we got disconnected to call me back or to fly on over for lunch. Montibelli then said that he needed to change locations. Sharron as he called Salinas's mom was driving him nuts. She's a good looking women alright but a bitch he said. I told Montibelli that Sharron's photo was in the dictionary. Look up the word bitch and there he would find her photo. Montibelli laughed and asked how many times Sharron's photo was in there? Montibelli said that he got several calls yesterday afternoon about my Fairbanks visit. Montibelli said that G.D. had been tight lipped with the state departments inquiries. I asked if he had heard about the encounter at the Fairbanks airport Montibelli said yes and that too. He said he heard that the Director had complained about the shooting of one of his best men. I wonder if he was told that his best man pulled a knife I asked? Montibelli said that the Director said, Christina being on assignment and not handing over the case, could have gotten her hurt. If so I said, things would have gotten really bad for the Director and his men. Montibelli said that they were most likely listening to our conversation. I agreed. Montibelli said he'd like to move to Costa Rica where he said he would be more comfortable. I knew he meant a better choice of women. I said that Fernando had returned last night and he had missed his ride. Montibelli said he had already made travel arrangements and would be in Limon within three days. While still on the phone Bob called. I said my good bye to Montibelli and took Bob's call. Bob said that our cargo ship had been boarded in Miami and they had found drugs and illegals. I reminded Bob that the captain was responsible for the ship. Bob said the search was because of something that had pissed off the state department. I told Bob that I wasn't going to be treated unfairly but if that was the way they would play, that two could play that game. I asked Bob about the captain and Bob said they hadn't arrested him as yet. The ship would need a bond of Five million dollars to leave port again. I asked Bob where he wanted the money.

I then called the Colonel and he also gave me heads up about the Director not being happy over the airport thing. I didn't mention Bob's Nassau ship being seized, but said that I would deal with the Director. The Colonel said to be careful. The Colonel said that our business was doing good and he appreciated our continued support. It seemed, The Colonel was at the moment trying to distance himself from the Director.

My next call was to the state department, the Secretary of State couldn't be reached. I though surly he thought I was calling about Bob's ship, I was not. I did not return any calls from the Director's office. I then made a few calls to a few old friends before heading to see Lori.

CHAPTER XIX

FRIENDS IN THE RIGHT PLACES

Christina and Evette would go shopping the entire day, they had a lot to buy. I checked Lori's schedule and today said she was having personalized scuba lessons. I drove over and watch quietly with Chubby until Lori spotted me. The instructor said Lori was ready for an Ocean dive.

From there Lori wanted to go sailing. I told Chubby that I'd have her home by tomorrows lessons. Lori and I stopped by the store and purchased what we would need. This trip should work out for me so that I could spend time with Lori and not run amuck with Christina.

Once on the boat Lori took over. She handled our departure like a pro. We sailed into the bay then out through the Key Biscayne channel and out to the ocean. We headed south, me not asking Lori where we were going. Lori again asked about my summer plans and when we could take that long sailing trip. I said that tentatively it would be July. Lori smiled showing those now sparkly white teeth. Lori was in her one-piece bathing suit and asked me to take the wheel while she changed. Lori said that wherever she went she carried an overnight bag hoping I showed up. For me the one piece looked great but what she came up in was like wow. The only thing she was wearing was one of my shirts.

We sailed down to the Ocean Reef Club where we would dock and have a late lunch at pool side. The only change in clothes Lori made was to add a bathing suit bottom. It wasn't easy but somehow I kept my hands off. We took a fresh water swim in the club's pool, then returned to the boat and sailed north until reaching Caesars' Creek. We passed through the creek and sailed on past Elliot's Key Park. Lori headed somewhat into the wind and from the cockpit rolled in the jib. Then she headed into the wind and ran up to the bow taking down the mail sail and then letting down the anchor. She then rolled up the main sail and came back to the cockpit. Lori then pulled off my shirt and took the bottom part of her bathing suit off and dove over. When she came up she waved me in. It wasn't 30 seconds before my clothes were off and I too was in the water.

We spent the night there getting reacquainted with Lori saying she had passed her high school entrance exam and would start at Miami High late August. Lori asked about Pa'me and said she missed her. I told her that Pa'me had resigned from the CIA and was now working with our group, Lori asked if she and the children could come down and visit with Pa'me during the summer. Lori said without me saying a word that she understood if she must share me with Pa'me. I didn't say a word to that comment.

The next morning at 3:00 a.m. while Lori slept I pulled up anchor and headed on back. I remembered my promise to Chubby. Lori woke up when I started the motor to head into the waterway where we docked the boat. It was now 6:45 a.m. Lori would be home on time.

As we drove down Chubby's street closer and closer to the house I could see that Lourdes had completed another of my odd request. There in the grass was parked a 1951 Wills Jeep just like the one that I use to have. Lori jumped out of my car and went running to the jeep. Starring at the jeep she was jumping up and down. Is this for me she yelled? Yes, I said it's yours once you have a driver's license. Lourdes had searched the country to find the jeep, it was the same model and color as mine had been. By now Chubby came out with the key and I took Lori for a ride around the block. Starting Monday Lori and Pa'me would start driving lessons together, Lori asked does this mean that Pa'me will be here this week? I said that Pa'me would be on loan for two weeks starting tomorrow. I hadn't planned it this way, it was a last minute change I made. I told Lori that Pa'me should be here by the end of the day. Lori kissed and hugged me and said how much she had enjoyed the sail and how much she appreciated the car. She kissed me goodbye while telling me she loved me, and I was off.

I drove home and found June at the table eating breakfast with Christina and Evet. June, our daughter and her two helpers had come in the day before, now staying next door at Jena's apartment. Of course, I wanted to give that hug and greeting kiss to Christina but ended up giving it to June. June asked if I had seen today's newspaper. I said no, June then walk over to the couch and said that her maid had picked up the morning paper from the down stairs lobby. It was the Herald's front page that read "Three Major US shipping lines found with drugs aboard" The paper listed the shipping lines names and ports. Three separate lines in three different ports. The article said it had been a long DEA investigation that would end up jailing hundreds of people and costing the lines millions of dollars in fines. DEA divers had found one ship with a false capsule attached to it's bottom that could hold well over two tons of the drugs. This was a massive find by the DEA at a time that the drug business seemed to be moving without anyone paying the price.

As I read the paper Bob called saying that maybe I had gone too far. Why Bob I said, what on earth are you talking about. Bob might have had that cigar in his hand but he wasn't laughing.

June knew I had been out all night and asked where I had been. I asked her to go back to her apartment and that I'd be over after I showered and changed. I walked June to her door and came right back. Christina was right there waiting for her kiss. Christina and I showered and I told her that she was going to stay a few weeks with Lori. The motive was for her to learn how to drive and get her driver's license. First a Pa'me license and then when I came back a Christina licence. From my room I called Lourdes and asked her to get Cat to call me. I was thinking of taking Cat and Evette back with me to Costa Rica. Cat for only two weeks. This would give Cat and I some well-deserved time together. Lourdes said that Cat had been looking for Jacob and had hired a Miami PI that had located Jacob in a rehab location down in Mexico. Lourdes said Cat was on her way to Mexico to see Jacob. Lourdes said that Salinas and Betty had all five of the children.

I would drop Cristiana at Chubby's telling Christina that she would be also taking a gun course from Big Ted or from one of his hot shots. I told Christina that I'd be in Nassau for the week and should be back in Miami after that. Christina said she would be worried about me the entire time I would be without her but that mostly she would be jealous. She had me stop the car blocks before Chubby's house and for the first time I saw a tear rolling down her cheek. Please she said don't let this change anything that we had, I need and love you.

From there I returned and spent the night with June. June said that she was sure that Cat would return with Jacob. When June was in Nassau, the three of them would sail together almost every day. The three being Salinas, Cat and herself, they had greats times. June said that life in Nassau was good but that she would also like to have a home of her own here in Miami. Maybe something by her mom's house she said. I told her to look for a house but that it would be put into one of the company's names. June and I slept good and the next morning I left early for Nassau.

Salinas didn't know I was coming before I showed up at the house. Salinas was out in the stables with her horses looking like she did the first time I saw her. She came running into my arms crying with joy. I asked where she wanted to go? To the shower she said. No I said where like where to. I'd like three days in Paris she said. Yes, three days in Paris. Without me she started running toward the house. I didn't dress like I used to, now I wore shorts and a Hawaiian shirt. While in the shower I asked Salinas if I had any clothes here in the house and she said that my black suit that I used for our wedding was here and pressed. I said it was at least a start. Salinas and I packed lightly as we would go clothes shopping in Paris. Betty spoke to me and said she was worn out with all these kids. I told her to hire more help. I'm getting to old for this she said. Betty said she wanted to retire in my Miami apartment while she could still find a man. I laughed, she didn't. Betty said she didn't know what I was gona do ifin Cat came back with that no good thing some called a man. What will you do Betty asked? That will be Cat's decision I said. I hope crazy doesn't run in the family I said.

Salinas and I were in the air with Tommy on the way to Atlanta when we got the call that the White House was looking for me. It wasn't the Secretary it was The President. We made the change of course and headed to DC. From the time we received the call until we were on the white house steps, only spent about four hours. We had a privet limo pick us up as I would need my guns with me until we walked into the front doors of the White House. I carried a gun case that would hold both guns and could be locked so that no one could open it, at least not without me knowing.

After we arrived we waited another two hours in the parlor. The limo driver had of course two or three news papers. I took the Washington Post into the white house and finishing reading what I had started in the limo. The Headlines read," DEA Fails to make arrests in Smuggling Sting!" The article said that apparently the busts were made from an anonymous call from a phone within the Langley walls. The newspaper article was critical of the DEA and noted that the drug movement could have had CIA involvement. It appeared to be a whistleblower that had made the call. The shipping lines ship that had the secret compartment was said to have originally been built with the compartment. The compartment was welded shut and that Shipping Line was fined $50,000,000.00. The other two lines were fined $10,000,000.00 each. The only major US line that wasn't effected was Mr. Crowbe's. When they came to get me from the waiting parlor, Salinas had my arm like she didn't want to let go and asked if I was sure to return. I smiled and said I'd be back and for her not to worry.

I was escorted to the Oval Office where the Secretary was already sitting. We stood when the President came in, he sat without the smile I had seen on my last visit and there was no hand extended to shake. Well, Jim, the President started; looks like my people could be right about you, he said. You may very well be more trouble than your worth. How so Mr. President I asked? The Director says you're behind this DEA trouble, is this true? Its cost our U.S. based shipping companies millions he said. Sir I said, I'm figuring you mean what I've seen in the news the last few days. The President looked at the Secretary and then back at me and said yes. I looked at the President and said that the only information I had is what I read, if it was the Director that said it was me, maybe it was his way of shifting the blame. The News said the call made to the news alerting them came from Langley not Miami. I continued saying that yes it was true that I had shot one of the Director's men some days ago, but that the agent pulled a knife on my wife. The President looked at the Secretary in surprise and asked if he knew of the incident? The Secretary said no. I also said the whistleblower had also made the call affecting a ship that I have a small interest in that runs from Nassau to Miami. The DEA down in Miami said that call also came from Langley. The drugs found on our ship were carried aboard by what was said to be an illegal alien, but my people later found the man who was released from the Miami jail. The man was released without any bond or charges, and after some conversation with a few of my people, the man stated that he was a US citizen and was paid to move the drugs and told beforehand that he would be arrested once in Miami. I told the President that I had a video tape and signed confession from that same man. The man was paid in cash with new $100.00 bills that were traced being delivered from the U.S. mint printing office to an official government office. I also have these records, as well as most of the cash. The President then looked at the Secretary and asked if the Director was in the building. The Secretary said yes. The President said he wanted to see him. I said that if he didn't mind I didn't want to see the Director.

I then told the President about my agreement with G.D. using the technology that I had to make his Starr Wars dream a working system. G.D. will develop a system that will be able to launch and guide a missile to any GPS located site. The system when activated could shoot down any incoming missile and or damage its guidance system. The system will allow us to shoot down any satellite we chose. The agreement that was reached is that the US Government would fund the work and G.D. will build it for you. This is your contact, and I handed the Secretary the G.D. Chairman's card. The President looked a bit surprised at all this and asked how long before there could be a working model? I said the guided missile part, I believed 6 months to a year and the other, two to three years. The President looked pleased.

The Secretary asked if there had been any progress in Costa Rica. I said that I would share the news with them and warned that I believed the Director's office had leaks inside.

We now have a girl living with the Russian; the girl is working for us, I said. Of course this will only work out if it stays within these walls. The conversation got still and the President asked about my wife. I said that my wife and children were all doing good. The President stood and offered his hand. Jim he said please keep up the good work. I stood and reminded the Secertary that he still owed me the difference of the $20,000,000.00 which was $9,000,000.00. The Secretary didn't respond but I was sure he knew exactly what I was talking about. As I walked out, I was sure The President thought he knew who blew the whistle and why. I was sure, no matter what, that the Director was in for an ear full.

As I walked into the waiting room parlor, Salinas stood and I told her to kiss me like she did that first time.

The limo driver said that two men had come by and checked the car. I asked if they had touched my case, the driver said they had picked it up and tried to open it without success. I was sure they somehow had installed some kind of device; I was a bit paranoid. I told the driver to head to the airport, I put on a pair of latex gloves then opened the case, took out my guns and asked the driver to stop. I put my window down and threw out the empty case. The driver looking in the mirror just smiled.

Once back in the leer Tommy said to call Lourdes back. I told Tommy not to rush as we had missed our Atlanta flight connection. I called Lourdes first asking her to make new reservations and then asking what was up? Lourdes said that Bob had called since she first called asking for me to return his call. Lourdes said that she had contacted young Malcolm's mother and that we have a graduation invitation in 10 days; Malcolm's mom noted that Malcolm would attend the UM in Miami starting in late August. I told Lourdes that I was not to miss that graduation and to get someone over to Carson's house to put things in order. The security detail at the house was to supervise any work. Lourdes said she did talk to Diane and she said she would contact me directly. Jena had called and said that she was almost a month without smoking. Mr. Crowbe called giving his regards. I knew why he had called; he was grateful that none of his ships were involved in the drug sting. Montibelli had called saying only that he, was at his new spot. That meant that he was now situated in Limon.

I called Bob and he said he would like to see the tape that was mentioned at the White House. I told him that he or anyone could view the tape, I would trade it for the return of my $5,000,000.00 that the release of his ship had cost me. I added that for Bob to communicate to the Captain of his ship that I was going to take that $5,000,000.00 from his pay. Bob said I was a SOB, I said yes, I knew what I was.

By the time I finished with my calls we were landing in Atlanta. Our new flight wouldn't leave until 11:00 p.m. that night so Salinas and I got a room at the airport.

We caught our flight and flew first class nonstop to Paris. After checking in at the hotel, it was to the stores shopping then Dinner. Salinas was slim but could eat like a horse. She loved the food and the attention.

We were treated like royalty everywhere we went. Salinas said she was in heaven! Salinas loved Paris, her speaking French made all the difference. The Eifel tower was her favorite. Our three days went by quickly, and before we knew it, we returned to Atlanta, then Nassau.

CHAPTER XX

CAT'S CHOICE

The news on Cat wasn't so good. Cat was still in Mexico working to get Jacob out of rehab, seemed he just didn't want to get out. I thought he might be worried what would happen to him if he showed back up in Nassau with Cat. This I thought, with good reason.

Back in Nassau, I spent some time with the children, my three and Deanna's two. Salinas and I were good, she reminded me that she was ok with the other girls and that I could send for her at any time no matter where or with whom I was with. Hers was the best offer I had. I didn't spend time in Nassau other than at the house and left late that night for Miami.

Evette was the only one home saying she had picked Christina up from the Hialeah gun range and had taken her out to dinner. Seemed like I was gone for weeks and not days. Evette said that Christina was worried about me. I didn't knock on June's door, I wanted to go and pick up Christina but I didn't. I thought about taking Lori and Christina out sailing for the weekend but decided that I couldn't do it. The next morning Evette and I got an early start for Limon. Tommy flew us directly to Limon and we were checking into the Malibu Caribe by 11:00 a.m. Our land Rover was at the port but hadn't cleared customs as yet. Evette and I walked down to the beach and had lunch. Evette asked me to sit separate from her as she was fishing and had the chum out. The chum was that she was talking about was that next to nothing bathing suit of hers. I wasn't chumming but I too was getting some attention. I wished that Christina could have been here. At about 3:00 p.m. Evette and I would catch a taxi and go back to the hotel and change and take the same taxi into town. If Peter was at the bar, then Evette would attempt to contact Silvia. Sure enough Peter was at the bar, so was Richard and Montibelli. I walked in and sat with Richard, Richard hadn't mentioned or maybe didn't even know why I was in Limon. Richard was a talker, he mentioned that he had met Peter and didn't like him. Richard pointed out Montibelli as Richard said he heard that Montibelli had purchased the run down building next to the Park hotel. Richard said that Montibelli was staying at the Park hotel while his building was being reworked. Richard said that Montibelli had a young girl living with him that was built like a shit brick house. I asked Richard if he'd like to get to know Montibelli. Richard said why not. I got up and walked over and asked Montibelli to join Richard and I. Montibelli surprising said no thanks. Montibelli said to sit, but it would have been rude so I didn't. Peter looked occupied with the same girl as before. Looked like Peter had a late model ford passenger van. A local man was driving the working girls here and there in Peter's van. I figured that Peter was renting the van out on most likely a daily amount. The driver of Peter's van was named Dookie.

It was 6:00 p.m. when Cat walked into the bar and sat at the table, it was a complete surprise. She didn't hug or kiss me and looked like she hadn't slept in days. Before I could say a word Cat said we had to talk. I got up and we walked across the street and she sat on the park bench. I've made a terrible mess of things she said. I found Jacob in a rehab center almost dead and wanting to be. We did this to him, Cat said, Deanna, you and me. We turned a perfectly good man into mush. Cat was now crying and as I went to comfort her she pushed me away. No she said no more mistakes she said. I came to tell you not to come for me or look for me, I will be with Jacob somehow bringing him back to a normal life. Salinas will take care of the children, I will send for Wendy Michelle and Johnny just as soon as I can. She said she had money but that she would need more. I said just to say where she wanted the money. Cat said to make the deposit into her Nassau account. Please take good care of our Jimmy, he's so young she said. When we're all good she said I'll ask you to send him for a visit. I know you will think bad of me and maybe hate me but this is what I must do. Janie said she will carry on at the shelter, please continue to support the cause. Cat asked if she could catch a ride back to San Jose with Tommy? I said of course. She opened my hand and put in her rings. I looked at her and told her that I would always love her. She turned and then looked back and said she knew. She walked a few steps and jumped into a waiting taxi. I stood there watching until the taxi disappeared. I sat back down on the bench and thought about what had just happened. I wasn't there two minutes before Montibelli walked over and sat down next to me. At first he didn't say a word, we just sat there for another few minutes and then he asked what I was drinking. We both got up and crossed the street back to the bar.

Richard was still there looking like he wanted to hear the whole story. Montibelli and I sat at Richards table with me introducing Richard to Montibelli. Richard asked if we knew each other? Montibelli not saying a word just nodded his head. Richard then asked if that was the wife? I said she was one of my best friends. She came on the bus just to say a few words and will return on that bus Richard asked? Yes, she came on the bus but Tommy will take her to San Jose I said. I then went to the phone and called Lourdes and said for her to contact Tommy, he was to fly Cat wherever she wanted to go.

Back at the table Richard said she looked pissed, she was I said, as pissed as one can get I said.

The longer I thought about it the worse it got. It was probably exactly like Cat said about the three of us especially me pushing Jacob over the edge. I knew what I was doing when I sent him to Miami. I just wasn't counting on Cat going after him. Cat making that choice, Jacob over her one and only child was just unthinkable. My brain just couldn't make sense of it. I would somehow deal with it.

Evette caught my eye walking along the side walk. I excused myself and walked into the park. Evette met me there and said that Silvia had done well, making a copy of Peter's military ID and she had sketched over a map that Peter had marked. I told Evette that this could be something really important. I told Evette about Cat and she too was sad. Evette would to go back to the hotel and I returned to the Bar. Richard wanted to hear more about Cat. I told them how I had met her when she was 15 and working at a ruff bar. Cat at the time was working for and living with man what would sell her out. Eventually I would shoot that man three times while he attempted to retrieve her from her sister's house. I was young then and full of fight. One night in a bar Cat had saved my life when a man broke a chair over my head knocking me down and out. When I opened my eyes the man had taken my Beretta and was about to shoot me when Cat came running at him like a crazed linebacker. Cat hit the man at about his right side arm and chest but the man flung her aside. That had given me time to get out my leg gun and get three shots off. My eyes where blurred, my first shot missed him but the next two connected with his two knees. Richard asked what had happened to the ex-boyfriend that I had shot the three times? The ex-boyfriend was killed in that same bar in a knife fight while the other man that was wheel chair bound was thrown from an air plane. Richard said it all sounded like a move.

Richard and I walked Montibelli to the Park Hotel and I walked with Richard to his house meeting his wife and young son.

At Richard's house, while his wife was making us all a drink, Richard wrote on a piece of paper that he knew why I was here in Limon. I asked if he had a map of Nicaragua, he left the room and came back with such a map. I placed it on the table and started searching for the area on the sketch that Silvia had given to Evette. Richard was the one that located the spot. Richard said it was just some 300 yards from the San Juan river that separated Nicaragua from Costa Rica. I asked if Richards airplane was in working order? Richard laughed and said we could fly over the area tomorrow morning.

Richard and his wife were heavy drinkers, after a few drinks and lessening to several stories from them both, I excused myself, staying with the agreement that we would meet at the airport at 8:00 a.m. the next morning. The thought did cross my mind that Richard could forget about the trip or just not be able to get up.

I caught a taxi and went back to the hotel. Although I was tired I just couldn't sleep. I just kept thinking about Cat. I somehow knew that I had made Cat's life miserable. Here too, I thought about Salinas, from a short time of just over two years ago when I first saw her in that barn at Paix, brushing her favorite horse, to now having two of her own children and taking care of three more. This while I ran around with at least three other women and was never home. As I sat out by the hotel pool on a lawn chair, I noticed the sun starting to peek through the clouds. The hotel was up on a bluff and the wind was blowing at about 25 MPH. I stood and looked at the surf and though about Bernabe and Tony. It had been years since I'd heard from them but the size of those waves made me think of them and how they loved to surf.

192

a bluff and the wind was blowing at about 25 MPH. I stood and looked at the surf and though about Bernabe and Tony. It had been years since I'd heard from them but the size of those waves made me think of them and how they loved to surf.

CHAPTER XXI

THE DOWNING OF RICHARD'S PLANE

I could hear someone speaking softly, someone from the kitchen asking if I wanted coffee.

I got a cup then went to my room and without changing, picked up a few items to take along and put them into my tourist pouch that was also my gun bag. I wore my usual, a Hawaiian shirt, shorts, my high top boots and of course my Bahamian wide brimmed straw hat. I hopped in a taxi and went to the airport.

When arriving I was pleasantly surprised to find Richard there checking the plane. As I pulled up he said he was ready to go. Richard's gear consisted of two life jackets, one the automatically inflatable type and the other the blow up kind. Richard had an Icon hand held ship to shore radio. We were on the runway and up in the air by 8:15 a.m. Richard proudly said he was making 2 to 3 trips a month to Blue Fields where he would purchase fish and lobster to bring back for Ian to sell to the ships that called Limon and Moin. He said that we had a contact in Blue fields that would also feed him with information. Richard said once in a while he would also deliver messages.

We flew north along the coast until we got to the San Juan river and then headed west for about two miles while hugging the river. Richard said we were coming up on the spot on our starboard and as he turned north and crossed the river into Nicaraga, I began to hear thumps like hail was hitting us. It wasn't hail it was bullets. Richard's reactions, was to say oh shit! and turn the plane to the east and then back to the south. Within seconds the windshield was covered with oil. I though Richard was going to put us in the river but he said he was going to put us down on the beach. I couldn't see a thing from the windshield, Richard was looking through his port side window and I guess he was being guided by the ground view. As we crossed the end of the tree line, I wasn't surprised to see that the waves, about 10 footers were breaking at the tree line. There was no beach to land. Again Richard's reaction was oh shit! Richard started to bank to our starboard to return to the river. Me, I was using the ship to shore calling a may-day and giving our position. As we turned the engine stopped with a load bang. With another oh shit from Richard, the plane dropped into the sea. One of those hugh 10 foot waves grabbed the port wing and the plane swang to the port and the front of the plane went right into the center of one of those inbound 10 foot waves. The impact crushed the front of the plane and then broke the plane's back, breaking the plane in half. Still strapped to my seat and now under water I was being hit with all kinds of material. I managed to unbuckle myself and then Richard. I somehow pulled on Richard's life jacket to get it inflated. We were both still being rolled around in the cockpit, I made my way to the open area to the rear and made it out and up through the debris. By now the waves had broken off both wings, I saw Richard pop up but couldn't get to him. The next thing I knew I could touch the sandy bottom. Still being pounded by the waves and debris I made my way to shore. Richard was still mixed in with the moving debris so I went back for him. When I reached him I could touch bottom, grabbing him by the back of the life jacket pulling him up on shore. When I say shore, we were at the woods edge.

I looked at Richard and asked how bad he was? He said he'd live. Me I had a bad hit and cut on the right side of my head near my right eye that was badly bleeding and a nasty cut on the back of my left leg starting at my knee going down. I stood going to help Richard so we could move a bit back into the pines and saw that Richard's right leg was broken. I think we both saw it at the same time as Richard gave me that same oh shit thing. Richard was bleeding from several spots. A notable cut on his face, his left arm and left hand. His wounds, besides the broken leg weren't quite as bad as mine so the first thing I did was to stop my bleeding. Some of my Hawaiian shirt was used as the tourniquet and bandage. I only had my left eye kind of clear of blood and could tell by feeling and by what Richard was saying that my head wound wasn't good. I had my swift army knife that I cut several small branches and made a half ass splint for Richard, so far neither of us seemed in a lot of pain. I knew with my may-day calls that it could bring help but I also knew that the Nicaraguans also would have heard the calls. I was sure we were in Costa Rica but wasn't so sure the Nicaraguans wouldn't send a helicopter to pick us up or finish us off. We had to move to the south. It was pathetic to see the both of us slowly moving through the trees. It wasn't 30 minutes that a soviet helicopter showed up flying over the wreckage that was still trashing the shore line. By now we were a good 100 yards to the south and when we heard the copter and the direction from which it was coming we took cover. The Nicaraguans must have thought we couldn't have survived the crash. They didn't hang around, maybe because they could have picked up our rescuers that I hoped were on the way. When the soviet copter left, Richard and I knew we didn't have to keep moving. Richard while sitting was pushing pine needles into a plie while I got out my water proof match container from when I was a boy scout. The small screw top container held matches and I lit a fire. Richard moved back and I started putting on some small dead stuff. I quickly cut several small green branches to be able to throw on if and when the rescuers would show up. Even before I was completely ready two jets flew over coming from the south. I quickly starting throwing the green branches on the fire to produce more smoke. The smoke mostly blowing to the west and into the trees, did catch the jet pilots eyes on their return swing. One jet swung around and waved it's wings to let us know they had spotted us. Now, we at least knew that help would be on the way. I had attended Richards wounds the best I could. The face wound was the only cut that I couldn't stop the bleeding on. Richard was applying pressure with a part of my shirt. My head wound was in a location that the wrapping, in order to have any pressure required to be wrapped covering my right eye. Seemed that my jaw could be broken as well, some of my teeth on the right side were also lose. We both looked a mess.

Richard then started to cry. I asked if he was crying because he was so ugly? He said it was for his airplane. It hurt so much when I laughed.

It would only be another 30 minutes before a Navy helicopter came our way. We again threw green pine branches on the fire and they came right at us. A navy man was lifted down and Richard was put in a seat and hulled up into the copter. Then me and then the navy man. Richard was dropped off at the Limon hospital and once the Doctors were attending him we continued on. I was flown to the US Panama base and then put on a navy plane and flown to Miami. Of course on the way they changed my so called bandages and gave me some medications. We landed at Miami international where I was taken via ambulance to Jackson Memorial Hospital. I was taken right into surgery and didn't open my eye until about 2:00 a.m. Christina was there holding my right hand with Lori on my left with her head on my chest. I tried to talk but my jaw didn't want to move. Christina said for me not to try to talk. I motioned her closer and whispered, for her not to alert anyone. Christina said I know, Jim, I know. With my right hand I patted Lori's head. I had this terrible head ache. With my only unpatched eye, I kind of looked at myself taking inventory to see if I was all there. Only seeing with my left eye, that my left leg had bandages from the mid thy to my ankle. My left hand, head and face were also bandaged. I was relived to be all there. Christina said the Doctors said to rest and that by tomorrow I should be able to talk.

Through early morning some, several Doctors and nurses came in and out of the room, but Christina and Lori never left. When morning came I asked how they had found out about me being here. Christina said she had received a call from Evette. Christina said Evette had called, saying that Richard's wife had come to find her. Evette then made some calls and found me at Jackson Memorial. Evette called Christina. Chubby had driven them both here.

A Doctor from John Hopkins eye center came in to give me the bad news. I would be blind in my right eye. The accident had caused irreversible damage to the right eyes optic nerve that normally would send information to the brain. The Doctor said the nerve had been severely damaged. As the Doctor walked out, I asked Christina to help me into the bathroom. Once in there I shut and locked the door. I looked in the mirror and started unwrapping the bandages that covered my right eye. The last thing to remove was a white pad over the eye. I removed the patch and just as I though, my vision was just as it was before the crash. The rest of my face was a different story. My upper lip on the right side had about ten stiches holding it together. My nose was again broken and the top of my right jaw was so swollen that my mouth wouldn't open. There were stiches all over the right eye brow, lid and tempal. There were also stiches here and there but just above the eye was where all the blood had been coming from. Of course it was all quite swollen. Needless to say a was happy that I could see and thought that some salt water would heel me up the rest of the way.

I unlocked the door and walked into Christina's and Lori's arms. While still holding them both I said to get that Doctor back in here. Of course I told the girls that I could indeed see with both eyes. The Doctor did come back and was surprised to see me with the bandages off. The Doc said that he was sure that my vision was temporary. It could last and hour, a week or even a month, but it would go. The Doc said that I shouldn't have taken the bandages off as that was the protection against infection. Be particularly careful of that cut that looks like your eye lid that exstends to the tempal as that was the cut that was the deepest and did the most damage. I asked when I could get these stiches out and the Doc said in two or three weeks. I asked them to check me out of here, the eye Doc said that the other Doctor would be in shortly and he'd make that decision. I thanked him and said I'd let him know how it went.

I thought about sending Christina to pick up some clothes but then remembered that my guns were missing. I asked Christina to go see if she could find a good size hat as besides the stiches some nice Nurse had also given me a haircut just on one side of my head. Lori said it didn't look so bad. I then called Lourdes, Lourdes didn't even miss me as I was only out of contact for about 48 hours. What surprised her was that I was in Miami. I told her that I wanted Tommy to meet me at Opa-Locka just as soon as he could. I mentioned the accident and told her to check the Limon Hospital for Richard's condition.

The other good Doctor came in about 30 minutes later. He too was surprised with my vision and also said he thought it was most likely temporary. The Doc noted that he had noticed that my left leg had recently suffered a large cut before this one, I hadn't remembered until he mentioned it. Yes, I said the first was a bullet hole that broke the bone and a nasty cut that took 100 stiches. He said that he had only put in about 80 but that he did see where there was quite a bit of scared tissue in there. I looked at him and mentioned that I must be accident prone.

Two hours later the three of us reached the apartment. We came in as quite as possible as not to let anyone from June's next store apartment hear us. The first thing was to open the safe, I felt naked without my guns. I took a gold cup 45 that I hadn't even fired, this along with a small 9 mm browning. I called Christina to come into the safe, Christina had never seen the inside of the safe and was amazed of how big it was. There was stacks of cash and jewelry everywhere. I locked it up and we were just about ready to leave when we heard that knock on the door. I hoped it wasn't June and it wasn't; it was Evette; Christina opened the door with her finger over her mouth. I had decided that Christina, Lori, and I were going to Harbor Island, the house should be finished, and if not, we'd stay at the Pink Sands. Evette said she bused to San Jose and hopped on the first flight out. Evette had arrived this morning going straight to the hospital and finding that I had just checked out. Christina took me in our room and asked if Evet could come along. I walked out and told Evette not to unpack. We were not going to stop by Chubby's so we got some clothes together and would head out. On the elevator I asked about the driver's licenses? Lori got hers and Christina did not. When we reached Opa-Locka Tommy was there waiting. Tommy said I looked like crap and asked what happened. It was the first time I had told the story. Tommy then said that after hearing the story I didn't look so bad after all.

We arrived on Eleuthera and taxied over to Charles and Madilyn's, Charles was out looking at property but Madilyn said that the house was finished but that it needed lots of items including food. Of course Madilyn assumed I had been in a car wreck and asked what had happened. I just said I was doing something that I shouldn't have been doing. Evette said yes and it was without permission. I volunteered Evette to take Tommy and go back to Miami and go shopping, Evette asked Christina if she would to go along, Madilyn said she too would go with them as Madilyn thought the list would be quite a long one. Madilyn left a note for Charles and we all took the taxi I had waiting. The taxi dropped Lori and I at the Eleuthera dock on the way to the airport.

Lori and I caught a water taxi and crossed the bay. Once on Harbor Island we caught another taxi and headed for the house. The taxi stopped at the gate and Lori and I got out and unlocked the gate door paying and sending the taxi on back. When stepping in the gate we could hear only the waves on the beach. I called the road side the back of the house. We were now on the back porch where I unlocked and opened the door. It was Lori's first time here, as we walked in she latched on to me not letting go. She then broke down and cried saying how grateful she was that I was alright.

I stepped back and picked up the two bags. The day couldn't have been more beautiful, from the door there was a clear view of the beach and ocean, in fact each room had the same beautiful view. The view and the house were breathtaking. The house had the basics but stuff like sheets, pillows and towels were missing. We walked through the house and then onto the front porch. It was amazing. We changed, me taking the rest of the bandages off and putting on my speedo. Lori had put on one of Christina's bathing suits bottoms and wore a shirt top. We walked out to the beach and with my arms around Lori thanked GOD for getting me to this point. I knew I wasn't on his favorite people list and I promised to double up on my charity work and be ready whenever he called on me. Until then I said I'll be returning to revisit those Nicaraguans to give them something HE said was HIS, Revenge.

While lying in the hospital, I had already planned my return visit to Nicaragua.

Lori and I then walked into the water, I only got wet and returned to the sand where I sat and Lori came and put her head in my lap.

We were in and out of the water until I thought my scars had enough sun. We then returned to the house and I started exploring and investigating. Not that the house was so big, it was not, but the space that it did have was well planned and used. The kitchen had everything we could think of, everything except pots, pans, cooking utensils, dishes etc., etc. There was now a small outside pool that had been added and of course a below ground generator that when the electric went off it would come on. There was underground fuel and water storage, this separate from the cistern that the original house had that had now been cleaned and reactivated. Rain water was still the only water source on the island unless you shipped it in and then trucked it to the house. There was also a small two car garage on one side of the house and a one-bedroom gest house on the other side. Both had been added but not attached to the house. There was a security system in place but not activated as yet. There were hand written notes everywhere explaining how everything worked. In the master bed room there had been back in the day, two fair size closets. Neither closet had space for one of my super safes. One such note that

Charles left was found in one closet. The note read, "see what you can find in here". I backed out and then looked at the other closet. The one with the note was smaller than the one without. Looking at them both I figured where to look but still didn't see it. It was Lori that found it, I was looking for something locked, it wasn't nor was it designed to lock. You pushed on the panel twice and a door opened. Behind the door was a set of stairs going down then a large safe door at the bottom. There wasn't a lot of room but certainly it looked secure. The keys, two of them were in the safes door and another note said not to touch the combination dial as it was not set as yet. The safe door was about 4 inches thick and had small holes drilled that only pierced the first 3 inches of the door. On the floor was a box that had another note. It read, sorry old friend you'll have to put this together. I looked at it knowing that putting on my locking device would take at least two hours and that I wasn't going to do it now. The doors edges had 4 monel one inch diameter pins that were inside a stainless tube that once my setting was in place would lock the door and it couldn't be opened until the 4 pins were pulled back into the door. Was this safe impossible for someone to break in, no but they would have to be down there working on it for some time. Time is something that they wouldn't have. Miami Safe and I had developed something that if the Safe door didn't open within 60 seconds from when the second key was put in and turned then a set of protocol would come into place that the safe door would not open for 24 hours the first time, then 48 hours the second and finally 72 hours. So if the safe door couldn't be opened within the 60 second time limit, it would take days before one had all the time they wanted to figure how to open it. Once inside the safe there was plenty of room. There were two unconnected batteries with an electric and small solar charger that was on the roof. The safe room was incased in 12 inch poured concrete plus a 1/8 "stainless steel liner. There was also oxygen and water inside. No, no food as yet. Lori was by my side the entire time and was impressed with what she learned.

At about dark we heard a horn beeping and then the gate ringer. Evette, Christina, Madilyn, and Charles with the delivery truck and extra help. Evette said that Tommy had to remove the 4 last seats to get it all in the leer. It took about 30 minutes for the truck to be unloaded. Madilyn said she 'd return the next day at about 10:00 a.m. to help sort things.

The only thing that needed to be done now, she said was to get the food that needed refrigeration in the frig and for someone to fix her a cocktail. Madilyn looked at me and asked, you do have a cocktail hour here don't you? Charles had come with them and started singing that Jimmy Buffet song Margaritaville. It was then that Charles showed me the sound system in the house. The only tape he left here was one with Jimmy's best. It was 10:00 p.m. before Charles and Madilyn left the house. The taxi had waited all that time. The water fairy was no longer running but Charles had come across the bay in his own boat.

Part of the time that Charles and I were sitting on the porch the women were fixing up the two bed rooms. Evette had filled Madilyn in on what was going on with Cat. I too had told Charles; both were saddened by the news. Charles had told me that he had found some property on Eleuthera that he was interested in building a few houses on. Charles said he had enjoyed working on this house and would like to continue working. We'd be partners 50/50, I'd put the money and he'd take care of the work.

After Charles and Madilyn left, I would then get one of those great showers. Evette cooked something that I thought was breakfast, beef steak, eggs and Cuban bread.

Getting under those new sheets was something I was looking for but feeling just a bit uncomfortable, I was thinking one of the girls was going to bend and go sleep with Evette. It wasn't to be. The smell brought me back to another time that I slept on new sheets, it was Deanna's 16th birthday aboard the "Johnny". I know, but it was just one of the many things that would take me back to those times.

I had to then feel my new scars to come back to reality. It had only been two days since Richard and I were shot out of the sky by the Nicaraguans.

CHAPTER XXII

MALCOLM'S GRADUATION

We would spend the next two days in and out of the water, letting my wounds heal. All three girls seemed to get along as sisters. The second evening we all walked down to the Pink Sands for dinner. Mrs. King was happy to see us and wanted an invitation to visit the new house.

I had decided that I wanted all 5 of the girls to go to Malcolm's graduation. We weren't planning to spend the night, so I wouldn't or shouldn't have that obvious problem. Salinas and June were informed that I wanted us all to go. All were to be on their best behaviors.

Tommy dropped Evette, Christina, Lori and I in Miami and the next morning at 6:00 a.m. picked up Salinas in Nassau, then came back for the 5 of us at Opa-Locka. The Graduation was scheduled for 3:00 p.m. This gave us time to have a family lunch.

At the graduation, we were not special guests, and I believe not even noticed by Malcolm or the family; the girls, however, caught several eyes, if you know what I mean. Not noticed until Malcolm's name was called, then everyone saw us. We clapped, yelled, and screamed Malcolm's name. The family sitting much closer turned and saw us, and so did Malcolm. Malcom looked our way and raised his scroll acknowledging that he saw us.

After the ceremony was over, people were gathering for family photos, and Malcolm walked to us to thank us for coming. As I got my hug, with my congratulations, I handed him two envelopes. Malcolm looked excited to open the envelopes but first asked what had happened to me? I pointed to my face and asked, you mean this? Its nothing I said. Malcolm first opened the one marked "Malcolm from your Grandfather." Malcom opened that envelop so fast that two keys dropped out onto the grass. Lori retrieved the keys. Inside was a small note that read "Son sorry I couldn't be by your side today but I am here in spirit. I'm so proud of you; remember to stay on track; I'll be watching; I love you, your Grandfather Carson" Behind the note, attached with a staple, was a bank statement with Malcolm's name on it. The amount was now $242,000.00. Lori then stepped closer and handed Malcom the two keys that he had dropped. Lori said that one was the key to his Fathers sailboat that was moored at the Coconut Grove Sailing club, the other his Coconut Grove home, both are now yours. I then stepped in closer and said to open the other envelope. Malcolm did; there was a note and a keyfob. The note read push my finders button. Malcolm did, and a horn started beeping from the parking lot. Malcom started running toward the beep. It was a brand new BMW. As he ran off, his mother walked up to us, thanking us for coming. Once she thought she had me by myself, she sarcastically asked, "did you have to bring all your women?" I looked at her and said Yes.

We were invited back to the house but we did not go. Malcolm had played high school football but wasn't offered a scholarship by the UM; he would be a walk-on. Malcolm needed to report to training camp by August 3rd and planned on being in Miami two weeks before. I was sure Malcolm's mother would have preferred him to live on campus, but I promised to keep an eye on him. Malcolm's mom again sarcastically said, "oh, that makes me feel better." Malcolm thanked us all and said he'd see us in Miami about mid-July.

Salinas and June weren't too happy about not being informed about my accident. That's what the story would be, that it was only an accident.

The girls seemed to get along good, I guess that was a good thing that we weren't spending the night. I hadn't yet spoken to Salinas about the kids but was sure that Salinas had a good idea what was going on with Cat and Jacob. From Miami only Salinas and I would go on to Nassau. I would stay two days with Salinas. Of course Betty said I had screwed up again. Betty now had two more women to help with the children. Five children, three being so young was a tuff job. Three having the same father and two only being weeks apart, two of the three could have passed for twins. Salinas now had 5 children and today asked for another. She said she wanted that boy and it wouldn't hurt me any as I wasn't going to settle down any time soon anyway, she'd be the one taking care of him, as she put it. I didn't say yes or no but Salinas took it as a yes.

While in Nassau Jack and the divers met with me and talked me into them starting up the treasure hunting again. They would move the two barges to our latest ship site and start diving at once.

Peter whom was on his third child with Ida would now transfer and head up the treasure group. I trusted Jack, the others were good men but. Jack was now the only single man of the four. With Jack's percent of his treasure he had purchased a small water front home on Eleuthera. Jack's girlfriend looked like your typical California beach girl with that tan, blond hair and blue eyes. Cindy had been working with Peter on the tourist boat since Jack brought her to Nassau. Peter's brother Billy also had been working with Peter and would now take the lead with making the tourist happy. We would miss Cat but the tourist and over at the Women's Center that kind of missing would be different.

Christina having again spent more time with Lori, suggested that I take Lori and the kids on a sail before we returned to Limon. Christina cared for Lori and it seemed was willing to share my time with her. Christina also reminded me that I had promised Lori a summer trip on the Morgan.

I did take two more days and a night sailing with Lori and the kids. We all had a great time with us just anchoring in the shallows of Elliot's Key. The kids were now good swimmers and said that they too would like to sail the Caribbean during the summer. Lori talked a lot about Pa'me and asked if we could take her along as well. It looked like our next trip would be in July.

The very next day I revisited the same Doctors that had stitched me up to include the eye Doctor that warned me that any knock on my head could trigger a complete back out of my right eye.

The next morning, Christina, Evette and myself returned to Limon. From the Airport we taxied to customs, our Land Rover and house hold goods were now here and free from customs. We hired three trucks and six men. The girls would take a taxi and have the trucks follow them to the house. The girls would supervise the labor unloading and placing the furniture in the house.

My first stop was to pick up Richard. Richard was home building some kind of water tank thing to have enough water so that his wife could do the wash for the cargo ship's crews. I was now driving my new Land Rover and I told him to come to take a ride with me. Once I had him in the car he complained about the scar on his face. Him sitting on my right he looked at mine and then said well maybe his wasn't so bad and laughed. By the way, Richard asked, where we were going? I told him that we were going to take my plane and go back to Nicaragua. Richard said to stop and let him out.

As we reached the airport there was a plane sitting where Richard's used to park. We turned onto the airport road, and I drove right up to the airplane. Damn I said looks like someone already took your spot. Richard not getting out of the car said that was the nicest airplane he had ever seen. The plane was a single engine Cessna Grand Caravan. Get out, you old fool I said, take a look. Richard looked at me and asked if it was mine? Nop I said, its ours, your uncle says they will replace yours, you can use this until you get yours. The door was locked as the plane was checked into customs waiting for a temporary permission. Who has the keys, Mr. Tolafio, Richard asked? I said yes, Richard said Tolafio would need something to grease the wheels. I told him that was taken care of. I told Richard that the back 6 seats had been removed and a refrigeration section added that could maintain 1,000 pounds of product such as Lobster and or fish. Their lobster was our Crawfish. I wanted Richard to keep up his trips to Blue Fields. Buy all the lobster he could to sell to the shipping lines. Limon now had 8 to 9 ships calling per week. Presently the ships only got maybe 15 pounds of lobster and that it wasn't so fresh. Richard and I would be partners 50/50, Richard was now happy. Richard didn't know that the G.D. technical support group had installed an addition power source. This source would be required if and when we ever got some of the new technology that G.D. was working on for all my planes.

Even for Richard it was too early to go to the bar so I took Richard back to his house. I then headed to the new house where the girls would be hard at work directing the unloading of three 40-foot containers that cleared customs and were now parked in our side yard of the house. Miami Safe had built a new safe for me which consisted of 10 major parts that would all bolt together from the inside. Once put together it would weight over 3,000 pounds. Since it wasn't my house we couldn't anchor it to the ground so we just made it too heavy to move. Of course it had one key, a combination and my added lock. The house security wasn't very good so we would have to require four of our Haitian army personal to be moved to Limon.

Evette and Christina looked different in their work clothes. I hadn't seen either work up such a sweat. When I mentioned the same to the girls Evette gave me something that she had learned from Karen, the finger. Seemed the air conditioners would be installed sometime during the week. Right at 11:00 a.m. the help started to disappear, it was siesta time, the crew would all go to their homes to eat and then take a short nap and return at 2:00 p.m. I thought what a life. Christina didn't waste any time to drag me to the pool. Our clothes were still at the hotel but as you can imagen that didn't stop us from jumping on in and cooling off. Hot water in the house would also take a few more days but that cool shower did the trick.

From their I went to the hotel to change, Lourdes had called and said that things were moving right along in Panama and looked like we were on for three days from now. Lourdes said the G.D. personal had arrived with their equipment and the C-130 was on the way back from an Iran delivery. Lourdes also confirmed that Fernando and a small group had been dropped off at the south eastern tip off Nicaragua. Fernando was to physically check the base that the Nicaraguan army was building or had built. This was the site from where Richard's plane had taken the gun fire that had brought us down.

I was counting on Tilofio giving us the permission for the Cessna so that Richard could fly me to Panama within the next two days. If not Tommy would need to fly on in and take me on over there. I was planning on paying a short visit to the Nicaraguan site that had shot Richard and I down.

Two days passed, our Limon house was now in living and working order. Fernando and company had come from Nicaragua with the news I was waiting for. Silvio came through with the Cessna permission, and Richard would drop Fernando, two of his men, and myself at the US Airbase in Panama.

CHAPTER XXIII

THE BIRTH OF TESS

In Panama, our C-130 was loaded with twenty-five 55-gallon steel drums of gasoline. The Russian gasoline had been sold on the black market from Cuba to Panama. Each tank was clearly marked as being from the Russian oil giant Youks.

Once at the base in Panama I first met with the two G.D. technicians and was given instructions on how to use the two pouches that they were delivering. Both pouches were strapped on, one to me the other to Fernando. Once in the air, both would need to be plugged into the other and one plugged into a newly installed power supply on the C-130. Each of the pouches had a kavlar barrier plate between the instruments and our bodies. The technicians said that in the case of any interference during the mission that the pouches could be destroyed without us being killed or at least not badly wounded by a small blast. We were shown how to detonate the pouches by pressing a button on the outside of the barrier plate. We were shown how to unstrap each pouch. Should the pouch be removed without following the instruction to the "T", then a timer of 15 minutes would activate a larger explosion.

We would fly the 25 drums of gasoline that were loaded in the C-130 north along the coast until we came to the San Juan River then turn west along the river. We had cordiated with one of Mr. Crowbe's ships that would be on its way north, just exiting the port of Limon. Just before we had made that westerly turn toward Nicaragua I connected the two pouches and connected the pouches into the new power source of the C-130 and then turned the device on. At the moment the devise was activated, our C-130 crew turned looking at me with thumbs up. This meaning that the device was working. The captain from the Container ship radioed alerting us that they had lost all navigational assistance, also noting some electrical instruments malfunction. Our C-130 now still flying west at a high altitude along the River would now move into Nicaraguan air space. Once over the small Sandinista base the captain of the C-130 opened lowering the ramp and lifted the planes nose. Out rolled all 25 drums of gasoline.

We would now make a 180 degree turn dropping down in altitude and would pass the drop area using our port side rapid firing cannon to ignite the gasoline. As we exited we could see the ground lite up with fire causing several major expositions including two soviet helicopters that never made it off the ground. That we knew of there were no attempts to bring us down.

The copilot noted that we were flying with visual contact with the ground as he had no directional electronics nor compass service giving out reasonable data. The copilot also noted that his fuel sensors had stopped working showing that we were out of fuel.

We continued flying at a low altitude flying east until about five miles off shore with no following aircraft. Fernando and I then turned the devices off and unplugged the pouches from the power supply and then from each other. We then banked the C-130 to the south returning to base.

We were gone less than two hours without even receiving a scratch. Richard was still there on the ground in the Cessna not even knowing that we had gone and returned.

The G.D. technical men only asked for one of the pouches back, noting that one pouch would return to Costa Rica with me, having Tommy pick me up traveling back to Fairbanks. The pouches would need to be returned separately. I understood what they meant. The Technicians would take one pouch and meet us back at Fairbanks. The Technicians didn't even ask how things worked out. I figured that wasn't a part of their job.

Richard would fly the 7 of us back to Limon. Tommy was there waiting, but I had to go and get Christina. Fernando had given his pouch to the other G.D. technician in Panama while I was still wearing mine. Fernando and his two men would drive me to the Limon house. When we arrived to the house Christina and Evette were sunning at the pool. With

Christina wearing next to nothing I had her throw something on and pack a small bag for the both of us. Both girls asked about my funny looking pouch. I was only at home for less than 15 minutes and the five of us were off to the airport. Richard was still there looking a bit dazed by the whole thing. Richard asked what was going on with my funny looking pouch? I told him not to fly within 5 miles of Nicaragua. Richard said he'd have no problem with that. The five of us boarded the leer with Tommy and we were off to Fairbanks.

Fairbanks wasn't in my plans and I didn't like it too much how it was all arranged. I guess I went along with it because I knew how important what we had done today was. Not just getting my revenge but the testing of the new system. I didn't know that the CIA had somehow been aware from the get-go.

Christina changed on the leer and there was a limo ready and waiting to transport the five of us to G.D.

Once dropped off at the front doors of G.D., we were escorted into a side room where the Colonel along with a top CIA man, that I hadn't met as yet was waiting. The Colonel hadn't previously met Christina and cordially gave her a hand shake. That wasn't so for the Colonel and Fernando and Fernando's two men. All 4 men greeted each other with a hug and pats on the back. All had fought together in Nicaragua the time that the Colonel had gotten into a bind down there. The reunion was short as the Colonel, the CIA man and myself were called into the next room.

With CIA present in the building I had asked Fernando not to let anyone take Christina anywhere without him going along.

I still had my part of the pouch on, the other pouch hadn't arrived as yet. We were now only seven hours from returning from our mission.

Once in the briefing room the Colonel said that the Sandinista base had been eliminated. Their defense battery plus two soviet helicopters were destroyed and they had suffered several casualties. The Colonel said the Nicaraguans', Cubans and Soviets would now think twice about settling into that zone again. The Colonel said that the new system worked even better than they hope for as both US cargo ships and a Navy destroyer were affected by the device. I wasn't trying to be smart but asked why the CIA was present, and why I had been asked to attend. It was the CIA man that spoke. Harris as he had introduced himself said that the CIA wanted to take over the project and move it from the G.D. control. Up until then I had been seated while he was talking but with that I stood and said absolutely not. I looked at the Colonel and said that I thought he should have known not to waste my time with this. We have a common enemy and we sometimes use each other in fighting the enemy but we are not partners I said. My agreement is and will continue to be with G.D. I said. Harris said that the decision had already been made and that I would be out of it from this point on. Me still standing, Harris then also stood and ordered me to hand over the pouch. I looked at the G.D. man and asked if they were in agreement with this? The G.D. manager said that he was in agreement with me that the project was privtely owned and should have no CIA involvement. The G.D. manager said he had warned the CIA men that the devices were only in trial and are Volatile! There were two other men in the room that then stood. I looked at the Colonel and said that this would mean an end to any cooperation between the CIA and my group. The Colonel then stood and said that he believed that the CIA should stay out of it. Harris then said that if I didn't give the pouch up it would be taken from me. And the other pouch I asked? We have it Harris said. I glanced at the G.D. personal and then began to take the pouch off. I took it off and put it into the open arms of Harris, armored plate to the outside. Still standing I turned and headed for the door not looking back. When I arrived back at the waiting room I found the agent that I had shot in the airport standing next to and talking with Christina. I waked right up and told him to get away from my wife, the man still in a shoulder sling said he was apologizing. I pushed him back and he resisted the push and said I had him at a disadvantage with his injury. I took that as him meaning that I had two arms and he only having one. My reaction was to tuck my right hand behind my belt and walked toward the man. Once in striking distance my left fist caught him square on the right side of his jaw. His knees buckled and he went down.

I motioned to Fernando toward the door, took Christina by the hand looked down at the agent on the floor and said one more time, "stay away from my wife." As we made it to the door the limo pulled up and as before one of Fernando's men sat up front with the driver. Fernando asked how things went and I looked at my watch and said seven minutes.

As we walked through the airport there was something going on the TV, seemed there had just been an explosion at the G.D. plant. In a non-related story, it appeared that three people were killed when a Limo that had crashed through a barrier wall on a local overpass. It was not known if there were any accident casualties at the G.D. plant. We had stopped to see the news flash but then hurried along. We reached our gate door and went through the door to find Tommy still there. I was concerned until we were in the air. Christina had my hand not letting go the entire time. Fernando and I knew Christina knew that we had something to do with the explosion and maybe the accident but we hadn't mentioned anything. I told Tommy to get out of US air space ASAP and to head for Eleuthera. Tommy would drop Christina and Myself off there and then take Fernando on over to Andros where Fernando and his men could lie low for a few days. Tommy could refuel and check the jet.

Cristina and I would be dropped off on Eleuthera after dark, we taxied on over to Charles and Marilyn's where Charles would take us in his boat across the bay to Harbor Island. Being late and not having anything but a small bag, we ate dinner at the Pink Sands hotel and then walked along the beach to the house. The house was now 100% finished and stocked. It had been a long day, we showered and went to bed.

The next morning, we were on the beach jogging, yes it had been a while but with things the way they were, I felt the need to get back into shape. My cut on my left leg was 100% good to go. Once back from jog we were greeted by a young boy sent with several pages of a fax that Lourdes had sent. The Washington Post said that two explosions that had taken place the day before were connected and that there were three deaths in the limo and one at the Fairbanks facility. The news said that three of the four men killed were working for the CIA. This meant that the Fairbanks explosion had also taken a life. I didn't feel good about anyone being killed but I also knew I wasn't to blame. I wondered what the consequences would be. The fax that Lourdes had sent also said that the Colonel, Bob and Secretary of State had called looking for me. I couldn't call from the Island as the phone call would be too easy to trace. I decided to stay the day without making any calls not even to Lourdes letting her knew that we had received her messages.

It was a good time to see how good Christina could handle a gun. We spent most of the afternoon getting her acquainted in the way I used a gun. Carson had said anyone worth shooting was worth killing. I didn't agree. I would shoot to stop the aggressor, so far that had worked with the exception of my first kill. I told her that there were always exceptions of the rules. Christina said she recalled the boarding house rule. She then said she was happy how the exception worked out.

The next morning after our run we returned to Eleuthera and Tommy flew us to Andros. Andros was one of our strongest spots.

I used the phone and called Bob first. Bob asked if I had seen the morning news? I had not, the Post reported that a cell from the CIA had attempted to steal some kind of Top Secret device and three inside the group had been killed and six more arrested. I asked Bob if the story was true and Bob said that the Secretary and the Colonel had called him personally confirming the story. The Colonel said you had saved the program, Bob said. Well the problem with that is that the Colonel was there with the CIA I said. Bob said that the Colonel had just met Mr. Harris whom was conveniently killed in the explosion. We'll never know I said. Bob said that the G.D. personnel said that if it weren't for the actions of their man and myself, the theft would have gained someone access to the most significant new device in years, not to mention its military advantages.

I then called The Colonel and his first words were, that the CIA agent wanted to know where I had learned how to throw that left? I said to tell him it was the boy scouts. The Colonel laughed and said he like to meet me somewhere and explain all that had happen. I said there was no need, that the explosion could have killed him too. I told the Colonel that I was going to lie low from Costa Rica and that Evette and two of Fernando's men would be there watching things. The Colonel said he understood. I also told the Colonel that to please give my apologies to the Secretary as I wasn't going to return his call at this time. Tell him to send me a check. The Colonel said he'd pass the message.

After my calls I gave a big hug to Christina and said that it looked all would be ok. We then flew to Nassau where Christina stayed on the "Cat" and I with Salinas and the kids. Salinas was good with everything to include she would take Christina for a sail while I visited with Jack and his men out on the barges. Jack and his crew were still pumping sand from the ship's hull not finding much of anything of value but a large broken sword that Jack said he wanted to give to me as it was something that didn't look like anything of much value but something I might like.

CHAPTER XXIV

DRAKE'S SWORD

Jack said that if there were anything down in the hull, they'd find it within the week as by then, the sand would be all but out. I had once told Jack about the small boat that Carson and I had found and he said that if the ship didn't bear any more treasure, that they take a look at the area that I had mentioned before heading back to Andros.

I was pleasantly surprised how well Christina and Salinas got along. I did notice that Christina had removed her wedding bands. It was something she had done on her own. I was there for 8 days. Christina had made friends with Salinas and said it was time for me to take Lori out on that sailing trip. She pushed me to go and said she would be here in Nassau keeping busy visiting the children and maybe even going out pulling traps or diving the wreck with Jack watching out for her. I said my good buys and took off for Miami.

Lori was happy to see me and was ready for our trip. We would first sail to Key West and from there to Andros and from there sail to Nassau. I sang the song, trailers for sale or rent, no food, no phone, no pets, aint got no cigarettes. I was happy but I did miss Christina. It was the first time I had missed anyone since Carson.

Once in Nassau I just couldn't act that I didn't have those feelings for Christina. Lori was also happy to see Christina. I had told Lori on the trip that Pa'me was now Christina acting as my wife down in Costa Rica. Lori didn't ask anything further.

It was Lori's idea that Christina join us on the rest of the trip. At this point I was just as concerned how Christina would feel as I was how Lori would feel. Christina and Lori took off early one morning on the "CAT" not returning until dark. I thought I would need to go looking for them but they came in with the evening tide. That night Lori told me that it was all set, the three girls and I would start off on our Island trip that next day. The three being Salinas, Cristina and Lori.

The next morning it was so, the four of us set sail in the "CAT" leaving the "Lori" docked. We would head to the western tip of Current Island, and then change heading toward Gregory Town. At first it was a bit strange, being with the three girls, but after two days and nights it began to feel like everything was going to work out. By the third day my attention was leveled out between the three.

On the fourth day we or at least I got a surprise visitor. It was June, the girls had contacted her before we left Nassau but June was in the middle of moving into her new Miami house. June joined us at Governor's Harbor. June and Salinas would stay until we reached Exuma, then they would return to the kids.

Now being back to Lori, Christina and myself, we had now decided that we would sail to Haiti. I had once, a long time ago sailed almost through these very same waters. It was in 1974 during the time that Janet and I made the daring exchange of her for the Cuban General's daughter. Janet was CIA, my part of this was as a favor for Bob. I remembered that terrible storm Janet and I passed through along the way. The "Cat" had a radar dome on its mast that these days allowed us to see any storms that approached. We still couldn't outrun the weather but we could attempt to change our heading. It had been some ten years since I had talked to Janet, I wondered how she was doing and thought if she was still working with the Agency surely she had heard my name once or twice. Thinking back to that time brought back lots of memories. Christina must have seen my face and came and kissed me, bringing me right back to where I was.

Being on the boat with all the girls was good, but for some reason, I felt more comfortable having just Christina and Lori aboard.

Once we reached the Paxi Château, Salinas's mother attempted to take over the show. It was Christina's and Lori's first time at the Chateau and meeting Salinas's mother. Sharron was her typical self, showing her displeasure with me bringing the girls into Salinas's house. Sharron told the girls how I had come to the house and fallen in love with her daughter at first sight. I told the story a bit different mentioning that I had first visited several times then spent ten days here taking a break from what I called the real world, later getting the news that Salinas was pregnant with Michelle. I then took Sharron aside and told her that these girls were also friends of Salinas and that they were our guest. We didn't see much of Sharron from that point on, we would have Tommy pick us up the next day and fly us to Port-a-Prince for a day trip. During the trip the girls asked if we could visit Cuba, that was a NO. The three of us talked some about Cat and her situation. Christina noted that Salinas had told them that Cat had been back only once to visit the children and only stayed one day. Salinas had said that Cat didn't look good. Christina said that Salinas said Cat was pale and was almost skin and bone. Christina said that Salinas said that she was now the mother of all five children mentioning that all were calling her mom.

The three of us would leave the next day for an almost straight sail to Nassau. Both girls especially Lori could hold their own behind the wheel. I was proud the way the Lori handled herself on the boat and around the other girls. She seemed as Deanna once said that she was now, well almost, a grown woman. I had said it before and would again that I felt sorry for those high school boys.

During our short stay at Paxi we had received word from Jack that they had completed the sand removal and there was no additional treasure. The broken sword that Jack had given me was the only thing of any value that was found.

Durning our sailing trip back to Nassau, Lori asked what were the chances that she and I would ever marry. I repeated that I would not be the one to change our relationship and reminded her that it was her that had decided to take the other girls along. There would be no talk of marriage until she graduated from the UM. Lori said I might have 10 children by then. And if so, I said we'll have another four. Lori asked if I could marry her and stay married to Christina? Lori said that it would be ok with her if we kept Christina as a part of our family. I told Lori that it was her that I was depending on to manage the fortune that I was amassing. I told her she must keep on tract with her learning.

By the time we arrived back in Nassau Lori wasn't the same girl. Her confidence was something that she had gained this trip. Our trip wasn't over as we would have two more days aboard the "Lori". Christina asked if I wanted to spend these last days with just Lori? I said no.

I spent the night at the Hill Top house seeing Salinas and the children, Christina, Lori and myself planned to leave the next day sailing the "Lori" back to Miami.

When Jack had given me the broken sword that they had found at the wreck, I had taken it and placed it on the counter of my Nassau apartment. Christina and Lori had slept at the apartment, and I would meet them there. As we walked out of the apartment I noticed the sword sitting on the counter. Not wanting to open the safe I took the sword and positioned it through my belt.

The two boats sailed very differently. The hunter seemed much faster and would respond with just a touch of the wheel. The girls tanned skin had now turned two shades darker. The difference between where the sun didn't shine and what did was night and day. Lori had filled out more and in no way now looked nor would she ever again look 16. I thought about what my Dad once said about me being fickle. The truth was I thought I could be happy with any one of the four girls, but it was now Lori and Christina as my favorites.

The girls and I anchored our first night on the west side of Andros, about a half mile off shore. We were early enough for me to get several crawfish for dinner. What we didn't eat we bagged and put on ice for the next day's sail.

That night I once again realized that it was going to be difficult to leave Lori again at Chubby's, this time I had just spent almost a month with her.

The next morning the sky was clear and by sun up we were on our way. We reached Biscayne bay that night at about 7:00 p.m. and decided to go on into the dock. We would arrive at our Coral Gables dock at 9:30 p.m. We had called to have a taxi pick us up and arrived at the apartment by about 11:30 p.m., we were happy to be home but the reality for Lori going home wasn't so pleasant. During our hot shower the shower didn't seem to stop moving. We all had been on one of the boats so long it seemed that we were still moving with the sea.

The next morning, I wasn't in any rush to take Lori home, I went down to the lobby and got a newspaper and the mail. Right away I saw

Cat's hand writing with my name and address on one of the envelopes. Right off, her hand writing bothered me. I opened it on the way up in the elevator. When the elevator door opened I didn't get out as I was reading the letter over and over, the news was as bad as it gets. The letter read, "My love, sorry to bring you this news but feel that it's the only way I could let you know. Jacob has passed away. I actually helped him go. You see Jacob had contracted full blown Aids and was suffering. It's no matter how he got it, he just did, I too am dyeing as Jacob unwilling passed it to me. You won't be able to find me and even if you could I don't want you to see me like this. I'm in a privet clinic and they are doing what they can but they only give me days to live. I got to see the children about 6 weeks or so ago, Salinas and Betty are taking good care of them. Jimmy looks so much like you. Please take good care of them all as I know you will. Enclosed are some papers that Jacob had signed granting you custody of Wendy Michelle and Johnny. It's funny but its I that leave you everything. I'll be seeing Deanna soon and we'll be waiting for you on the dock. All my love Cat". I looked at the date on the letter and it was two weeks old with no return address. Once I came to my senses, I went into the apartment and called for Jerry, my reaction was to find Cat. While I waited for Jerry's return call, I thought about it, all it should take to find her would be to follow the money trail and maybe back track on her last travel to Nassau. The Jerry call came within minutes, I informed Jerry of Cat's letter and asked him to find her, do whatever it takes I said. I mentioned my thoughts about the money trail and her latest travels. Jerry said that he would get right on it.

Lori had gotten up and asked what was going on, I told her it was nothing. I walked into the kitchen, wet down Cat's letter and sent it down the deposal. I took the two documents and would make copies, then put them into the safe. I opened the safe and while putting the original documents inside remembered the broken sword. I would also put the sword in the safe. Still being a little off from Cat's letter with the news, I reached for the sword that was on the table and it slipped off the table on to the tile floor. The sword cracked the tile and a piece of the sword also came loose. I picked up the sword and the small chip that was on the floor. In looking for where the chip had come from I noticed something strange of the handle. The handle tip was a red ruby that looked like it too had come loose. I got a hot rag and twisted the ruby counter clock wise, to my surprise, the sword's Incased ruby unscrewed and came off in my hand. Now there appeared a thin layer of cloth in the void that looked like paper. I was careful with the cloth as I took it out of the handle. It wasn't a map like I first thought, it was dots, just dots on a cloth. Only one dot was a bit larger than the others. I got a magnified glass and found that the dots, all but the biggest one had been poked into the cloth. To me this cloth could have been placed under a chart and marked with a sharp object, then removing the chart and then marking the indented spots on the cloth. My attention then shifted to the sword. It was definitely English. Maybe an officer's sword that had been broken in battle. Bob then came to my mind so I called Lourdes to locate him. My mind being as it is, thought it could have been Drake's sword, I knew from history that Drake had lost his last battle at Puerto Rico before taking refuge in Panama's waters. Drake had paid the Panama Governor handsomely to let Himself and his men refuge there while Drake sought medical attention for his wounds. Drake would eventually die of his wounds aboard his ship. Maybe Drake had managed to bury his treasure before he died. While I waited for Bob's return call I made a rough copy of the dots withholding only the big one. I then put the cloth back into the handle and the sword back as it was. I then placed the sword into the safe. Sadly, once the sword was into the safe the thought of Cat sitting somewhere alone waiting to die came back hard.

I would take Lori back to Chubby's, the children were so happy to see her. Chubby and Lilly were just waiting for Lori to return so they could take the kids on a small vacation.

I told Lori that I may stay in town and that she should call the apartment when they returned.

From there I went to the sailing club and again called Lourdes. Christina was at the apartment when Bob called, she told him I would wait down at the sailing club. Bob called and I told him about the sword. I wanted to look at any late 1500s maps of the east coast of Panama. Drake was said to have died just north of Colon. Bob laughed that hardy laugh of his and asked if I didn't have enough problems. I didn't return the laugh and Bob said he bring a professor or two over with some old maps and charts. Bob asked if Betty would be there to cook up some fritters. No fritters I said, Bob said some Russian caviar and some good champagne would do. See you at 8:00 p.m. Bob said.

I hadn't noticed Robert before I got off the phone. Robert was there waiting to say hello. Where's the girls Robert asked? I hadn't noticed but Robert noted that I was almost as dark as he was. Robert said that people were talking about their fishing trips over in Nassau. Robert asked when he could go, I hear the whiskey on those trips are served up by a beautiful white girl. Robert was talking about Jack's girlfriend Cindy. I told Robert that he was always welcome, to include I'd have our Leer pick him up on a Friday afternoon and bring him back on Sunday. Robert was grateful and noted that the bar wasn't open as yet. I left the sailing club and drove on by the Big Daddy's liquor store. I purchased a case of Busch beer in cans and a pint of his favorite Jim Beam whiskey. I didn't dare buy more than a pint as I didn't want to get Robert fired. At the same store I purchased 6 bottles of Don Pieriron, four bags of ice and a small case of caviar. I went back to see Robert, he put 6 of the canned beer in the ice machine and the bottle under the launch seat. Robert was grateful and said he'd be making his rounds, with a big smile, got in the launch off he went.

I would go back to the apartment and put the champagne in the frig. I then sat out on the balcony with Christina, thinking about and remembering Cat. We sat out there until Bob called from the lobby. Christina would need to go down and bring them up. Bob brought two professors of History. I had the sword out for them to see plus two copies of the paper with the spots. Both men brought along maps and charts.

One professor was looking at the sword while the other looked for something to match with the dots. The second chart that was looked at got our attention. With that chart on the table, the paper was moved until one spot marked the city of Colon and the other spots marked several outter Islands. The professor proclaimed he had solved the puzzle. By now Christina had popped open one of the champagne bottles that were on ice. The champagne and caviar were severed and the Professor proposed a toast, to the most beautiful tan he'd ever seen.

The professor told the story of Drake's last defeat and him barely making it to Panama. As the story goes the professor said, Drake's ship was badly damaged. Drake transferred what he told the crew was all of the treasure to one of the two good ships they had. Once the treasure and

Drake's personal belongings were transferred, Drake's ship plus one more were burned. Drake and the few remaining crew watched as the two ships burned to the water line and then sunk.

Panama hadn't heard of Drake's recent defeat and was bribed into giving himself and his men safe harbor. Drake offered a Kings payment for the service. The Governor played it right as within the month Drake developed a fever and died. Upon Drakes death his two ships and men were taken prisoners.

The Governor didn't fare so well with King Phillip, when the King heard the story. The rest was history as the first treasure we found was part of Drakes payment to the Governor. We had confirmed this as we had found a broch that the Queen had given to Drake. We also had found what was left of a seal that we believed to be of the spanish Governor.

The Sword was found on the second ship. Both ships had met their fates just 300 yards from each other less than 20 miles from Nassau.

By now on the third bottle of champagne the second professor had found where queen Elisabeth had 12 such swords made, all 12 swords were passed to her most favorite captains. One such sword was indeed given to Drake. The professor speaking had found a match drawing of our very sword. Before leaving the professors now having much too much to drink both said that they were sure the original paper was marked where the burned ship had gone down. They said they figured that Drake had most likely kept the major part of his treasure aboard that ship before sinking it. Both men said they would love to further assist in locating the treasure. Bob and the professors would leave at midnight. Christina would escort them to the lobby and make sure they left in a taxi, none of them were in any shape to be driving.

While I opened and placed the sword in the safe, Christina had returned and removed what she had on and put on the female match to my red, white and blue bath robe. Lord only knew how many girls had used that robe but none of them looked so good in it. I had purchased that matching set when I was 19 years old trying to get ready for Michelle to come to Miami to live with me. Michelle died less than a week later. That was 16 years ago. As I locked the safe Christina came up behind me and turned me around and kissed me. She then took my hand and led me into the living room sitting me down on the couch. Christina then stood in front of me and began to talk. She started out saying that she was in love with me, not in the way that was work, in the way like, love of her life. She was in love with me. She said she could no longer share me with the other girls including Lori. Christina said I should cut Lori lose; you will never marry her like Lori believes Christina said. Three years of high school and four years of college. How many more Lori's will you run across during that time. Let her go Christina said, let her enjoy high school dances and parties. You plan on taking her to the first school dance she asked? What about the Senior Prom? By then you'll be all most 40 years old Christina said. Then Christina started on June. Christina said that June was going back to work. June, Christina said was missing a social life. June said men asked her out all the time and she was tired of waiting around. Christina said that June said that she had hoped that I would chose her over all of us. June said she had now given that idea up. June said she had seen how you looked at me and touched me. I too see how you looked at me, on the trip. Christina said that she was the only one that I put my hand under her clothes, grabbed her butt and pulled her in to kiss her. I was the one you looked for and watched, she said.

On the other hand, Christina said every day; it became harder and harder to see me kiss and or touch the others. She said her just thinking about me being with one of the other girls made her want to vomit. Now she asked, do you love me? It would be impossible to tell her no. But, there was a but. I had to ask the question. I asked if she was giving me some kind of ultimatum? Christina paused and said no but that if I didn't love her in the way she wanted me too, she would only stay until the Nicaragua war was over, win or lose she would then go. To go would kill her she said, but to stay would do the same.

What about waiting at home for me? What about my children? What about Salinas? I said she hadn't mentioned Salinas. Christina said that Salinas would be the caretaker of all my children except the ones that we would have. I said that Salinas was again pregnant. Christina said she figured that Salinas would be her toughest hurdle. Ok Cristina said, Salinas can stay but I don't want to ever see you even touch her. What about waiting I again asked? If I can't go with you I'll wait, it won't be easy but I'll wait. Christina then said I hadn't answered her question. I stood and with my right hand, raised her robe in the rear and took her by the butt, pulled her in close and said, Yes, I love you. I then scoped her up and carried her to our bed. The conversation didn't stop there. I told Christina that I would not stop seeing any of the three of them. I said that I would not be the one to break with Lori. If she can stay the course, then yes I would one day marry Lori. What are the chances that happens, very slim I said. I would not be taking her to all those school dances, but she will go. I told Christina that I too loved Salinas and that I would never abandon her. June, if June choses to move along I don't blame her just as long as she understands that our daughter will grow up knowing her father, sisters and brothers. We talked more about Lori and life in general. I told her about Cat and that I didn't know how it would end but that I just didn't want her to die like that.

I said that I would not encourage Lori to go out with boys but I also wouldn't in anyway discourage it either. Christina said that her wedding rings wouldn't come off again not for anyone. We finally got to sleep at about 4:00 a.m.

It was still early when I called Lourdes to have Jack call me just as soon as she could find him. I asked Christina how far she had gotten with her scuba lessons and got that look. Christina was to get to the YMCA today and get signed up again. I told Christina to get Evette here to join her getting her reacquainted with her diving too. I said that there was a good possibility that we'd soon be doing some diving. Christina asked if it had anything to do with that broken sword and I said yes. Christina said she liked that word and that I could keep right on saying it.

It wasn't until that night that Jack called back. Himself and the divers had been checking out the location where I said that Carson and I had seen that small boat on the bottom. Jack said they hadn't seen anything in two days of searching. I told Jack to put that on the back burner for a while that I had something new that we could all work on. They should get the barges moved back to Nassau and all come to Miami.

It would take us several weeks to buy a new boat and outfit it the way we wanted. We purchased a 1986, 54-Foot Ocean Supper Sport. My brother Bob's shop would build all the rigging that we specked out. In the meantime, Christina would receive her scuba certificate and we made several dives out by the Fowery Rock light house with Jack and his men. Evette was of course with us.

Evette had all along been receiving letters from her ex-husband, three weeks ago she had returned a letter and this week had visited him in prison. George would shortly be up for parole. Evette said that George had been a good boy in prison and she was planning to attend the parole hearing to ask the panel for his release. Evette asked if we could get George's old job back? I said I would look into it when the time came. Evette said it would help at his parole meeting if George had a job lined up especially if it was his old employer. I told Evette to watch the old part. I told her to have Lourdes wright the letter. Here, the thought came of us losing Evette.

It was weeks before we heard back from and then saw Jerry. Tommy had delivered Cat to Mexico City the time she had visited me in Limon. It took Jerry time to track her down. Cat had told the truth, both Jacob and Cat had since passed away. Their bodies were at once cremated do to their illness. Jerry brought back their remains.

It almost killed Jacob's father whom had already blamed me for most of Jacob's problems including him leaving Nassau. The Judge received Jacob's ashes at his door crying like a baby. Ida was there to comfort him.

Cat's father had now lost three of the four daughters he had. The only one left was Janie.

Jerry said there wasn't much money left in Cat's Mexico account and said that one of the Nurses had said that Cat had mentioned leaving it to a nearby children's home. The Nurse told Jerry that Cat had died two weeks before in her sleep. I would make sure the Children's home would get that money and more.

I took Cat's ashes and with her Father and Willy looking on, poured the ashes into the outbound tide at the end of Nassau's city docks. All three of us sat there drinking and remembering old times until the tide had turned back.

I received lots of calls, cards and telex's, I even got a call from Karen. Karen said she was sorry for my loss. Karen said she had heard that Cat had just recently given me my first son. She knew how much Cat meant to me. It was good to hear from Karen although I'd wished it had been under different circumstances.

Carson's son Malcolm showed up in Miami and moved into Carson's old house. Malcolm was trying out for UM's football team and looked to me like he had a good chance to make the team. We had hired a full time house lady from Nassau to cook and clean for Malcolm. Before Malcolm arrived, I had moved the old Mercedes in the garage on its north side to the south side. I told Malcolm that the Mercedes was mine and that one day I would remove it.

Lori having her drivers lience would drive the jeep to her first day of high school. Since Cat's death I hadn't moved closer to one girl or another.

With a prod from Christina, Lori had invited Malcolm for a sail out on the Morgan. Malcolm had his sailboat moored at the sailing club, but Malcolm didn't know how to sail. Malcolm had picked up Lori from Chubby's house early one Sunday morning and returned her just after dark. Lori said that Malcolm was nice but only talked about football.

Lori entered tenth grade at the same high school that my Mom, Dad, all three of my brothers, and I had gone to. Mr. Spreen and Mrs. Turtelow were no longer there at the school. I was hoping at least one would still be there to meet Lori and see that jeep. I could just imagen Mrs. Turtelow seeing that jeep parked in her front yard early one Sunday morning! I would have loved to have been there for that.

Malcolm took Lori to her school's opening football game. Malcolm was late picking her up because of his UM practice. Malcolm also took Lori to the after-game sock hop at the school. Lori was home by midnight and again the next day; Lori said Malcolm had boarded her talking about football.

Malcolm made the UM's football team, but I wouldn't get to go to his first game. I sent Lori as my representative. Lori, whom went with Evette said she didn't understand a thing that was going on. She said Malcolm wasn't good enough to play and was like her, sitting the entire game.

Fernando had parachuted into Nicaragua with 30 men to secure and repair our old landing strip. This was to get ready for two of our C-130s to return, one which would land and drop off two armored tanks and the other to drop off another 30 men. Fernando would remove the remains of our first C-130 from the westernly end of the runway. Photos of our burned out C-130 had made their way to congress. The only identifiying marks that were recognizable on the burned aircraft was a emplem on the tail of the C-130's carcass. The emblem, on the plane's tail looked like some kind of animal with a nap sack over it's shoulder, of course it was my Father's emblem of a Traveling Cat. Yes this was that same emblem that had been on the sail of the boat Rusty and I, then both at age 15 had sailed to Nassau.

Fernando's group now with the Contra's would control the southeast end of Nicaragua. Our small group were well armed to include 25 powerful hand held heat seeking missiles that were called Stingers. The cost of just one of these missiles was about $40,000.00 each. Our group started off carrying 25 of these missiles into Nicaragua. The stinger had a range of 5 miles which made almost any aircraft especially a helicopter almost sure to be brought down. The tanks, Fernando's men and our supply line, insured that the Rebels were well supplied. Fernando had started to train the Rebels. Working together as a group the contras had the ability to strike things like electrical plants that were located well into Nicaragua's interior. The stingers could and were used for ground to ground missions too. Fernando's and his men played havoc with the Sandinista's capital. With Fernando's group in control of the south eastesterly tip and the apparent new contra advances, the US congress had now approved $100,000,000.00 in military aid to the Contras. Jerry with our two C-130s had no problem keeping the rebels well supplied.

Richard had done his part with him making two trips to Blue Fields in our Cessna. His first trip produced the information to help get Fernando's men into Nicaragua, plus a bonus of 350 pounds of lobster. On Richard's second trip, Richard brought back 900 pounds of lobster and more information. Seemed that the Sandinistas had to know it was Richard's airplane that they had shot down, but somehow decided to permit him to fly in and out of Bluefield. Maybe it was the fear of the retaliation like what they got from his plane being shot down.

Silva was now living full time with the Russian agent in Limon, Costa Rica. Her information on the Soviets planning in Nicaragua had proved priceless.

Montibelli, living in Limon had purchased the only cold storage and ice plant in town and had built a live salt water tank that could hold lobsters until they were sold.

Jena had sent me two messages that she now had three months of no smoking under her belt. I told Christina about Jena wanting to help her have a child. Christina said it would have to be artificial insemination. Roy said I was as crazy as Jena. Roy said that if I fathered a child with Jena, at any time, I could receive a parenthood claim that would cost me millions. Jena who was becoming richer by the day, would have to agree to take 15 million of her trust money and put it aside to be used to fight or pay off any possible suit for parenthood. Jena said that she would sign that or any agreement to have my child. Jena would have to wait three more months, but I still didn't think she could or had quit smoking.

We had done over a month's planning and ten of us were now ready to head for Panama in the new boat, yes even though it was 54 feet long, I still called it a boat.

There was that possibility of someone already coming across the sunken Drake ships, but for me, one way or the other we would find the ships if they were down there. If Drake did indeed sink his own ship thinking to one-day return for his treasure, he wouldn't have sunk it in very deep water.

I had seen Lori several times during the last month and things weren't going exactly the way that Christina wanted but Lori and Christina remained very close. I had promised that I would either come back and visit Lori soon or send for her.

The ten of us pulled out of the Miami Marina on Saturday morning with Captain Mike at the wheel. Captain Mike looked at Christina and I and said that this was going to be quite the adventure. We were headed to a Panamanian Island group known as Boca de Toro. We were looking for the lost treasure of Sir Frances Drake.